Kara — this is how we knew Embassy 50 years ago — Enjoy.

Leora Potter

Sad Eyes

LEORA POTTER

Sad Eyes

A novel

by

⁂

LEORA POTTER

HOT PAGE PRESS

Printed and Bound in Hong Kong
ISBN 0-9745652-9-6

ACKNOWLEDGMENTS

⁂

My heart felt thanks to Tiffany Whitehead and Christie Hansen, the outstanding editors that have polished this manuscript.

I also want to thank JoAnn Arnold, Penny Hamilton, Carol Cail, Paula Wilson, Arita Evans, Gail Nelson, Susan Potter, Paige and Bruce Bennet for reading, and critiquing my manuscript.

A very special thanks to my wonderful husband, Stan Potter, for his suggestions, and his willingness to read and edit Sad Eyes.

Another very special thanks to my wonderful son Dr .S. Steven Potter for reading, re-reading, critiquing, and editing the manuscript even though he had a heavy work load, he took time for me.

I want to thank both my husband and son for their encouragement to go forward, keep trying and to publish this novel.

Dust cover portrait by photographer Becky Hansen, phone 435-656-6969

Book dust jacket design by Josh Bevan, at Design to Print,
phone 435-674-4033.

Thanks to Mark Behrmann, a professional artist, for the sketch on the book cover. Mark paints portraits as well as scenes and whatever his clients desire. We have paintings of his in our home. His phone number is
303-362-1113.

Thanks to Gregory Zarcoff for putting the finishing touches on the MS and for publishing the book. Phone 702-458-7782

Chapter One
Asunción, Paraguay, 1959

Sleep would not come. Lana searched for Brian's hand in the dark. "Are you awake, Brian?"

"Do you have a problem?"

"Yes. I'm haunted by what I saw today."

"Where?" Brian asked sleepily.

"Caroline and I searched for the best place to use our Charity funds."

"What Charity funds?"

"The money raised by the Embassy Wives Club to benefit the less fortunate in Asunción," Lana replied. She was wide awake. Lana had been appalled at the neglect and lack of bare necessities that she had witnessed in the facilities they had visited.

"What did you find?"

"So many needs that we can't begin to fill all of them. The people were forlorn. The facilities were terrible. Stinky, over crowded, not enough food or medical care. What really stuck in my craw and made me absolutely sick to my stomach, was a small, pathetic, sad-eyed girl at Sanatorio del Ruiso."

"Tell me about her," Brian said, his voice filled with sleep.

"She's tiny, just skin and bones. Caked on dirt, sores on her face and big brown eyes that reached out and grabbed my heart and won't let go," Lana lamented.

"Why?" Brian, tried to be patient.

"She looked so alone, sitting on a log slowly dragging one bare foot through the dirt, raising it up and letting the dirt filter through her toes and back to earth, with a sad faraway look on her face. Her clothes were dirty and too large; she had no shoes–just bare feet to walk on that hot dirt."

"Paraguay is a poor country. Why has this one little girl torn at you?"

"She's an individual; she's not one of the masses I see down at Chaco Land. She looked forlorn and desperate," Lana said.

"Did you talk to her?" Brian showed more concern as he realized the hold this little girl had on Lana.

"No, but she got up from the log and followed us as we toured the facility. That place is so barren! There isn't a blade of grass in the yard. It houses lepers, tuberculosis patients and orphans. I had no idea humans lived like that. The facility is shameful."

Brian slipped his arm under Lana's neck, stroked her hair and said, "Lana, you've lived a rich and abundant life. Of course this shocks you."

"That little girl is human. She's begging to be loved, to belong and have someone care." Lana could not get the vision of this sad-eyed little one to fade from before her.

Lana thought about her plentiful life. She had been born with the proverbial silver spoon and raised in the lap of luxury. She could not imagine sick people existing in such filth and hunger. Even here in Asunción, Paraguay, where she and Brian now lived.

Brian turned over and soon started to purr. Lana gave up talking.

As she lay there sleepless, tortured and distraught, she shifted gears in her thinking. She remembered what Brian had told her of the phone conversation with Washington which had brought about this great change in the Carter's life. It was the one that meant Brian, Lana and their son Patrick, would be moving to South America. Her husband, a nuclear physicist involved in research in Maryland, had a call from Todd Martin of the State Department, in Washington D.C.. Telling him how impressed he was with Brian's scientific knowledge and his leadership ability shown when they toured Nuclear Defense Lab a couple of weeks prior to that. Then he asked if the Carters would be interested in a diplomatic assignment for a few years.

Brian found out he could take his family. The most important assignment to be filled right then was in Asunción, Paraguay.

The Carters met with Todd Martin the following Tuesday in Washington D. C., as he explained more details about Paraguay and what would be expected of them.

Fear had gripped Lana as she thought about the drastic change this would be in her life. Strange country, strange customs and so far from her precious parents. Lana also imagined the new life would present many wonderful opportunities to meet interesting people. That was exciting. She loved people. Her emotions were so mixed. She wondered how Patrick would adjust to this strange new country. She Remembered Brian's conversation with Patrick, their seven year old son, about the move. "Patrick it would be to a country that is poor. The people will speak a different language. The customs are different. How would you feel about adjusting to a completely different life for a couple of years?"

Patrick had asked good questions about the change. He had asked if there would be some people that spoke English, what would the schools be like, would they live in a hotel or have a house? Then added, "I think it would be interesting, Dad. But I'll sure miss my friends."

Brian added, "I've heard you can have your own horse in Asunción."

"Wow! That would be awesome."

Lana was glad that Brian had not used this as a bribe to sway Patrick's thoughts, but as icing on the cake after Patrick had agreed to the change.

Brian said he thought a complete change from research on nuclear weapons to a diplomatic assignment would be fascinating.

These memories relieved Lana from thinking about Sad-Eyes and allowed her to drift off to sleep.

Chapter Two

Next morning Lana Carter was waiting for Franco, their handsome gardener who doubled as a chauffeur, to pull into the circular driveway in front of the house. He was to take her to a board of directors meeting.

Lana was surprised at the charisma Franco exhibited, being a gardener. Where did he learn this charm that was so much a part of his personality when he tended bar for their parties? It was necessary for someone knowledgeable to tend bar as Lana did not drink and could not train someone to mix drinks: she didn't have a clue how.

Franco was very valuable to the Carters. He wore several hats: this morning he would return home and take Patrick for swimming lessons at the American club.

Lana was dressed to impress even the elite of Asunción, in her beige silk suit, pink blouse and brown shoes with matching handbag and gloves. Her short blond hair was smartly styled. She always had a pleasant countenance that helped people feel at ease.

She thought back to life in Maryland, USA and the day she had received the call from Brian inviting her to go to Washington. She recalled the conversation and the feelings of excitement mixed with fear. She agreed to go and find out more about the assignment and what was involved. Lana didn't welcome a giant change in her steady, organized life. Her life now was rewarding and she was quite content. She had heard if you're comfortable with your life, you're not growing. Maybe she needed new challenges. Also this might be a growth opportunity for Patrick, having to adjust to new surroundings and customs. She hoped it would not be too big a change and cause problems. His welfare was very important to her.

Franco stopped the car in front of Lana. He jumped out and opened the door helping Lana into the car. As she rode along her thoughts returned to that day in Washington that set the stage for her life now.

Brian and Lana met with Todd Martin and a couple of other State Department people as Todd explained, "We have a request from President Stroessner to have a top notch scientist come and oversee installation of a research unit at the University in Asunción."

"Paraguay is one of the land locked countries of South America isn't it?" Brian asked.

"Yes. They are a little behind the rest of the world in many aspects of their achievements and trying to catch up."

"What would my responsibilities be?"

"You will work for President Stroessner setting up and staffing a research unit at the University and assist in getting some worthwhile research started. You will be attached to the Embassy. You will have an office there with an assistant and secretary. You'll have access to the Embassy pouch, commissary and a chauffeured Embassy staff car will be assigned to you. You will be paid by both governments."

"Why?" Brian wondered what would entitle him to pay from US government if he was to work directly for President Stroessner.

"You will be expected to do some undercover work for us."

"Intelligence work?"

"Yes. You have been cleared for top secret for your research at Nuclear Defense Lab so the FBI won't have a problem clearing you for work with the State Department. We will expect you to inform us on aspects of the Paraguayan government happenings, also what is happening in the rebels camp. We understand there is still much unrest and that the former government is trying to regain power. Being part of the Embassy crowd you will have access to power people and information valuable to us. This information will be dispatched in the Embassy pouch, which is sealed when it leaves the Embassy and is sent by air. Available also is a ham radio station where things come immediately in code."

"Is it dangerous work involving situations you read about in spy novels? Putting me and my family's life in danger?"

"No, this is more information gathering and passing it along. However if for any reason the situation does get sticky, you will have a code to send us and we will evacuate you immediately. We care about you and your family."

"What do you think, Lana?" Brian asked.

"I'm baffled. So much thrown at us–so sudden. What are the schools like in Paraguay? We have a son in grade school." Lana was not only confused, she was fearful of the new life's impact on her and on Patrick. He needed good schools and friends in this formative part of life. The Carter family was very close and did many things together, like golfing, movies, etc. She didn't want this stability to be torn apart with too many social demands.

"There is an Embassy school for all Americans. Some of the children of the elite Paraguayans also attend the school," Todd answered.

Lana wondered if there was a church for her to attend in this Catholic country. "Is there a Mormon group meeting there? I don't want to miss an extended length of religious training for Patrick, or myself," Lana inquired.

"I don't know but I'll find out," Todd replied.

"When do you need an answer?" Brian asked.

"Today if possible," Todd answered.

"How long is this assignment?" Lana asked.

"Two and a half years. Join me for lunch and you can ask further questions."

"That sounds good to me," Brian agreed.

After lunch Brian requested, "This is a big decision, let us sleep on it and discuss the situation with Patrick, our son. He is an important part of our decision. We'd like to have a twenty-four hour think session before rejecting or accepting."

"That's agreeable. I'll expect a call from you tomorrow afternoon. You still have my private phone number?"

"Yes. I'll call around three," Brian promised.

"If you accept, we'll start your paper work. Clearance takes several weeks even when we put rush on our request."

"You mentioned diplomatic passports. Do you prepare those?" Brian asked.

"We'll take care of all the paperwork after you fill out the tons of forms we give you," Todd agreed.

"When would our assignment begin?" Brian asked.

"Soon after the holidays. Could you manage that?" Todd replied.

"Let's discuss it tomorrow," Brian said.

Todd reported that there was a Mormon church in Asunción. Two in fact. One on each side of the capital city. The Carters accepted the assignment and the wheels of preparation rolled forth for departure. They were given an extensive list of things to bring that would make living easier; items that were difficult to get or were not available in Asunción. They were also asked to send money to stock their bar. Liquor was ordered from Europe by the case and that took time. Part of the assignment was to entertain and attend official functions.

Excitement mounted as the time grew near. Lana shopped for new formals to wear on the Luxury Liner going to South America and the many social functions they would be expected to attend in Asunción.

Lana's thoughts returned to the present. Being here for nearly two years now still seemed like a dream. Life in Asunción was interesting and in many ways rewarding, but so different. It had been an education for sure.

It was difficult to realize customs from one country to the other could differ so much.

Franco stopped the car, jumped out and opened the door for Lana and asked, "What time should I return?"

Chapter Three

Brian, dressed in his usual business attire of suit and tie, was sitting at his desk in his office at the Embassy and had a minute to relax. He thought back to 1956 in America when Todd Martin, from the State Department, called to report, "Your clearance is nearly ready. I didn't expect a problem."

"Good. What's the next challenge in getting out of here in less than six weeks?" Brian asked. He was getting excited about the new life style ahead.

"I don't anticipate any delays. Everything is falling into place even better than we expected," Todd assured Brian.

"The house is sold and we have our shopping completed." Brian said.

"I don't think I mentioned it before, but I was impressed with your wife. She will fit the mold of what we like for diplomatic wives. She is very attractive, but more than that, she is articulate, smartly dressed and has that well-bred attitude of confidence that is not stuffy."

"Yes, Lana is used to the political role. She is the daughter of Will Brahns, the senator," Brian responded.

"I discovered that as we did her background search. She will be a definite plus to you and to the Embassy."

"Her mother is quite a social lady. I think Lana inherited a lot of her flair for entertaining."

"That will come in handy as you entertain."

Brian realized in many ways Lana had adjusted to Asunción better than he had. This partying, playing golf, socializing so much of the time was interesting, but not as satisfying as his research where he could measure results and progress back at NDL. The research lab at the university was progressing slowly and no one seemed in a hurry to speed things up. The Latin American way, mañana-mañana.

Brian was pleased that Lana bonded with different groups, striving to make life better for the less fortunate. She had changed dramatically living here.

A real person had emerged, a person with depth of character. It was probably always there but not as visible as now.

Lana kept Patrick's welfare her number one priority. She scheduled activities with him to learn more about the country they lived in and to have fun together. Patrick enjoyed going on exploring trips into the countryside and downtown Asunción. Brian appreciated her efforts.

Brian was proud of the leadership Lana exhibited in her board positions at many of the clubs. The American Embassy Wives Club, the Centanario Country Club and the American Club board of directors. Lana was amazing.

Asunción Paraguay, 1959

Lana and her dearest friend, Caroline, were on their way to the Embassy Wives Club board meeting. Caroline was driving her Chrysler and chatting as usual in her adorable Texas drawl, stated, "Life in South America is fascinating."

"Fascinating, but also challenging at times. What's your biggest frustration here in Asunción?" Lana asked.

"Power outages."

"Yes, that's crazy, Caroline. Have you adjusted to the demanding social agenda?"

"Almost, I had a difficult time when we first arrived. Two socials in one evening at times was a bit much."

"The Embassy schedule commands most of our social life. I would like more freedom to enjoy close friends," Lana lamented.

"I resented the many official functions in the beginning. However, the Ambassadors and their wives are very gracious, informed, interesting and loads of fun. They're great. I love getting to know them and their countries better."

"I think my objection is the idea of being controlled," Lana responded.

"Agreed. I love the informal partying after command performances."

"Me too I like to communicate in English. Brian makes fun of my Spanish. When I dreamed in Spanish, I felt I had finally come to grips with my problem. But I still struggle with conjugations. My vocabulary is extensive, but I often slaughter verbs," Lana shared.

Fiery, energetic, attractive, Caroline Arnold and Lana Carter were inseparable. When the Arnolds relocated to Paraguay, the Carters were assigned to be their sponsors. Their responsibility was to help Arnolds get acquainted with people and places. Soon their friendship grew to an intimate family-like togetherness.

Caroline and Lana shared most everything. Their age difference was not a problem. The Arnolds were ten years older and didn't have children, but they adored nine year old Patrick and made a big fuss over him. Patrick reveled in their attention and was soon calling them Aunt Caroline and Uncle Bernie, at their insistence. It helped to have a near and dear adopted family when so far from biological family. Lana realized Caroline was the sister she never had. The one you share with, love and adore.

After raising money for charity, the committee chairperson and another selected member of the committee researched the community to determine where the funds should be spent. This year Lana chaired and selected Caroline to accompany her.

As they approached Sanitario del Rioso they found a barren spot of earth with no green vegetation, dilapidated buildings, in the middle of lush tropical Asunción. It looked completely out of place. It reeked of sadness and desperation. There wasn't a smile on a single face.

"Have you ever seen such a depressing place, Caroline?"

"It's difficult to imagine the sick survive in this forsaken facility," Caroline stated as they walked to the office to meet their guide.

"A little grass in the yard and paint on the building would improve the Sanitario's image." Lana said.

"Hanging the dangling shutters would help," Caroline agreed.

"No wonder the patients looks so forlorn. It's depressing." Lana observed as she looked around at the sad helpless look on the people's faces.

They walked in silence for a few minutes.

"Do you see our companion behind?" Lana asked.

"Yes, she has followed us since we arrived."

"What a pathetic little creature." Lana was captivated by her countenance.

Her eyes were big, round and piercing brown. Her little face was dominated by the eyes and by ugly sores on one side that testified to unhealthy surroundings. Long, filthy, matted dark hair hung in tangles to frame her face.

When she looked at Lana, all else faded and she captured Lana's whole attention. The child brushed the dirty hair away from her eyes, tucking it behind her left ear, revealing more sores at the side of her forehead.

Señorita Florentina was their designated guide. She was also the Social worker and manager of the facility. She greeted them graciously as they entered the office and gave them some background of the Sanitario. Next was a tour of the facility to see the needs first hand and evaluate what might be accomplished to make life easier for the residents.

As they toured, Sad-Eyes followed them step by step throughout the Sanitario. Her dirty bare feet paddled along on the hot earth, without complaint. Her dress was way too large, dirty and torn. Her facial expressions sad.

Florentina explained,"This is the sleeping area. The dining room is the next building."

"You can smell they had stew for lunch," Lana said.

"No air-conditioning in the building?" asked Caroline.

"Most of us do not have the luxury of air-conditioned homes. This is a poor facility. Our funds only buy the essentials," Florentina stated.

"Who pays for food?" inquired Lana.

"The government. It's scanty payment. Not enough to feed as we would like," Florentina responded. She seemed to want better for her patients.

The group left the interior of the building and went to the rear where they stopped to look at the lean-to shack the residents used for showers and toilet facilities.

The males and females use the same bathroom, they were told. Lana gasped at the thought of ever being desperate enough to go to this forsaken area to cleanse or go to the bathroom.

She understood why the little girl was so grimy and why body odor permeated the building.

They paused before starting back to the front.

Lana walked back and extended a hand to the frail girl, who shyly put her dirty little hand in Lana's. "¿Como te llamas?" asked Lana. (What's your name?)

There was a faint glimmer of appreciation in her sad eyes for the attention, but no words. No smile. A little of the dullness of the eyes vanished for a moment.

Long enough to let Lana see a person inside the facade. With her free hand the little girl pulled her hair out of her eyes and tucked it behind the left ear.

Lana let go of the little girl's hand and rejoined the group, "Señorita Florentina, do you know anything about this child?"

"She's an orphan. We're trying to find a home for her."

"Does she speak Spanish?" Lana asked, knowing many country people spoke only Guarani.

"Yes, some. She's from the country and they speak more of the Indian dialect, known as Guarani," Florentina said.

"I realized that and when she didn't answer me I thought she might not understand my Spanish," Lana replied.

Turning to the girl Florentina instructed the child in Spanish to leave them alone. Lana interceded.

"Please let her follow."

Lana wondered about the girl. What had Florentina not told them? Why would a small child, probably three years old, be in this Sanitario that housed lepers and tuberculosis patients? Then Lana remembered it also cared for orphans. How sad. What a forlorn place for a child to live. It was depressing to visit, it would be horrible to live in.

They continued their tour with Sad-Eyes following.

Funds were limited. The Embassy Wives Club could select one facility and then do only part of the job needed. If they accomplished their task at this Sanitario, in a first class way, this facility would have to be torn down, a larger one built, staffed with more people, the yard landscaped and better medical help provided.

The E W C contribution would be no more than a band-aid.

As they concluded their tour and were ready to leave, Sad-Eyes was standing at the curb. She waved her hand good-bye as Caroline and Lana drove away.

"Caroline, I can't get that little girl out of my mind. What a waste of a human life. Didn't she make your heart bleed?"

"Yes. So many people are deprived of basic needs here. I found early on I couldn't worry about them or I just about went berserk, so I try to shut my mind to the depravity unless I'm focused on doing something positive for them. Then

I do it with all my heart."

"Those sad searching eyes tell reams about her life. They shout her need for love. Did you see her tiny skinny legs and arms?" Lana asked.

"Yes, I couldn't miss them, they looked like toothpicks."

"How could any one be happy in that forsaken place?"

"If you let it eat at you, Lana, it can destroy you. You can't fix the whole country at once. That's why we take one project at a time and try to fix something."

As Caroline got out of the car, Lana called, "See you in the morning at the board meeting."

The Arnolds and Carters talked together, played bridge together, golfed and celebrated holidays together. They seemed to be of one cloth woven tightly into a friendly family type tapestry. Lana tried to take to heart what Caroline had said about not letting people in sad situations dominate her life here in Asunción, but that little girl's pleading eyes continued to haunt her. Lana wanted to get pregnant and have more children. She couldn't now; surgery had robbed her of that option. Why did the Lord give children to parents that couldn't take care of them–then deprive others of the joy of giving birth and nurturing a loved child? Why put children in such dire conditions that they didn't even have enough to eat? Her heart ached for the sad-eyed little girl. Lana so desired another child of her own to be sister or brother to Patrick. Unfortunately endometriosis had robbed her of that opportunity. The doctor called Patrick their miracle child and thank heavens for him. He was such a blessing to them. He was handsome, intelligent, a great sense of humor and a leader from day one. When Lana started hemorrhaging often, the doctor. advised a hysterectomy and that demolished their dreams of another pregnancy.

Lana looked at her relaxed husband, sprawled in his easy chair, looking like he didn't have a care in the world, with a lock of sandy hair falling on his forehead above his mischievous green eyes. She adored her beloved companion.

"Brian, the little girl in the Sanitario is on my mind constantly," Lana stated as she reviewed in her mind the sad eyed little one that looked so starved for attention and for food.

"We're Americans. We're used to better lives."

"Here some are blessed; others have absolutely nothing. Look at Estelle and Ruby, our neighbors. They have big cars, servants, lovely homes, a summer cottage at the lake and live the abundant life. This sad little girl was starved. She obviously doesn't even have enough to eat. It's terrible."

"Lana, this is not America," Brian stated as he dismissed the conversation.

After trying unsuccessfully to talk about Sad-Eyes, Lana went to bed. She tossed and turned trying to sleep. Sad-Eyes surely had a grandparent, an uncle or aunt, someone willing to care for her and take her out of that desolate place.

No sleep came, so Lana got up, slipped on her blue silk robe and paced the floor. Still restless, Lana stepped into her silk slippers and walked out onto the brick deck by the pool. She looked over the estate they had leased in Asunción for two and half years. The home was lovely with crystal chandeliers in every room except the kitchen and had marble floors and fireplace. The three acre grounds were immaculate–thanks to Franco, the gardener. The tropical flowers were colorful and the fruit trees were shady all year and offered beautiful blossoms in the spring and fruit later. The servants and Patrick loved picking and eating the fruit right off the tree.

Lana walked around the pool, then settled into a chair.

She again envisioned the stark deprivation of the Sanitario and contrasted it to the grand home where she had grown up. It was a wonderful estate in Phoenix, Arizona, complete with a heated pool, six bedrooms, five bathrooms, two family rooms each with fireplaces, library, formal living room and dining room, spacious kitchen, offices for each of her parents and servants to care for their every need. The servants' housing was in the rear of the property over the garage. Lana realized she had lived the charmed life during her growing years. Not many of Lana's friends had such a luxurious life even in the United States. However, they did have heaps more than this poor little sad-eyed girl. Lana's friends had nice homes, clothes, cars and opportunities. That was the lacking ingredient in this little girl's life...no opportunity. Where could she go from the Sanitario if she survived? School? Doubtful. Marriage, family and a nice home. Not likely.

The moon was bright and Lana could see someone coming from the servants' quarters in back.

As their maid, Maria, approached, Lana saw the concern on her face relax as she recognized Lana. "Señora, you're worried., What matters?"

"I couldn't sleep. Sometimes the fresh air clears my mind," Lana said.

"Would talking help?" Maria asked.

"Maybe. I saw a tiny girl in the orphanage today. She looked so defeated."

"Many, many, poor people in Paraguay, Señora. You a big help to my family and me. Many times my mother wouldn't eat if you no help us."

"You're a great help to us, Maria. Without you to manage our home, we would sink, not swim. With you, things are smooth and calm. We appreciate you. Thanks."

"De nada. Is the little girl sick?"

"I don't know. All I know is she's an orphan and very dirty, very sad and hungry."

Maria cleaned the main house each morning. Then she went to the kitchen in the servants' quarters to fix lunch for the servants. This was her obligation as Marcelena, the cook, was busy in the main house preparing food for the Carters.

Maria remembered she forgot to put clean towels in the master bath after cleaning. She returned to the main house. As she entered the master bedroom she found Franco rifling through some papers on Señor Carter's desk.

Franco jumped when he realized Maria had caught him snooping.

"What you doing, Franco?"

"None of your business," Franco answered with malice in his voice.

"Franco, why speak to me so bad? We're friends."

"If we're friends, por favor, don't tell señor. It's very important, but I can't tell you why."

"If señor asks, I no lie."

"He won't ask. Please don't mention this. Please, Maria."

Maria knew Franco was a valued servant as he filled many needs for the Carters. She didn't want to be the reason for his dismissal. His snooping split her loyalties. For now she decided she would play the waiting game.

The servants worked together and lived together. They were family for each other.

Marcelena, the cook, had worked for other Americans and had knowledge of American preferences. She was older and often played matriarch.

Maria, the maid, was new to American households, but eager to learn the ways of the Carters. She was dependable and had a great sense of humor. She was happy to accommodate.

Juana, the nanny, was energetic, enthusiastic and Lana thought she would be a great influence on Patrick.

In the United States Lana had a cleaning lady once a week and extra help for parties. Now she had servants to serve her every need. She could play golf when she liked. The nanny would be there to care for Patrick and the cook would have dinner ready when she returned home. Maria would be sure the house was clean. Lana's time now was divided between social events like luncheons, parties and bridge, or serving on the board of directors for different clubs, or committees at the Embassy Wives Club and enjoying her son. She loved it all. Her schedule was crowded, actually on overload much of the time.

Lana thought life in Asunción was rewarding as she had many opportunities to help some of the poor better their station in life. That was one of her successes, although having fun activities with Patrick was her very favorite part of life. Being a mother was exactly as her father had promised. Children are indeed the best investment in life. Watching Patrick grow and respond to exciting opportunities was her greatest joy. She loved his companionship.

The board of directors of the Wives Club reviewed the many facilities Lana and Caroline had researched.

They unanimously voted that the Sanitario del Rioso should have two bathrooms: one for men and one for women, with hot water, showers (each with a seat for residents who couldn't stand to shower), toilets and basins for their residents. They would no longer have to use a bucket to clean themselves. E W C would buy more beds for the sleeping area, get shutters repaired and hung, plus some landscaping and a paint job.

Lana was anxious to convey their commitment to Florentina. She called and made an appointment to go to the Sanitario.

There was Sad-Eyes, sitting on the same old log in the bare dirt yard, kicking one foot in the air after dragging it through the dirt wearing the same dirty, too large torn dress.

Lana thought she detected a slight lift of spirit as their eyes met. Sad-Eyes stood up and followed Lana as she went to the main administration building where Florentina's office was located. When Lana looked back before entering the building, she saw the little girl brush her filthy hair out of her eyes and tuck it behind her left ear.

Señorita Florentina was sitting behind her sparse desk in her cool cotton two piece navy blue dress, her hair pulled back into a neat knot at the back of her head. She looked prim and proper waiting for Lana's news.

"Señorita Florentina, we have decided to build two bathrooms one for men and one women, buy some more beds and get some repairs done, such as shutters hung, do some landscaping and a paint job if funds permit."

"All of that?"

"We wish we could do more. For now that is all the funds we have."

"When?" Señorita asked excitedly knowing what a difference it would make for the residents. She felt it would raise their spirits to have better living conditions. Señorita was frustrated with their limited funds at the Sanitario. She wanted better for her patients. This was great news.

"As soon as we can find contractors to do the work. We will get several bids. We'll check the Embassy's list of approved contractors."

"I could help with some suggestions."

"Please do," Lana agreed. Local knowledge about who to use would be valuable. Maybe Señorita Florentina could get more accomplished for their dollars than the Americans could.

"The residents will be thrilled with the club's generosity."

When Lana came out of the building to leave, accompanied by Florentina, Sad-Eyes was sitting on the warm cement near the portico. She got up to follow Lana to the car. Lana wanted to know more.

"Señorita Florentina, please tell me about this little girl."

"There is not much to tell. Her name is Tanya. She has one older sister and three older brothers. Two of the older brothers live down in Chaco-land and one sister and brother are here in the orphanage with Tanya. Both of her parents are dead. The older brothers built a shack out of salvaged material in the free land by the river, Chaco-land. They come visit sometimes. The boys have no money to support the younger children so the government is providing shelter for them here."

"How long have they lived here?"

"Nearly a year. Hopefully we'll locate a family willing to care for them. This is most difficult and not promising. As you know, Paraguay is a caste system country and the poor can't support each other. The rich don't want to mix their blue blood with the poor. It's sad."

"What was this girl's family like?"

"Her brother Juan, who lives here, is nine years old. The sister, Ignacia, is nearly seven years old and Tanya is nearly five years old."

"She's so tiny, I would have guessed three at most."

"She has not had proper nourishment so she is small."

"Isn't Tanya an unusual name for a Paraguayan?" Lana asked.

"Tanya's father was European and her mother was Paraguayan."

"Have good people applied to take her?"

"Not yet," Florentina answered.

"What happened to her parents?"

"Her father was killed by an unfortunate accident. Then her mother became very ill and died a year and a half later.

After returning home Lana kept thinking about Tanya. Again she walked out to the pool trying to clear her head. Life did not seem fair. What would Tanya's life be like in five years, if she lived that long? Lana couldn't bear to think of a tiny helpless child not having enough to eat.

Lana returned to the house and called Brian. "What would you think of bringing Tanya to our home for the weekend so we could clean her up and take her to the doctor?"

"Who? What?"

"The little girl I told you about last evening. She has the saddest eyes you have ever seen and sores on her face that need care."

"What kind of care?"

"She needs to see a doctor. She needs some loving attention. She needs a good meal. One to fill her small pot belly. Brian she is so pathetic, sitting on that log, staring into space and looking lost."

"Lana, you can't walk in and say I'm taking her home for the week end."

"Maybe not. But please let me call and see if it's possible. All they can do is say no," Lana said.

"Do you have any idea what the sores are?"

"That's part of what I need to find out."

"You are so impulsive sometimes. What if you bring some disease into our home?" Brian asked. "You said she was in the Sanitario with lepers."

"I can take her to the doctor on the way home. I've thought about this. If it is leprosy or such, I'll return her to the Sanitario immediately."

"I don't know. It sounds risky to me."

"Please let me at least try to get some help for her. You'll love her, Brian, I know you will. Someone has to care about her. She is just a throw away where she is."

"If you have your heart set on it, go ahead and see what you can find out. I know you won't let this rest until something is done."

"Thanks."

Lana was relieved that Brian agreed, even though hesitantly. She had to find out what the child needed and Dr. MacClanahan could help identify her problems.

Lana called Señorita Florentina, the stately social worker who seemed to be the boss at the Sanitarium.

"How can I make arrangements to bring Tanya home for the weekend? I'd like to have our doctor check those sores."

"It could be arranged if you like. We permit home visits."

"Yes! We would love it."

"How soon would you pick her up?"

"Thirty minutes."

"Very good, I'll get the paperwork started," Florentina promised.

When Lana arrived, Florentina told her the rules for home visits. Then she told her, "Tanya's parents came from a small village about thirty-five kilometers west of Asunción. Some of the neighbors wanted to help the family but couldn't accommodate all five. They, too, were very poor."

Lana agreed, "In Paraguay it seems you either have lots of money or almost none."

“Tanya's family and her neighbors barely survived.”

“How sad.”

"After Tanya's father was killed, things got even worse. The mother did the best she could but her health was failing," Señorita Florentina said.

"What caused her illness?"

"Tuberculosis. She suffered terribly."

"Who cared for the family?"

"The older boys tried. They worked picking up some day work around the golf club doing odd jobs; one even caddied occasionally."

"I admire their spunk in getting along. What a challenge to be left without parents and three siblings needing care. They must be very mature for their age."

"One of the neighbors wanted to take Tanya–she is adorable. But they couldn't take more of the family to keep them together. When the husband lost his meager job of gardening, they had to give up Tanya, too," Señorita Florentina lamented.

"Poor little soul. How devastating." Lana had a difficult time imagining the dire circumstances that surrounded this tiny bundle of humanity.

"Your paperwork is complete, Señora Carter. If you have any questions during the weekend please call."

Florentina explained to Tanya in Spanish, "Señora Carter is taking you to her home for the week-end. Have a fun time and we will see you on Monday by five in the afternoon.

Lana reached for Tanya’s hand. Tanya hesitated, then accepted and they walked to the car. Lana thought they might have to clean and disinfect the upholstery after Tanya spread germs from the sores.

As they rode along, Lana could soon see the emerging of a new human being. Lana tried to converse with her, “Tell me about your family.” Tanya didn't answer. “Do you like learning new things?” No reply.

Tanya didn’t speak a word but her countenance changed. Life could be seen behind those big brown eyes.

Lana decided to go directly to Dr. MacClanahan's office to check on the sores. She didn't want to take leprosy into their home.

Dr. MacClanahan checked the sores, took some samples for the pathologist, then assured Lana, "I feel certain the sores are not leprosy. I'll give you some medication that will help clear up the infection."

When Lana arrived home, Patrick, who was very tall for nine, asked a bunch of questions. Patrick was a handsome lad with curly red hair and deep blue eyes fringed with long lashes. He was naturally very curious and Lana had forgotten to tell him where she was going. Or why. Showing up with a dirty urchin of a child blew his mind.

"Who is that?" he asked scrunching his face in disbelief.

"A girl from the orphanage who needs care. Her name is Tanya and she is visiting us for the weekend."

He stared at her, giving Tanya the once over from filthy head to filthier feet. He couldn't believe his mother would bring home such a disgraceful human. Why?

"She's really dirty. You're not going to take her into our house are you?" Patrick asked.

"Yes. A good shower or bath will fix the dirt."

"But Mom, our home is clean. Maria will have a fit if you take her in and leave mud streaks."

"That's where the bathroom is, Patrick. That is where I can clean her."

"You could take her out to the servants' quarters and have her shower in their bathroom."

"She's our guest, not theirs," Lana replied.

"She doesn't look like other guests we've had. She's a mess."

"Wait to judge her, Patrick. I think a shower will do wonders."

"Does she speak English?" Patrick asked.

"No, but she does speak Spanish."

After the initial shock wore off, Patrick shrugged and decided to put it on hold. He walked away wondering who this filthy girl was and why his mother had dragged her into their clean home. For what purpose? Was she going to be made a part of the Carter family? His mother had said for the weekend, then what? Would she be returned to the orphanage?

Lana took Tanya by the hand and led her into the house. They went to the master suite bath. She undressed Tanya. Lana shuddered as she saw the frail frame of skin and bones. You could tell she had not been eating right; she had the little pot-belly that goes with starvation. Lana's heart went out to her; she looked so frightened. Lana wanted to hold her close and assure her things would be better.

Caked on spilled food and layers of grime covered the girl. Heaven only knows when she last had a shower. After having seen their shower facilities at the orphanage it was no wonder. Mud was caked between her tiny toes. Her right arm had a streak of clean, where water or juice had run down to her elbow. Her hair was tangled and matted. Lana wondered how many shampoos it would take to dissolve that messy mass in water.

Lana turned on the shower. Tanya's eyes opened wide, she was scared of the shower. She looked at Lana as if asking if it was safe. She backed up and Lana could see her fear, then tears. "Esta bien." Lana assured her. Lana reached out to take Tanya's hand.

Tanya pulled her hand out of reach, putting it behind her and backed up. She looked terrified.

Lana again reached out taking her hand and pulled her toward the running water. Tanya yanked her hand away and started screaming.

Lana tried to put her arms around Tanya to assure her, but Tanya pulled away and kept screaming.

Tanya backed further away, determined not to be touched and not to enter the shower.

Lana called for Maria to help.

Maria spoke to Tanya in Guarani, the country language. Lana watched as Tanya's face relaxed a bit and the terror in her eyes subsided some.

Lana took one of Tanya's hands and Maria the other, Tanya was stiff with tension, but entered the shower, scrunching her face as the warm water pelted her body.

That was Tanya's first experience of a warm water shower. She told Lana later, they had bathed with a bucket of water at their little shack in the country. There was only cold water from a bucket in the facilities at the Sanitario. Very cold in the winter, Tanya added.

Although Asunción is in the tropics, it does get very chilly in the winter months of June, July and August.

As the dirt dissolved, the brownish water ran off and down the drain.

Lana soaped Tanya and then rinsed. Tanya started to relax and enjoy it. Her skin became lighter and lighter. Soon it revealed a sweet little girl with olive skin, big brown eyes and long, almost black hair that had to be shampooed three times.

Tanya emerged squeaky clean and smelling fresh. Lana wrapped her in a huge towel and dried her hair before taking a comb to the natural curls she saw emerging. Tanya was lovely.

Lana couldn't bear to put those awful clothes back on her. Even when laundered they would not be acceptable.

Lana was frustrated. There were no department stores here to buy ready made clothes for this little one. In Asunción Paraguay in the 1950's you had to buy material for the modesta to make dresses, shorts and outer clothing. Stores did have underwear and shoes.

Lana couldn't wait. Tanya needed clothes now.

Patty, Lana's dear friend, had a daughter a little larger than Tanya.

She called Patty and explained the problem. Was there any possibility that Patty could lend Lana a few items of clothing that Barbara had outgrown?

Patty soon arrived with a bundle, "I have several outfits. I hope some of them fit your little one. They are not on loan. You may have them, They're too small for Barbara."

"You're wonderful Patty. Thanks."

"Thought you could use some sandals and underwear. I also threw in a swim suit. I know how you love the pool."

"I don't think Tanya swims. But maybe we can teach her. You're a life saver, Patty."

Lana hurriedly dressed Tanya in a cute red outfit and took her to the mirror on the closet door and said, "¡Muy linda!" (very pretty). Lana won her first real smile from Tanya. The sad eyes softened and Lana felt triumphant. Lana held out her arms to Tanya, but she declined and looked away.

Even though Tanya refused Lana's arms for abrazos (hugs) she did take her hand and they went in search of Patty and Barbara; Lana was anxious to introduce Tanya to her friends.

Tanya hung back, behind Lana. She was frightened of the strangers, but gave a half-hearted little grin in acknowledgment that she was being presented.

Patty, with her infectious personality, extended her hand to Tanya, saying, "Welcome. We're happy to have you with us" in Spanish.

Tanya grinned slightly , refused Patty's hand and slipped behind Lana.

Turning to Patty's daughter, Lana said, "Barbara, why don't you take Tanya and help her check out the play area in the back? I don't know if she has played on slides or swings so be careful. She may be frightened."

Barbara held out her hand. Tanya held Lana's hand like they were glued together. She would not budge from Lana's side or let go of her hand. Lana explained in Spanish, "Barbara wants to show you how to swing."

Tanya shook her head emphatically and held onto Lana's hand.

Lana could sense how terrified Tanya was of all these new activities.

"Why don't we all sit and visit. I guess Tanya needs time to get to know you. Thanks for trying. Patrick is in back with his dog if you want to join him, Barbara."

"Is this Tanya thing for keeps?" asked Patty.

"It's only a weekend stay," Lana answered.

After the Rogers left, Lana took Tanya to meet the servants. Gathered in the kitchen, they were chattering away in Guarani.

Marcelena, the cook, said, "Good to have you with us, Tanya."

Franco, the gardener, offered, "I help Patrick and would like to assist you. There are swings and slides in back. May I show them to you?"

"No. Gracias."

Maria said, "Let me know if you need something, Tanya."

Juana, the nanny, stared at the visitor in open curiosity and said, as she smiled, "I'll be caring for you."

Lana explained Tanya was there to visit for the weekend.

That was Friday afternoon.

Patrick and Lana had a wonderful time taking Tanya pool side and introducing her to splashing in water and having fun. Tanya was terrified of the water at first and it was difficult to persuade her to enter in the shallow part of the pool. Lana put her on a floater and pulled her from one side of the pool to the other. Patrick showed her how to splash the water to keep cool.

Brian joined them when he came from the office. They had Maria bring their dinner out to the deck by the pool. It was too nice to go inside. After eating and talking for some time they all, except Tanya, took a final dip. Then headed for the cabana to shower and dress.

After the children were tucked in, Brian and Lana sat quietly reading books for the evening. This was very unusual for a Friday night on embassy duty. Weekend parties were the norm. This was a marvelous reprieve and the Carters decided to take full advantage of it.

The Rogers had suggested a get together. The Arnolds had invited them to a small party, but the Carters had assured them they needed time with their family.

Lana put her book down, looked over at Brian sitting comfortably in his large club chair, with his feet on the ottoman, the usual lock of curly sandy hair falling onto his forehead. All six feet of his body, comfortable in lounging pajamas, stretched out relaxed as he read his science fiction book.

Brian felt Lana's stare and put his book down. He looked at her with his mischievous green eyes and asked, "You have something important on your mind?"

"Yes. Why don't we adopt Tanya and take her back to the States with us?"

"What? I thought this was for the weekend and to get medical help for her."

"To begin with it was. Brian, now I want to hold her close and assure her that her life will be better. I don't want to ever put her back in that awful orphanage."

"I don't know if adoption is a good idea."

"Why not?" Lana asked.

"We don't know anything about her background, what her family tree was like or what we'd be getting into."

"We don't know when we have a child what all we'll 'get into' as you put it. When they're family you deal with it."

"She doesn't resemble either one of us. You with your blond hair and blue eyes, me with sandy color hair and grey-green eyes. Tanya has dark eyes and black hair."

"That doesn't matter."

"I think Patrick would resent it. He's been the only child for nine years now."

"No, I don't think so. Have you watched him with Tanya? He's asked many times over the years why he doesn't have a brother or sister. I think he'd love Tanya. He might feel threatened at first. But I feel in the long run it would be a definite plus for all of us."

With a slight frown he admitted, "You may be right. You took me by surprise when you brought her home. Now you want to keep her. I've to get used to the idea. I don't honestly know how I feel."

"You know I can't have more children. Tanya needs a home–a home we can provide. I think it would be very rewarding and I'd like to do it. My heart reaches out to her. I feel a very special bond with her and I know she'd be a wonderful addition to our family. It would give her a chance at life."

"Let me sleep on it." Brian was not convinced that a permanent situation with Tanya was advisable. Lana often jumped before she thought. He didn't feel a special bond. Yes, Tanya was cute, but that wasn't enough to make her part of the family. He didn't like the idea, but decided to go slow and not rock the boat.

"At least let's look into it and see what's involved. Watch her over the weekend and see what you think. Search your heart for an answer that you'll feel good about ten years from now. Brian, I know we can't fix the whole country as Caroline puts it, but we can make a difference with one."

"I'll give it serious thought. But I need time."

Lana realized bringing an orphan from Paraguay would be a shock to her parents. The Brahns had not been too happy about Lana and her family coming to this "antiquated forsaken" country as they called it. The Britannica told about six short-termed dictators previous to President (General) Alfredo Stroessner who took power, two years previous to the Carter's arrival.

Brian and Lana thought it would be an adventurous change of pace for two and a half years, an education of different countries and cultures.

The move certainly had been a change and it had been adventurous. Lana recalled the first night in Asunción. The ambassador had given a "welcome to Paraguay" party for them. Ambassador Cassidy was exact on many rules to obey while in Paraguay. "You are not to wear curlers or shorts in public."

"No shorts even in this hot tropical heat?" Lana had inquired.

"Never. You are expected to have at least a cook, maid, gardener and nanny since you have a son."

"Our son is in school most of the day, I don't feel we need a nanny."

"It is the way of the natives, the image expected of the diplomatic corps. The system here is definitely caste and we are expected to live up to the standards of the upper social strata. Possibly you could have a nanny that served as a laundress also," Ambassador Cassidy advised.

"That sounds better. Where do we find a reliable staff of servants?" Lana asked.

"Usually the most dependable servants come from American families leaving," Ambassador Cassidy replied. "They have been trained in American customs, how to assist when entertaining and are honest."

"Do you have a list of Embassy personnel leaving in the next month?"

"Yes, I'll make that available to you. Another must, do not break the rules and laws of the country. I do not want to be notified that you were speeding or running stop signs. You will be shown the check stations. You are to strictly observe their demand to stop and show your embassy documents which you must carry at all times. The guards at these stations shoot to kill if you don't stop."

So many rules and so many people at the party made Lana's head swim. She was sure she wouldn't remember many of their names.

By the time the embassy limo had returned the Carters to the hotel, both Lana and Brian were deathly ill from the food they had eaten.

They didn't know which end to put down first. Diarrhea and vomiting vied for attention in the bathroom. What a way to start life in South America.

The Carters learned quickly many of the do not eat foods. Even at the Embassy cream was not pasteurized and many of the vegetables were not safe to eat until your stomach was used to the raw foods available. Most Americans spent a lot of time in the bathroom the first few weeks and referred to their dilemma as PT's or Paraguayan Trots.

CHAPTER FOUR

Lana watched Patrick with Tanya. He read to her and introduced her to his dog, Shadow.

She heard Patrick brag to one neighbor, "I have a new sister for the weekend." He had a positive feeling about Tanya now that she was clean and presentable.

Lana also watched Brian watch the children. Tanya came into breakfast on Saturday and her face registered pure delight as she looked over the food laden table. Brian showed her which chair at the table was hers. She was starting to feel more comfortable.

It was a thrill for Lana to watch Tanya's excitement knowing she could eat any of the food before her.

The night before Tanya had sat very erect in her chair with books stacked on it to make her high enough to reach the table. She had looked at the food on her plate and eaten very little. Lana thought Tanya's lack of appetite was probably the strange surroundings and different food than she was used to. She noticed Tanya ate mostly with her hands and a little with a spoon. Maria talked to her in Guarani and Tanya's countenance saddened and she stopped eating.

Lana noticed Tanya sneaked out to Maria later and was slipped a galleta (biscuit). Now she looked at the food as though she was starved.

After saying the blessing on the food, Lana filled Tanya's plate with some eggs, ham and biscuits. The juice was already poured.

Maria told her something in Guarani. Tanya took the fork and tried to eat. She didn't do too well; it turned sideways in her hand, food spilled and then she dropped the fork. Tanya was very frustrated and started to cry. She turned to Maria and complained in Guarani, "I've never used anything like this to eat with. I only had a spoon or my hands before."

Maria translated for them. Brian said in Spanish, "Eat how it is most comfortable for now. We will worry about using the proper utensils later." He then turned to Maria, "Get her a spoon please."

"Maybe that was why she ate so little last evening," Lana commented.

As soon as breakfast was finished Brian headed for the golf course and Tanya asked, in Spanish, "Could we go to the water again?"

"Why not? Get your swimming suits and we'll give the pool another work out. We do need to go shopping to get some shoes and underwear for you and your hair styled, but that can wait."

As the children prepared to go swimming, Lana called Estanalou, her favorite hair stylist. “This is Señora Carter. Could you possibly work in a small girl today and style her hair? She needs your professional touch.”

“I’m booked solid, sorry.”

“If you have a cancellation let me know.”

“Oh, I’ll work her in on my lunch break. Bring her in around eleven thirty.”

“Super, I’ll be there.”

Lana hurriedly put on her swim suit and joined Patrick and Tanya who were waiting impatiently on the back patio.

Tanya loved the floater in the pool after she got over being frightened. She would lay on it and bask in the warm sun. Patrick would splash some water on her as he swam by. She would squeal, then try to splash him.

Watching the two youngsters have fun together strengthened Lana's feelings of wanting to adopt her.

As the day progressed and Tanya felt more at home, she loosened up more. She skipped a bit, walked taller and smiled more often. Her response to loving care was exciting.

Early Sunday morning Brian made his way to Lana's dressing table where she was putting on her face for the day. Standing behind Lana he rested his hands on her shoulders, then massaged her neck. He bent down and kissed the top of her head.

"I think you have a good idea. Tanya does add a new dimension to our family. See what you can find out about adoption."

"Great! Fantastic!" Lana shouted as she jumped up and tossed her hair brush high and then caught it and threw her arms around Brian. Adoption it was. She knew with determination they could make it all work. They would have a larger, more wonderful Carter family.

Monday Lana had Tanya all to herself. They had a great time shopping and exploring downtown. They met Brian for lunch at Mikos.

"Very nice place," Tanya said. "I've not eaten in place like this. What can I have?"

"Anything. What do you want?" Brian responded.

"I don't know. It all looks strange," Tanya replied.

"They specialize in steaks and sizzled potatoes," Lana said.

"What's a steak?" Tanya asked.

"One of those," Lana said, as she nodded her head at the plate being served at the next table.

Another first for Tanya. Brian and Lana enjoyed the excitement of educating this child to a new lifestyle.

When the salad was served, Tanya ate it with a spoon. Then when the stake arrived, she picked it up with her hands. Lana explained that she would help cut it into pieces, then Tanya could eat the meat with spoon or fork.

At four in the afternoon Lana drove back to the orphanage with a shiny new Tanya, the medication, some new clothes, toys, new hair style and books.

Lana hated the thought of leaving her at the Sanitario and hoped she could fill out more papers and take Tanya back home while adoption was in the process.

Señorita Florentina looked in astonishment at the transformation of the girl that had left only three days earlier.

"Señorita Florentina, you mentioned you were looking for a

home for Tanya. We would like to be the family that makes a home for her. How do we go about adopting her?"

"For keeps?"Señorita Florentina asked.

"Yes. We want to take her back to North America. We want her to be part of our family."

"There is no adoption here in Paraguay at this time. You can obtain custody documents and then adopt her when you get back to the United States if all is in order. You do need an immigration certificate for her to enter the U.S.."

"Where do we get that? We're anxious to have her as a permanent part of our family. I can't have more children and we do want a larger family."

"You obtain the immigration certificate at the Embassy. I must ask you a few questions before giving custody documents. First of all, are you Catholic?" Señorita Florentina asked.

"No. Why?"

"Her mother's dying wish was that she be put with a good Catholic family and raised in her faith."

Lana's hopes smashed with the first question. Then her heart swelled with determination. Where there is a will, there is a way. Lana stood tall and asked, "Could we please talk to the board of directors and plead our case?"

"Certainly. They meet this Thursday. In the meantime Tanya must stay here."

Lana explained about the medication for her sores and turned to leave. Then she turned and went to Tanya and impulsively gave her a hug. Tanya slipped her arms around Lana's neck and squeezed. That was the memorable first hug from Tanya. She held tight, not wanting to let go. Lana held her at arm’s length and said, "I love you."

That hug strengthened Lana's determination and she left with tears in her eyes, vowing she would not leave Paraguay without Tanya.

Her heart was heavy as she was obligated to abandon Tanya in that awful place. Thinking of the toilet facilities she would have to use, the lonesomeness she would have to endure and the lack of food and care that would be her plight brought more tears to Lana's eyes. A big sob escaped, letting Lana realize how desperately she wanted to adopt Tanya. She would fight a good fight.

Lana slid behind the wheel of the car, tears flowing down her cheeks, she looked toward the curb as she put the car into gear. There stood Tanya with a questioning look, "Are you going to leave me here?"

Lana tried to smile and waved, then drove away, sobbing.

Brian and Lana were dressed professionally as they sat facing the board at the Sanitario to plead for the adoption of Tanya. Brian usually stripped off his tie the minute he came home, with a “that feels good” comment. Tonight he kept his business appearance, hoping it would help.

There were seven sober faces to contend with, three women and four men. All looking inquisitively at the Carters. Brian fidgeted a little in his seat under their scrutiny.

"Why do you want to adopt Tanya?" the man at the head of the long table asked.

"To be part of our family," Lana responded.

"Not to raise a live-in maid for your home?"

"Goodness no! To be our daughter and a sister for Patrick," Brian quickly answered.

"Tell me a little about yourselves," the lady to the right of the director suggested.

Brian said, "We are a strong family, comfortable financially and will provide love, family unity and a good education for Tanya."

"Are you Catholic?" the gentleman with thick lens in his glasses and black curly hair asked.

"No, we aren't Catholic, but we are Christians and will teach Tanya of God and Jesus Christ," Lana assured them.

"You have one son; is that correct?" the gentleman at the head of the table asked. He seemed to have the most say about what happened

. "Yes, Patrick, who is nine years old," Lana answered.

"Do you plan to have more children?" The lady in the scanty sun dress asked.

"Unfortunately I can't bear more children. But we want more children. Tanya would be a perfect answer for us," Lana said.

The questions continued, then the lady sitting near the end of the table smiled and requested, "Please wait outside in the reception area."

Thirty minutes later the Carters were summoned. The spokesman at the head of the table, the director, said, "We are impressed with your credentials and do not doubt that you would provide a good home. However, we must deny your request because you're not Catholic."

Brian stood and asked, "What would change your mind?"

"At this time we must look for a Catholic family to fill the mother's wishes."

Lana stood and looked each member of the board in the eye, not believing what she was hearing. "But we can provide a family with food and care. That seems very important to me and we are Christians."

"I understand that. Also as Americans you will sever Tanya from all of her family and heritage by removing her to such a far country. She will not see her brothers and sister often, maybe never. I'm very sorry, but we must deny your request."

As they left the office they saw Tanya watching from a distance, wearing her little red outfit, now soiled. Lana noticed her shoes were also missing. Tanya ran to greet them. Her eyes pleading, "Take me away from here and help me to be happy."

Lana stopped, stooped down and held Tanya by both shoulders, "We can't take you home yet. But we have not given up. We are fighting for you, little one." She then loosened her grasp on Tanya's shoulders and encircled Tanya in her arms for a tight hug and kiss on the cheek. Lana tasted Tanya's salty tears. She felt her sadness as they held each other. Lana knew Tanya felt the same bond of friendship she did. Lana desperately wanted to be sure Tanya was eating correctly, that someone was caring for her and that life was not too sad in the Sanitario.

Brian picked Tanya up and gave her a cheerful toss in the air which brought a big grin. He put her on the ground and reached his arms around her and gave her a hug.

Knowing they couldn't take her home with them, they proceeded to the car. Tanya followed. Watching their every move as she tucked her hair behind her left ear, Lana saw Tanya's tears, streaking down her cheeks as she realized they were leaving her behind.

The Carters waved. Tanya waved as they pulled away, tears making their tracks down soiled cheeks. Lana cried. It seemed so futile. The Carters offered home, food and care and were rejected. Corumbá.

"How can we convince them, Brian?" She asked between sobs. "That little bundle of human life needs a home and family. How can we make them understand what we offer is a life saver for her?"

"Good question. How can we make them understand the opportunity we can offer Tanya?" Brian answered. He was confused at the standard they had set. Surely they could see Tanya was not cared for in the Sanitario, but could be in the Carter's home.

"We must find a way to get custody. I feel in my heart Tanya was meant to be part of our family. I'm desperate to make it happen," Lana stated emphatically. She got control of herself. Lana stopped crying and started to deliberate possible ways to convince the board of their sincere desire to make a good home for Tanya. "Should we point out her lack of food and care?"

" No. That would only point a finger at the Sanitario. We don't want to cause trouble. Just help Tanya to have a better life," Brian said.

The next morning Brian had a great idea and they immediately called the Sanitario. "Florentina, we would like an opportunity to meet with the board of directors again. We have a new proposal," Lana stated.

"The soonest would be next Thursday."

"Very good. Please schedule us," Lana requested.

"See you at seven then."

"Gracias."

By the time the Carters had gotten out of their car they spotted Tanya running toward them. They ran to greet her, with big hugs all around. "So good to see you, little one," Lana whispered.

"You look terrific, Tanya," Brian said.

"Did you come to get me?" Tanya asked in Spanish.

"We are here to try," Brian replied.

The board of directors, all seven of them, looked at the Carters skeptically. They had already given them their answer.

"Please hear a new proposal we have for you," Brian pleaded.

"Yes?" The director asked.

"We have given this much thought. We want desperately to help Tanya find a better life and to enlarge our family. We love this little girl. We are not Catholic, true. We are willing to tell her of her Catholic heritage and that her mother did want her to continue in that faith," Lana advised.

Brian added, "We would be willing to send her to a Catholic school for the first few years until she decides what to do about religion."

"We will make all information available and let her decide. Would that make a difference?" Lana added.

The director said, "Would you please wait in the outer office for a few minutes?"

The minutes dragged.

After nearly an hour, Florentina appeared with no smile on her face and asked them to return to the board room, which was a bare room with a long table and a few straight back chairs.

"I know your intentions are good. But we still must deny your request for custody of Tanya. Lo siento. It is best for all," the director informed the Carters.

The decision had taken so long the Carters were encouraged that they were winning the battle. They were depressed at being rejected again.

Tanya watched them emerge. She waited patiently on the portico. "I come home with you?" Tanya asked with a twinkle in her eye and a big smile.

"Not yet, little one. But we are still fighting to get you," Lana promised.

Lana watched as Tanya's happy countenance changed to a sad one. Huge tears formed in her eyes, slowly trickling down her soiled cheeks.

"Brian, there must be some key to getting that girl. They would not have taken so long if it was a quick rejection."

"I agree. They must have had an intense discussion."

The Carters went to bed spending another restless night. At two in the morning Brian perked up. "Lana, Lana, wake up! I think I know the answer."

"I'm awake."

"Remember how we finally got our car released from Customs? It arrived and we were told it was under a load of potatoes that had to be unloaded, it might be three or four days before the car was available."

"Yes. I do remember a week later they still did not release our car. Two weeks later we still didn't have the car. More excuses."

"Carlos, my administrative assistant, gave me the clue on how to get it. Take a few bottles of scotch, a case of American cigarettes and some handy cash and tell Customs that you wanted to reward them for their many troubles."

"We had the car the next day. Maybe that is the secret now."

"Let's call Florentina. It's certainly worth a try."

When Lana thought Señorita Florentina would be in her office she hurriedly dialed. "We have a new proposal for the board. Please make an appointment for us next Thursday," Lana requested.

Lana knew her mom loved brussel sprouts and vegetables but Marcelena had never prepared them. She decided she would go to the market with Marcelena and see what was available. Supermarkets full of appetizing prepared food were not found in Asunción in the fifties. The fresh food markets were where all the farmers brought their produce early in the morning. The cooks came and purchased, then took home to prepare.

"Marcelena, I want to go to the market with you in the morning and see what's available. Mother is a real health food nut. I'll want lots of vegetables and fruits on hand."

"It's not necessary for you to go. Señora. I'll get them," Marcelena said.

Lana insisted, "I'll go with you."

"The market is best at four-thirty or five in the morning."

"I don't mind getting up at the crack of dawn one morning for the experience," Lana assured her.

"That's before dawn, Señora."

"I can do it." Lana was anxious to see where their food came from and what the selection was. Marcelena cooked the same foods repeatedly. Lana wanted to see what she was missing.

With a shrug, Marcelena agreed.

The next morning at five o'clock Lana pulled on a light knit top and a pair of slacks, grabbed her camera and joined Marcelena, who was ready and waiting. Today they took the car, usually Marcelena rode the tram.

The market was unreal! There were live chickens in cages waiting to be sold. Fish were lying on long wooden slabs with no ice to keep them fresh; vegetables were being freshened by dipping them in the gutter water and the stench was overpowering. Flies, lots of flies swarmed everywhere, especially on the meat.

"Marcelena, that meat is not safe to eat.

"It's good you bring your beef from Argentina packaged, frozen and on dry ice. It is much better beef and much cleaner."

"I understand now how Maria thought that first bunch of meat delivered in the back of a dirty pick up with flies all over it was quite normal."

"Si, Señora, we're used to it. We scrape the beef and wash it and cook thoroughly. Then it's safe."

"This is a real eye opener for me." Lana was shocked at the conditions of the meats and vegetables.

"I was worried about your coming to the market. The standards are not what Norte Americanos seem to expect."

"For sure." Lana decided to take some pictures of the Paraguayan market to show Brian and people back home.

The policeman spotted Lana taking photos. He ran to her and grabbed her arm and yanked the camera from her hands.

"No take pictures here!" he shouted sternly in Spanish. With that the companion officer opened the back of the camera and took out the roll of film and threw it in the garbage. He closed the camera, slowly, then handed it back to Lana.

Her mouth was still open and his grip on her arms still firm. "I didn't know it was illegal to take photos," Lana protested.

"It is forbidden," the policeman growled as he sternly faced Lana

"Sorry," she apologized.

"You take picture in the market again and I will arrest you. Understand me?" The police officer commanded.

Lana nodded. She was so shocked she forgot to protest and show her Embassy papers.

The sun was peeking over the buildings and the heat was already steaming. With the high humidity it felt hot. "Let's head home to some air-conditioning," Lana suggested.

Safely home Lana agreed, "You were right Marcelena, going to the market was a bad idea. I didn't find the vegetables I wanted. Now I'll smell the market when I eat."

Even though the Carter's table was always set on clean linen with candles and fresh flowers, Lana had a difficult time erasing the image and smell of the market for several days. She would recollect the stench and the dirty surroundings of the food and realize the food for their dinner came from the smelly market. Yukk!

There was such a huge contrast between the rich and poor in Paraguay. Some didn't have decent living quarters or enough to eat; they had only old clothes and many went barefoot. Some lived in Chaco Land, the river bottom where the land was free. They made make shift living quarters out of old crates or scrap lumber and whatever they could scrounge. Most springs they were flooded out. When the water subsided, they rebuilt. The more fortunate poor had small homes and lived on small parcels of land in the country working hard to grow produce or flowers to market and make life livable.

The well-to-do lived in mansions, had staffs of uniformed servants, fancy automobiles driven by chauffeurs and enjoyed life like royalty.

One group seemed oblivious of the other except the lucky poor worked as servants for the rich. They were furnished decent housing, plenty of food, uniforms, medical care and a salary. Some were taught to read and write.

The social life in Asunción for the Americans and the rich was fabulous. Invitational fashion shows were held in the President's gardens with courtiers coming from Paris, Rome, New York or Dallas to show what was new. Dinner parties with the power figures, including President Stroessner and his cabinet, ambassadors and members of the embassies of other countries were part of the normal routine.

Life on the whole was intriguing, fascinating and glamorous for the Carters.

With Lana's father being a senator, she had many opportunities to associate with power people. Here it was constant and not as Senator Brahn's daughter, but as Lana Carter. Also it was not optional; it was on command. They were actually told most social functions they were expected to attend, sometimes even being told the minute to arrive such as "You will arrive at four minutes after five to go through the receiving line at the Argentine Embassy on Friday evening."

Tonight Brian and Lana were on their way back to the Sanitario to present another plan to obtain adoption of Tanya.

When the Carters arrived Tanya ran toward them with arms outstretched. Her sweet hugs were worth fighting for.

"Hello, little one. It's so good to see you," Lana assured Tanya as she gave her a big hug.

With a joyful toss in the air Brian got a squeal and a big hug afterwards. "You're a sight for sore eyes."

"What does that mean?" Tanya asked.

"I love looking at you. I love you," Brian said. He no longer doubted adoption of Tanya was right for them. He thought it was a great idea. His problem now was solving the question of how.

Facing the board of directors for the third time Brian started his appeal. "We want Tanya as part of our family. We'll send her to a Catholic school and we would like to make a personal endowment of $3,000 American dollars, to fund needs at the Sanitario, also a personal gift of $200 American dollars to each of the board members and to Señorita Florentina, for your many good works. All we need is permanent custody papers."

After hearing Brian's proposal the director nodded to the lady at the foot of the conference table. She nodded back. Without further discussion the director requested, "Your generosity is appreciated. Please take a seat in the front waiting area."

A few minutes later they were summoned to the board room.

"We decided with your willingness to give her the Catholic schooling, we will grant you custody. In the meantime, you can take Tanya home with you."

Lana rushed over to Señorita Florentina, "Thank you! Wonderful! Marvelous! Oh I'm so happy! Thank you!" In her enthusiasm she gave Florentine a bear hug.

Brian headed for the courtyard on a run to find Tanya, with Lana running close behind. Florentina called, "You must sign some temporary papers. We will then prepare permanent custody papers. Please come to my office before you leave."

"Certainly. As soon as we give Tanya the good news," Brian replied enthusiastically.

Tanya was waiting as they expected near by. Brian scooped her up in his arms. “Good news! You can come home with us.”

Tanya put both arms around Brian’s neck and squeezed. Brian thought how rewarding that squeeze was. The fight for Tanya had been worth all the pain and expense.

Tanya’s dream of being with the Carter family finally realized, she beamed. Then she looked behind and saw Ignacia looking so sad. A huge tear had formed in her sister’s eye. Tanya realized she was turning a corner in her life, leaving her comfort zone, probably never to see her sister and brothers again. Her happiness turned to sadness and she let out a huge sob followed by quiet crying, wiggling to extract herself from Brian’s arms. When she hit the ground she ran full speed to Ignacia, throwing her arms around her sister. Repeating, “Mi hermana, mi hermana.” Ignacia stood stroking Tanya’s hair and hugging her. Both crying.

With their return to the states near, Lana decided to visit Dr. MacClanahan early the next morning and get Tanya's physical examination started. The paperwork for entrance to the States took a few weeks and Lana didn't want any more unnecessary delays.

Dr. MacClanahan was not available but the pediatrician, Dr. Taylor, was. He took the Embassy papers and proceeded to examine Tanya from head to toes. The doctor found disturbing spots on the lungs in her X-rays. "We'll have to study these further before we can sign the papers. Could you bring her back Monday?"

"My parents will be visiting from the States at that time, but this is very important to us. Yes, we'll come and let you see what you can do."

"Very good. Stop on your way out and confirm a time with Marian."

In the Baptist hospital most spoke English and had American type names. Many were Americans who had come to Paraguay originally with Point Four, a government program. They saw the great need for a sanitary hospital and returned to help the Paraguayans. They were dedicated people with a desire to serve others.

Celebration was in order with the return of Tanya and the Brahns arrival.

The plane arrived in mid afternoon. The Carters planned a grand welcome at the airport, complete with a band and friends.

"Come Tanya, it is time to go pick up Patrick from school and meet your grandparents."

"Today?"

"Yes. Right now. That is why Juana selected one of your new dresses for you to wear today."

They stopped at school to get Patrick then headed for the airport to meet the Brahns.

Lana wanted her party that evening for her parents to be her grandest of the year. Many of the exciting people she associated with in Asunción were invited. The Carters spared no expense in organizing this event.

Coming down the stairs from the plane, Vera, Lana's mother, looked majestic. Her imperial walk, smiling face and lovely lavender suit made her look the part of visiting royalty.

Lana took in a deep breath as she ran to meet her mother. She threw her arms around her and hugged. She didn't realize how much she had missed her parents until they arrived. "Hello, Mother dear, You look marvelous"

"Lana. We're finally here. Such a long flight. I'm dead on my feet," Vera said.

"Yes. It's long. It's so good to see you. I've longed for this moment, when I could talk to you face to face and hug you."

"Could I break into this intimate circle?" asked Will.

"Oh yes," Lana agreed as she turned to hug her father.

"You still smell like Chanel Five, Lana. So familiar."

"My favorite."

"Good, 'cause I brought you a fresh supply," Will answered.

"Dad, you're the greatest."

After hugging her father, she relinquished her spot so Brian and Patrick could greet her parents. Then little Tanya was introduced.

Lana wished she had not invited friends to let this be a family affair. Since she had, she started the introductions of their friends. The band was playing so loud in the background they could hardly hear the names. So Lana motioned the band leader to hold down the volume.

Back at the Carter's estate the servants were busy making preparations for the evening festivities. "The señora wants a perfect party this evening," Maria advised.

Marcelena was busy boiling monioca to be fried later and mixing filling for the empanadas.

The day was hot in December and the air-conditioner didn’t keep the house as cool as they had hoped with all the baking and cooking.

"When does the party start?" Franco asked.

"Guests are invited to arrive at seven for appetizers," Maria said.

"I should be in my white shirt and bow tie by six-thirty to set up bar. How can I help now?” Franco asked.

“Put some tables and chairs around the pool. Hopefully the storm will not come until after the party. Be sure the area is clean underneath the tables on the back patio," answered Maria.

Maria was busy and assumed Franco had gone back to his gardening, but heard a noise in the master suite. She went in to see if something was wrong and saw Franco rifling through some papers on Brian's desk. "Franco, what you doing?"

He jumped in surprise. "I’m looking for a receipt," he lied.

The bills and receipts were sent to Brian, who paid for them and Franco had no need to see them. Maria knew he was not telling the truth.

Maria scowled. "I think the señor would not like you in here. This is the second time you been snooping in the señor's desk. With what purpose?"

"Maria, I still can't tell you–trust me."

"That's difficult. You spying on Señor Carter for some reason."

"It's a good reason. I'll tell you later. I promise."

With that he returned to the garden and Maria returned to the dining room.

Maria wondered what Franco was really looking for. What was he involved in that he thought good, but so secretive? She was tempted to tell Señor Carter. She did not want to spoil this evening. She decided to sleep on it and decide tomorrow.

"Patrick you've grown so tall. You're taller than I am," Vera commented.

"I stretch tall every morning, Grandma." Patrick was proud of his height and wanted to be tall like his father and grandfather.

"You what?" Vera asked.

"I stand as tall as I can with my shoulders straight."

"That's good. Come stand with your back to mine. Let's measure."

"Patrick, you're a at least five inches taller than your Grandmother." Lana observed.

Tanya was not to be left out. She came and stood beside Vera and Patrick. "How tall am I?"

"You're about six inches shorter than your Grandmother," Lana told her.

"Tanya is adorable, Lana," Vera said.

"She is precious. Patrick is so good to her and helps her in many ways," Lana shared.

"Lana, I need my dress pressed for the party tonight."

"Sure. Give it to Maria."

In Paraguay in the 50's many things were frustrating, like no electricity at times. Sure enough, this afternoon, no electricity.

"Sorry, Mom. No electricity. Do you have another dress you could use tonight? One that doesn't need pressing."

Maria said, "Señora, no worry, I know how to make it work. I'm prepared."

"There's no electricity. How can you make it work?"

"Señora, no worry. I have a good answer. The dress will be ready when the Señora's shower is finished."

Maria went to the servants' living area and returned with an unusual iron. It had a lid to open on the top and no electric wiring. "What in the world is that funny-looking thing, Maria?"

"I heat some carbon (charcoal) in a bucket out by our house and you see. It works."

Half an hour later she returned triumphantly with a hot iron. She showed Lana how the lid of the iron opened and you could put hot carbon inside and it heated the iron to press clothes.

The national law in Paraguay was that the government had to furnish electricity at least four hours every day. The law didn't say when. When the supply of power was short, the four hours were often between midnight and four in the morning. It did keep the food in the freezer frozen. But it didn't pump the water, cook food or press clothes.

On days when they were without electricity they improvised. The Ambassador told the Carters at their welcome party that the Americans were innovative imaginative individuals and they should keep their creative minds working and not let little things frustrate them. Lana tried.

"I love Asunción. Your life here is exciting. We'll go home and think of all the interesting people we've met and this beautiful country you live in."

"Mom, thanks for coming."

"I wouldn't have missed it."

"You looked gorgeous in your mauve dress at the party tonight. I'm so proud of you. Several people thought you were my sister."

"They're used to flattery."

"Not at all. Remember that luncheon in Washington D. C. when the hostess commented that she was so happy your sister could join them also?"

"Of course I remember. That was a compliment."

"The truth, Mom."

The party for her parents had been a blast, even better than she had hoped. The conversation had been riotous; many danced away the night and Marcelena had excelled in the kitchen with marvelous Paraguayan delicacies.

Lana showered while Brian shaved and they were soon ready for bed. Kneeling by the bed Lana said her closing prayer of thanksgiving, crawled into bed and Brian's inviting arms. She snuggled with her head on his shoulder. He pulled her to him and kissed her forehead lovingly.

Lana felt warmth creep through her as Brian whispered, "Lana Carter, I love you. You're precious to me."

"Thanks, that love is important to me. So are you, Brian." She arched her neck and kissed him firmly on the lips. Brian tightened his hold. His hand reached up towards Lana's face. She could almost feel the caress it was going to give her cheek, when the hand kept going to his face and he scratched as if his nose itched. Lana felt disappointment burn as tears welled in her eyes. Her warmth chilled. Brian put his hand back around Lana's waist and relaxed as he slipped into a very sound sleep.

Lana was tired and frustrated. She wished Brain would kneel with her in prayer, he had never followed up on studying about her faith and she missed sharing this important part of life with her dearest friend, her husband. She soon felt drowsy, but couldn't help wondering how much of what had just transpired was automatic from Brian and how much was from the heart. When he had stirred deep emotions in her, his nose itched.

After a busy day of sightseeing, the Brahns and the Carters sat on the patio plotting the next day's activities as they watched the bright pink cotton candy looking clouds drift along the intense blue sky. The clouds gradually turned into a fiery orange, pink, red and gold sunset.

"I wish we could capture that gorgeous sunset on film," Will said.

"Let's try. It's spectacular, one of our prettiest," Lana agreed. She ran for the camera to shoot the sunset.

On her return Vera asked, "What are some of the specialties of Paraguay that we should shop for tomorrow?"

"My favorites are the beautiful nanduti lace, their hand made inlaid wood guitars and of course the beautiful Paraguayan harps."

"Take us to them," requested Will.

"We'll explore the best markets for them early in the morning. Remember you shop early and late in Asunción. Midday is siesta time. Everyone locks doors, eats a huge meal and naps from noon until three or four in the afternoon."

Vera bought lace, a guitar and a beautiful Paraguayan harp to be shipped back as a unique decoration for her music room and reminder of their visit.

The challenge of the moment was to get documents so Tanya could enter the United States.

Lana returned to the clinic for the third time to meet with Dr. MacClanahan and Dr. Taylor.

"The only problem is the spots, or scars, on Tanya's lungs that say either she now has or has had tuberculosis."

"What does that mean?"

"I can't sign the papers for clearance for immigration."

"Why?"

"TB scars have to be shown inactive for at least one year before the United States will grant entry. They look like scars, not active. But I have to prove it by tracking them for change."

Panic stricken, Lana asked, "What can we do? Brian returns home in a few months." She was on the verge of tears.

"I feel they are scars. Until I prove that I absolutely cannot sign the documents," Dr. MacClanahan replied. "I need time."

"But we don't have a year. Is there any other test to show inactivity?"

"I'm afraid not," Dr. MacClanahan answered.

"How can we convince Immigration that Tanya is safe to enter the states?"

"Maybe a special waiver. I would verify that Tanya doesn't show symptoms of active TB."

"Thanks. Please do. I'll take that to the Embassy and see what they can do for us."

Lana was sad; it seemed there was one challenge after another when trying to get Tanya to the States.

Going home was exciting for Lana. But with this new challenge it was also sad. She looked forward to the day she would return to the American way, department stores, clean super markets, relaxed neighbors that you could go visit on a minute's notice. Most important Lana wanted her children to know and benefit from knowing their grandparents.

She wondered if Brian was tempted to sign another contract, take home leave and return to the good life somewhere in South America, as many defined it. Lana hoped not. It was glamorous and exciting but so artificial, not what she wanted for herself or her children on a long term basis.

Lana's parents returned to the USA and things around the Carter home were getting back to normal. It was Ladies Day at the club for golf and Lana left early to practice a bit before starting play. The game didn't finish until shortly after noon and then they ate lunch, so it was usually mid to late afternoon before getting back to the estate.

Maria was in the servants' quarters fixing lunch; Marcelena in the kitchen and Juana was with the children in back. With Lana on the golf course, Franco decided to go to Señor Carter's desk and see what new information he could gather about the Carters. He had given much personal information to rebel leaders, even the Brahn's home address in Phoenix, Arizona.

A tropical storm rolled in curtailing the golf game. Rain came down by the bucket loads. Soaked to the bone, Lana returned home early. She went straight to the master suite to get some dry clothes and was shocked to see Franco going through Brian's papers on his desk. She stood quietly at the door watching. She couldn't believe her eyes. Franco first went through many papers on Brian's desk and then started to search through some papers left on the edge of the dresser.

Lana couldn't keep quiet any longer. "What are you looking for, Franco?"

He jumped, turned and replied, "Keys to the storage area in the garage."

"You'll find them on the key board on the back of the kitchen door," Lana replied.

Franco left. Lana wondered what Franco was searching for.

The Carters' two plus years living in Asunción had been exciting, but scary. Brian was working for both governments, Paraguayan and United States. A cloud always hung in a corner of their sky.

Brian worked openly for the Paraguayan government, managing the installation and staffing of the test unit at the University. He also gathered information about many strategic happenings for the United States government, information about the present government and the rebel contingency. He had it on good authority that the rebels were anxious to retrieve power again and that groups of the former regime were making plans for a coup.. This information was relayed back to Washington through the MARS station (ham radio) in code or through the locked Embassy pouch. There was always the question of, "did someone know of this second responsibility?"

Lana loved their Paraguayan home. Her favorite was the sunroom on the back of the house completely enclosed with glass overlooking the pool and terraced gardens behind which displayed lovely flowers year around. Lana used it as her private domain for partial seclusion. It was a little out of the traffic of the main house.

The home lent itself to entertaining. A competent and friendly staff of servants was the success of entertainment. Then it was a snap most of the time.

Even then things could go wrong, like the night Brian planned a surprise birthday party for Lana. It was her big three-zero birthday.

The party was a surprise and a howling success.

Most of the streets in Asunción were cobblestone and they ate your tires like rats eat cheese.

Paraguayan ice cream back in the fifties was not safe to eat. It wasn't pasteurized and it gave lousy stomach cramps and the trots. Marcelena baked a birthday cake from a mix bought at the embassy commissary. She found a recipe for ice cream, pasteurized the milk and cream and borrowed an ice cream freezer. Brian and Patrick headed across town to the brewery, the only place Brian knew to buy ice to freeze the ice cream.

Before they returned, people started to arrive. Maria and Franco were prepared. Out came the balloons, decorations and food. Lana was pleasantly surprised that Brian would plan a surprise party for her and invite their friends to share in the her special day.

Brian had hired a small band for the back patio but since it was pouring rain, the band was transferred to the big entertainment room. Soon everyone was dancing and making merry. Everyone except Brian. He had not returned from his errand.

The crowd finally ate the cake without ice cream and Maria admitted that Brian had gone for ice

Rain in Paraguay comes down in sheets, in a few minutes you're soaking wet. In this tropical storm the cobblestone streets decided to eat a tire. The rain was so thick Brian could hardly see across the street.

A galley of natives gathered under the awnings and watched Brian and Patrick change the flat tire. The crowd found it amusing that the gringos were getting soaked.

The spare tire on the car, they put the flat in the trunk and headed for the ice.

With the delay of the flat tire they arrived as the brewery was being closed for the night. The last man was locking up and heading for the tram. Brian stopped him.

After explaining his plight Brian pleaded with him to unlock the big chained gate and get some ice.

Brian paid for the ice and gave the man two 100 Guarani notes for a tip. The man smiled. That was about a third of a week's salary for him.

Feeling triumphant Brian and Patrick headed home.

Big problem!

Now the cobblestones ate another tire and there was no spare. Asunción is built on hills like San Francisco. With inadequate drainage, the tropical storms flood the streets creating rivers running down the hill.

Again a crowd gathered under awnings to watch the gringos.

The water in the street was halfway to Brian's knees and when he pulled the tire and wheel off the car, it got away from him and started floating down the hill in the river. Running after it was not easy with water so deep.

The natives, being a fun-loving people, thought it was great sport to watch Brian chase the tire. They chuckled at first and watched with smiling faces. Not one stepped off the curb to catch the tire for Brian.

As he tried to move faster to catch the tire, he lost his balance on the slippery cobblestones and fell into the water. They changed their chuckle to an outright laugh. Hooting, clapping, yelling and shouting, it was real entertainment.

Brian yelled in Spanish, "Please stop the tire for me." They kept laughing.

After the second plea for help, someone took mercy and stepped out and held the tire until Brian could get there.

By the time they found a station that would fix the flat and get it back on the car several hours had passed. Paraguayans are seldom in a hurry.

Brian and Patrick arrived home in time to say goodnight to the last of the party guests. They were soaked to the bone and laughing like it was the best time ever.

What a memorable birthday! Lana had a wonderful time at her surprise party and her men had an unforgettable adventure in the tropical storm.

The extremes of the living conditions for people in Asunción were depressing, one group lived so luxuriously and the other barely survived.

Maria came from a deprived background and had been taught to read and write by a neighbor. She was fortunate. There were many illiterate in Paraguay.

Maria was a wonderful maid. She had a sense of what was needed in their home and a keen sense of humor. She was honest and dependable. Lana learned how far Maria had progressed when unacceptable meat was delivered to the Carters. The meat arrived in the back of an open pick-up covered with flies, so unappetizing. Lana instructed Maria, "Throw this out."

"Why, Señora?"

"Food poisoning."

"Could I please have it?" Maria asked.

"What for?"

"My mother is very short of food and it would mean a lot to her. With proper cleaning and cooking it will be fine."

"Maria, this is dangerously dirty. I don't think it a good idea for anyone to eat it."

"It'll be okay. It's much better than what she has."

"If you want it, yes, of course, Maria."

"May I have enough freezer paper to wrap it. On my day off I'll take it to her?"

"Certainly. Freeze it. Maria, you should wash it well before cutting and wrapping."

"Si, señora. I will scrape and wash it thoroughly. Mother provides for seven children and food is scarce. She'll be very happy with so much good beef."

"Mark each package carefully, then put it on the bottom two shelves of the freezer apart from ours and I will take you and the meat to your home on Tuesday."

Maria said, "No, Señora, it wouldn't be proper for you to drive me. I am your servant."

Lana assured her, "It's all right for me to drive you. You can show me the way and it will be a fun excursion. We'll take Patrick and admire the beautiful Lapacho trees that are in full blossom now. I've been wanting to get out and see more of the countryside."

"Gracias, Señora. Mother will be happy to meet you. I will be happy to show you the country. You're very kind."

The trip was an education. The countryside was dressed in the brightest purple and pink as the Lapacho trees showed their most beautiful finery of the year.

Transportation in the country was overloaded buses with live chickens in crates on top and some people hanging on the side.

Other transportation were ladies sitting side saddle on burros and men riding in small carts filled with vegetables and fruits pulled either by a horse or donkey, usually a donkey.

The small shacks that dotted the countryside were rather depressing. People with only essential clothing, most of them barefoot, tended the vegetables or flowers.

"How do these people live, Maria?"

"Most raise flowers or vegetables to market in the city. They are the women you see on the donkeys selling door to door to the servants."

"That's where you get flowers for our table?"

"Usually. Some from our yard."

"Do you also buy fruit and vegetables from the street vendors?"

"Only special foods or if Marcelena forgets to get it at the market."

"That is their only means of support?"

"Yes, for many. Most men ride carts. The ladies ride backs of the animals," Maria answered.

When Lana arrived at Maria's home, she was shocked.

"This is where your mother lives?"

"Yes. This land was given to Mother by her father when I was born. Relatives built this house for her."

"It's only one large room. How many children does your mother have at home?"

"Seven. I'm oldest–eight all together. Four of us are negro. Four are light. We have two different fathers."

"Your mother never married?"

"No. As you know, in Paraguay there are seven women to every man. People with no money, no marry. Only people with lots of money marry and men with money often have mistresses. Otherwise many women would not know love or have families."

"Now I understand why the mistresses of the gentlemen are acknowledged. That was a big surprise to me at the New Years Eve Party at the Centenero Club. Many of our friends had their families that we knew at their table. Their mistress and her children sat at a nearby table. Both families seemed friendly."

"That's usual. In the country we grew up without fathers in the home and without bathrooms. Mother still does all her cooking in the yard on a barrel, cut down with a grate on top. Carbon (charcoal) cooks the food."

"Your life must have been challenging."

"Yes. We had lots of love from Mother, from father and other relatives."

"Are you close to your grandparents and cousins?"

"Most of them."

"Is your mother bitter that your father doesn't help more with your support?"

"No, she is glad to have had love and children to share her life. Many never have that."

At home later that evening, Lana gave Maria a big hug. "Thanks for all you do for our family, Maria. You are one special person."

"Thank you. My home here is good. Thank you and Señor Carter for your kindness to me."

Needless to say, Maria got a sizable raise the end of the month, as did the other wonderful servants in the Carter home. Even though Ruby, their neighbor, lamented that the Americans ruined it for the natives with their unreasonable generosity.

Ruby declared that Americans came to Paraguay and paid their servants too much, thus stealing the cream of the crop of trained maids, cooks, gardeners and nannies, leaving the natives to train new servants and pay more or they can't keep them.

Señorita Florentina called. "Would it be convenient for me to come by for a few minutes and visit this morning?"

"Of course we'd love to have you. What time?"

"We'll start immediately. Be there in about twenty to thirty minutes."

Lana's mind was in a whirl. What was this unexpected visit all about? She notified Maria that Florentina was coming and to show her right in. In Paraguay a visitor did not approach the door of a house and knock or ring a bell. The person calling rang a bell at the gate, a servant met them and announced who it was to get permission to open the gate. Only then was a person permitted to enter the estate.

Lana checked Tanya to see if she was presentable.

Then Lana remembered that Florentina had said we'll start immediately. Who was we?

Lana thought about telling Señorita Florentina they were having difficulty with the documents for Tanya, but decided she still had hopes they could find a solution, so why bother her with their problem.

When the car approached, Maria quickly permitted Florentina to enter. She didn't wait for the bell to ring. Lana saw both Ignacia and Juan were in the car with Florentina. What in the world?

"Good morning," Lana called as she approached the car.

"Thanks for making time for us on the spur of the moment. I want you to get acquainted with Tanya's brother and sister. I believe you saw them on a couple of occasions. But I wanted you to see what dear children they are."

"What is the purpose of this visit? I'm completely confused," Lana inquired.

"I hope you and your husband will consider taking all three of the children, keeping part of the family together. It would be good for the children to have each other. Both Juan and Ignacia are older and it will be impossible to find good homes for them here."

"But that was not our agreement."

Lana was not only surprised, but rather annoyed at Señorita's plan to force two more children on her, or make her feel guilty for not taking them.

"No, but you may not have thought of it and I wanted you to get to know the children better. Ignacia doesn't have the beautiful features of Tanya, but she is a dear little girl. Please, let the children play together."

"I don't see a problem with that," Lana replied.

Tanya spotted her brother and sister and ran to greet them with hugs and more hugs and lots of chatter in Guarani that Lana didn't understand.

"Maria, please take all the children out back. Ask Juana to call Patrick and involve all of them in some activity. See how they get along," Lana requested, not knowing how to handle the situation gracefully.

"Don't you need me here to serve refreshments?" Maria asked.

"Yes, please return and assist here as soon as you get the children situated."

"Si, Señora."

Lana watched as the children played. Ignacia was truly homely and shy, yet a sweet child. Juan was a lanky boy with a hesitant smile, nervous and a bit clumsy, but personable. He had many nervous habits, such as rubbing his hand along his thigh, biting his lip and smoothing his hair often. Lana watched carefully as she thought of the many problems it would present to take two more. An adjustment for her, yes, but more importantly there would be the three of them together and Patrick would be the outsider.

Lana noticed Patrick was pushed aside often as Tanya's family mingled, talking excitedly together in Guarani, the native Indian language, which Patrick couldn't understand. He stood alone baffled at what was going on with the three of them.

Tanya, anxious to share her new life with her brother and sister, was telling them about all her activities. They seemed so excited to be together and share, an unexpected pleasure for them, but isolation for Patrick.

Patrick was obviously the outsider. Lana didn't like that.

"Do you notice how Tanya, Juan and Ignacia are the family and Patrick is standing alone?"

"That will pass as they get more comfortable with each other." Señorita Florentina assured Lana.

Lana decided to get her camera and take photos of the group. Later she would show them to Tanya when she was older and asked questions about her family back in Paraguay.

Adopting all three did not seem possible. Lana didn't feel she could cope with the challenges it would present.

As Lana approached with the camera and asked the children to pose near the pool, Juan pushed Patrick aside and said, "This is of our family. Move over."

"No, this is of all of you," Lana said.

Juan permitted Patrick back into the group.

When Juan and Ignacia were not there, Tanya and Patrick were brother and sister as it should be.

"You see what happened?" Lana asked.

"As I said before, that will pass."

"I don't think I can handle it. We want a family, not fragmented groups."

"Please consider what it would mean to Ignacia and Juan."

"We will consider it," Lana agreed.

Lana followed Florentina and the children to the gate. There were tearful hugs and kisses between Ignacia and Tanya. The scene tugged at Lana's heart. Maybe it would pass and be all right to have the three. Lana resolved she would talk to Brian.

She needed to talk to a good friend before Brian. Lana called her beloved sister, Caroline, "Care to play a round of golf this afternoon? I need to talk."

Caroline always had her head on straight and would be good medicine for a confused soul. She was family in a foreign land, away from biological family. She was a valued sister. Lana needed to find peace in this gigantic decision. She knew the opportunity for Ignacia and Juan to be taken out of that orphanage and to the states. Yet Lana also knew the challenges involved for herself , Brian and Patrick if they did adopt all three.

"Give me about an hour to rearrange my schedule and I'll be ready," Caroline responded.

As they drove to the club, Lana explained the happenings of the morning. "What would you do, Caroline?"

"Lana, you know this is a decision you have to live with for a long time and only you and Brian can make the choice. I can see your problem. I can also see the great opportunity for those children to be taken from their present surroundings. What chance do they have for a decent life living in the Sanitario?"

"Why does life have to be so complicated?"

"To make us strong. To help us grow."

Arriving home from golf, Lana found Mela, the seamstress, very proud of the clothing she had completed for the Carters cruise home.

"I love the beautiful dresses for Tanya, she'll be thrilled," Lana said.

"Yes, she saw me working on them and exclaimed that she never dreamed she would have clothes so pretty. Señora, she is most fortunate."

"We are very fortunate to have her. She's a doll," Lana stated.

"Do you think Patrick would like a tuxedo jacket to wear for evening?"

"What a marvelous idea. He has grown up so much. I think he would adore having his own formal wear, like Dad's."

"We need to go over some of the sketches for your wardrobe. I found some beautiful French brocade in a rich blue. It would be exciting for a dress with shoulder straps and a short jacket, similar to this," Mela said as she showed Lana a picture of an elegant dress in Vogue.

"Gorgeous!" Lana agreed. "Please get the material and let me know when you need more money in the clothing fund."

"There should be sufficient for the dress and the material for Patrick's jacket. Then I will need more."

Going home by luxury liner would be Tanya's first cruise and they had two long dresses made for special evenings, along with lots of casual wear for both Patrick and Tanya.

That evening while Brian and Lana watched, Tanya and Patrick modeled their new clothes.

Seeing Tanya in her long dresses tugged at Lana's heart, knowing she might not go to the States with them. Lana was fluctuating between hope and despair. One minute she rejoiced, the next minute she didn't see how they were going to cope with Immigration and get permission for Tanya to enter the USA.

As Lana watched the two children playfully vie for attention in their new attire, her determination again took charge.

Lana called her father in Phoenix, Arizona. Lana told him of their dilemma. He agreed Tanya needed to come to the States and have a better life.

Lana felt better after talking to him. He always had great ideas and was creative. Maybe he could think of something they hadn't.

Brian and Lana decided for the moment they wouldn't drop the bomb of misfortune on their children. They would let them believe everything was okay.

That evening they went to bed feeling defeated, not knowing how they could overcome this new obstacle, or what was right about adopting all the children. Brian held Lana in his arms and she let all her frustrations dissolve in tears. She settled down and snuggled on his shoulder. He comforted her with, "Lana, it will work out for the best. You must have faith."

The glamorous social life of the Embassy group that a few short weeks ago had her wrapped up in what to wear where, was insignificant. Number one priority was to take this tiny girl home as part of their family. The big question was how.

CHAPTER FIVE

Two weeks passed. Life was running smooth as could be expected, even though immigration refused a special waiver offered by Dr. MacClanahan. Which stated the spots looked like old scars not active TB and that Tanya did not show any symptoms of TB at present.

There was a special cocktail party to attend at Tyne's and it was a must-attend affair. Lana had to put her worries on the back burner, dress and go. She was not in the mood to socialize.

When Brian arrived home from the office he seemed uptight and asked, "What are you wearing tonight?"

"I haven't decided. Any preference?"

"No. Let's take a ride before dinner. I want to run out to where Lady is stabled."

Lana knew something was wrong. Lady, Patrick's horse was fine. Franco saw to that. Lana knew it was more than checking on the horse–something that couldn't be said in front of the children.

"Before dinner? I think Marcelena has dinner ready. You know how she hates it when her meals aren't eaten while they're hot. The children are in and scrubbed. I think Maria is in lighting the candles."

"We'll come back and eat before we leave for the party."

"Okay," Lana replied as she read the note Brian slipped her that read, "Important, please come now!"

Lana called into the kitchen to have Marcelena hold dinner. Marcelena hurried out of the kitchen, "Dinner is ready. Don't you want to eat first?"

"No. Please hold it. Or better yet, have Maria serve the children and we'll be back as soon as possible." With that Lana followed Brian to the car.

As they started out the long driveway to the street, Lana asked, "What's wrong?"

Brian, holding his finger to his lips, said, "I wanted to check on Lady. That horse has been restless lately."

Lana resisted pursuing it, though she was curious. Brian hands were clenching the steering wheel until his knuckles were white. His jaw was firm and set.

Why? Brian was usually very relaxed and casual.

Brian pulled in near the stable and parked. He came around and opened the door for Lana.

As they headed for the stables, Brian asked, "You know that my assignment has a dual purpose here?"

Brian slipped his arm protectively around Lana's shoulders. Trying to soften the impact of what he had to tell her.

"I know you collect information for our government while fulfilling your obligations to President Stroessner."

"Lana, today I found out more than I wanted to know. I know there's going to be a coup attempt at ten o'clock tonight. I know who some of the opposition leaders are."

Lana's stomach knotted, "Are you in danger?"

"Yes, I think so. This afternoon I got advice from a friend who should know. I was warned to not take any chances on whom I trusted with information."

"Who told you that?"

"Lana, you know I can't divulge the identity of my sources."

"Of course. What else were you told?" Lana was so confused by the new developments and wondered how frightening it really was. Evidently Brian was worried. He was a basket case. How could they cope with a revolution on top of trying to get out of Paraguay, get documents for Tanya and keep their sanity?

"I was told not to talk on the phone about anything sensitive and to be careful when and where I talked. I trust my contact. I must be careful. Please be careful also. You must not talk to anyone about my intelligence work."

"Why so careful of where you talk?"

"The house, the car, the phone and who knows what else are wired to eavesdrop. Either of the Paraguayan political groups would be furious to know I collect information for the United States government. I feel like I'm walking a tight rope."

"You say there is to be a revolution at ten? Is that a rumor or fact?"

"Fact. Yes, full blown. Not a threat, but a crazy battle for power. Killing, prisoners and the works."

"Oh, heaven forbid! I'm not going to the party tonight. I'll stay home with the children."

"No, no! You can't do that, It would look suspicious. We'd all be in danger."

"How can I go knowing what's happening? I need to be with the children. Besides I don't feel like partying."

"You have to go, Lana." Brian had needed to share his information and discuss it with some one. Lana was the only one he could trust. Now he questioned if that had been wise. It might be their undoing if she slipped and said the wrong thing at the wrong time.

"I don't know that I can," Lana stated honestly.

"Lana, believe me, if you don't, then you really foul up my assignment and it could be horrible. These people play for keeps. We'll all be in danger."

"Something that has me concerned is Franco. The other day golf was rained out and I came home early and found him snooping through the papers on your desk."

"Did he take anything?" Brian asked.

"No I don't think so. But he sure looked guilty when he saw I was watching him," Lana replied.

"For now let's not concern ourselves with that. We have enough on our plates."

"Tell me what's going to happen tonight," Lana demanded. Not really wanting to know. Every nerve taught and her stomach getting in tighter knots.

"The Blue Party is going to try to retrieve power from the Red Party and dethrone President Stroessner. They want to kill him or send him into exile."

"He'll be at the same party we are tonight. Do you think the rebels will storm the Tyne's home?"

"I don't know. I hope not. The worst part is that Ramero, one of the President's most powerful supporters isn't going to be at the party. His son's twelfth birthday celebration is this evening. I hear the rebels are planning to attack him and his family at home. They think if he's out of the picture it'll weaken President Stroessner's government considerably."

"Warn him," Lana begged.

"I can't warn him, his phone and house are bugged and his home is being watched. Attempting to get in touch with him would not rescue Ramero and would be a dead giveaway of me."

"I like Ramero. What can we do to save him?"

"I don't know. I feel helpless. I can't think of a way to get word to him and I'm not sure he would believe a message if I could get it to him."

"Why wouldn't you take me in the bedroom and tell me all this at the house?" Lana asked.

"My double life has been discovered. Our home, our car has been, or soon will be wired. The only way we can discuss any thing sensitive now will be when we're completely out of hearing range of anything that might be bugged. Or by writing notes to each other and answering by notes. When we use notes we must be sure they're destroyed."

"This is scary."

"Very. I have a code to send an SOS to Washington requesting immediate withdrawal to the United States. It'll take a few days and some help on your part."

"What can I do?"

"Be sick at the party tonight and before the evening is over let someone know, preferably Lorie Foster, since she's a gossip, that your remaining kidney is giving you a lot of trouble."

"Then what?"

"I'll take it from there. Let's get back to dinner and get ready."

"Not yet. Tell me more of what to expect tonight."

"Exactly at ten all hell will break lose. The Blue Party will attack. There will be shooting and the works, the beginning of a horrible coup attempt."

"What will we do?"

"Try to be calm. Get home to our children as fast as possible. If things get too messy, the Embassy will evacuate the American families to Buenos Aires. We only have one plane so everyone can't go at once. The camionetas (the large vans) will pick up the children and women first to take them to the airport and fly them out of danger. Then the plane will return for the rest of us. There's room for all the children and all but four of the American women to go in one flight."

"We're so near going home. How were you exposed?"

"I'm not sure. The only clue I have is the warning I was given. Intelligence work is crazy. It is necessary to trust some people to get information. Sometimes you trust the wrong people.

"Brian, do you think your life in danger?"

"Maybe. I think it's time to return to the States. Let's get back to the house. You must not tell the children or the servants about any of this. You must not talk to me about it. We don't know who is listening. Please act as normal as possible."

"Normal? How can I be normal when my whole world is crazy right now?" Lana felt drunk with tension. Her world was exploding and she had lost control.

"You have to be courageous. Put on a happy face and we'll go forward."

"I still have a dozen questions."

"They'll have to wait--for now we need to get going," Brian realized they had lost control.

"How will this affect our getting documents to take Tanya?"

"I wish I knew. We'll have to work as fast as possible to get things in order to leave here soon. Actually we won't be able to do anything while the revolution lasts. I'm sure we'll be restricted. Remember how we were confined when there were rumors of a revolution?"

Before leaving for the evening, Brian gave Maria unusual instructions, "Maria, do not give anyone permission to enter the estate under any condition tonight."

"Why, Señor?"

"Please, just follow instructions."

"Yes, sir."

"Advise all servants to stay in the main house until we return," Brian demanded.

"All? Even Franco? No matter how late you are?"

"Si. Stay here with the children, all of you."

Brian rang for Franco and instructed, "If anything sounds strange, Franco, put up the American flag and if any soldiers approach they should be shown our official Embassy papers. Do not let anyone enter the premises."

"Si Señor. What if they are friends?"

"Don't permit anyone in tonight."

"I can't leave our children. I cannot leave them here alone," Lana whispered to Brian.

Brian put his fingers to his lips to hush Lana then wrote. "You must. Remember, if you don't act as normal as possible we will all be in danger."

Lana was nauseated and scared. Lana wrote back, "I can't."

"This is one of the most difficult parts of my assignment. But we must carry it off as professionally as possible. Lana, we'll be home soon." Brian scribbled hurriedly.

"Ten o'clock is nearly two hours away. It will be an eternity waiting and wondering how Patrick and Tanya are. They'll be scared to death when all the commotion starts," Lana responded on her note.

"I know. That's why I have asked all the servants to stay inside tonight. That'll help them to feel more protected."

Communicating by writing was troublesome. Talking was much faster and more effective.

"What if we don't get back? What if we are detained? We are going to be with the President."

"Lana, please don't be pessimistic. Think positive." Brian wrote. "Ready?" Brian asked resorting to talking, instead of writing.

"Yes, I guess."

The notes were gathered and torn to pieces then torn some more to be sure they were not readable if found.

Lana smiled, radiating confidence she didn't feel. Her gorgeous blue cocktail dress helped. Brian tucked his hand lovingly beneath Lana's elbow and guided her back into the kitchen to say goodnight to all.

Lana slowly walked to the car. Brian opened the door and she got in. As he started around the car to get in, Lana jumped out and ran back and hugged Patrick and Tanya. Turning to Patrick she begged, "If things go crazy tonight don't panic. We'll be home as soon as possible."

"What do you mean, Mom?"

"I hate to leave you tonight. Something inside me says I would rather be with you."

"Go have a good time, we'll be all right," Patrick promised.

As they started out the driveway for the second time, Brian slammed on his brakes and said, "Wait one."

He ran back toward the house. Lana saw him talking to Franco in the yard, give him a pat on the shoulder and a firm handshake. Then he returned to the car.

"Care to share what that was all about?"

Brian held his fingers to his lips reminding her the car was bugged. "A couple of last minute instructions."

When they arrived at the Tyne's there was already a small crowd gathered.

President Stroessner's limo arrived as the Carters entered.

Señora Stroessner, his wife, was not with him. He often didn't bring her to these small intimate parties. She seemed to have difficulty communicating in the more relaxed atmosphere.

Soon the jovial mood of the group took over and Lana nearly forgot the witching hour was near.

A few minutes before ten, Lana noticed Brian talking seriously to someone she didn't recognize in a far corner. The intensity of the expression on his face reminded her of what was going to happen soon.

She froze. Lana felt like she was sitting on a time bomb, waiting for it to start ticking, then explode.

It was difficult to be involved in the banter.

Lorie sensed that all was not right. "Aren't you feeling well this evening, Lana?"

"As a matter of fact I'm not. I've had a lot of pain in my remaining kidney. I'm hounded with a urinary tract infection again. Dr. Martinez doesn't seem to be able to help."

"Had you thought of going to Buenos Aires to see one of the urologists? The medical staff at the University Hospital has a good reputation. I hear they . . ."

The last part of Lorie's statement was completely lost as pandemonium broke lose. The atmosphere seemed to literally explode. Shots, sirens and rapid fire filled the air. Thank goodness the shots were outside, even though near, not in the Tyne's house.

The excitement of the party abruptly changed to total quiet. All lights went out, both on the street and within the house. Devastating darkness! Lana's heart nearly stopped, even though she knew what was happening she wondered if they would storm the Tyne's home and try to kill or capture President Stroessner. The shots seemed so close, the darkness so ominous.

After a few minutes the inside lights came on again. But the street lights remained blackened.

President Stroessner turned pale even under his bronzed Paraguayan complexion.

Lana had never seen him move so fast. He ran without hesitation for the phone, dialed, then spoke so rapidly she couldn't understand him. He listened a few seconds then, with an authoritative voice, again spoke rapidly. The only thing she understood was "State emergency." After a few more seconds he suddenly stopped talking and looked at the phone. Obviously it had gone dead so he couldn't continue.

He ran for the front door. His chauffeur had risen to the emergency and was there waiting with the limo.

They swished off into the night with no headlights. Thank heavens for the moon. Excited whispers started again as if everyone was in shock.

Ambassador Cassidy instructed, "Obviously an attempted coup is in progress. Go directly home. Do not leave your homes until you get further word from the Embassy."

Brian and Lana ran for the front door, not waiting for the maid to hand them their belongings. Lana grabbed her evening bag from the table and looped her arm through Brian's and they were off, running for their car.

The United States Ambassador called a quick announcement, "If this gets too ugly we'll come evacuate you."

No one answered or asked further questions.

The Tyne's home was vacated within minutes. It seemed the ambassador knew what was coming and was ready–or maybe he thought fast.

Brian opened the car door and Lana jumped in.

Lana was speechless.

There were shots all around. "Lana, get on the floor. I think it might be safer."

Finding her voice again she whispered, "Good idea," and she slid down. She was shaking. "The children are going to be so scared."

"Yes, I'm sure they will be. We'll scoot for home as fast as possible. We can make it." Brian's voice was calm and assuring as he jammed on the gas and started homeward.

Those shots sounded so near; home was nine miles away.

The streets were deserted. Minutes before, the trams had been clamoring down the tracks, full of happy jovial people. It seemed someone had flipped a switch and changed the world. Now it was more like outer space darkness void of humans, not at all like lively Asunción.

Even though the Ambassador had warned them not to get speeding tickets, Brian thought a revolution was adequate reason to speed. He floor boarded the gas pedal and went as fast as cobblestone Mariscal Lopez Boulevard would permit.

For a minute Lana's attention was diverted from the immediate fear as she recalled a bit of history about Asunción. Maricsal Lopez Boulevard, named after the great dictator that put Paraguay in the forefront of all of South America, when he built the first rail road, put in a mail delivery system and was so in tune with what the people needed and wanted. The Triple Alliance war wiped out the progressive Paraguay mentality as it nearly wiped out its manpower. The country struggled for years to get back on its feet and was still behind its neighbors in the fifties when the Carters lived there.

Blinking lights reflected in the window above brought Lana's thoughts back to the present danger. "What's that?" She inquired. Sitting on the floor made everything seem so far away and detached.

"I don't know. But I want to get home to Patrick and Tanya so I'm going to ignore it."

The blinking light car speeded up. A man on the passenger side pointed a gun through the rolled down window at Brian and demanded, "*Halto, o tiro*" (Stop or I'll shoot).

Brian slammed on the brakes and pulled the car to the side of the road and parked. Out jumped four rebels. All with guns waving them at Brian.

"*Porque not se paro*?" (Why didn't you stop?)

"We are trying to get home to our family. They are going to be frightened," replied Brian in Spanish.

"Get out of the car with your hands held high."

The rebels had no uniforms, just blue bandannas around their necks to let others know they were the Blue Party. They had flyers to hand out, declaring the rebels represented the people, stating they wanted to return power where it belonged, to the Paraguayans.

Brian objected to being stopped and questioned. He showed them his official papers and said, "We're with the American Embassy and have diplomatic privileges."

"This is a revolution, Señor. Your papers mean nothing to us. Get out and stand beside the car." Then they spotted Lana on the floor. "Who are you hiding there?"

"That's my wife. She's not hiding, I felt she would be safer on the floor with all the shooting."

"Both of you get out of the car," the leader demanded.

Brian helped Lana out to stand beside him.

"Now give me your papers," The leader demanded.

Brian decided dead diplomats don't get to make many complaints. He handed the rebels their documents, hoping they would be returned.

The men of the Blue Party proceeded to search every possible nook–the trunk, under seats and even under the car with a lighted mirror on a long handle.

Street lights were out so the only light came from the rebels' glaring flashlights. It was stone quiet. There were no pedestrians. Everyone had taken cover in a hurry.

With guns being waved in their faces, Lana stood like a statue, speechless, waiting for the next order from the rebels. After a few minutes, having received no harm, she regained her senses. Lana quietly prayed that the rebels would let them proceed home. She also prayed for the Lord to look after their children at home.

If documents meant nothing during a revolution, the rebels or soldiers might invade their sanctuary, their home. Patrick and Tanya would be terrified. Lana felt a serene and peaceful glow seep into her chest and she knew the Lord had heard her silent prayer.

Finally, the Carter's documents were returned and the rebels gave them permission to proceed. Lana let out a big sigh of relief.

"Man, they're a scary bunch."

Brian held his finger to his lips, reminding her their car was wired and they had to be careful of what was said.

Lana's relief was short-lived. Again they were stopped. This time by a roadblock of soldiers in uniforms a half mile or so from where the rebels had stopped them. The blockade was lit with lanterns.

The soldier in charge ordered, "Get out of the car with your hands held high."

Brian replied, "We are with the Embassy and have diplomatic privileges. Here are our papers."

He thought the uniformed soldiers would honor their papers.

Wrong!

"Señor, Get out of the car! We must search you."

As they crawled out of the car the soldier asked, "Where did you come from and where are you going?"

Brian answered, "We have nothing to hide. We are anxious to get home to our family. With all the shooting and noise our son and daughter will be frightened. We left a party at the Tyne's where your President was also. He left in a hurry."

That seemed to soften the soldiers a bit and they gave the Carters more respect.

As Brian was standing there to be searched he couldn't get Ramero off his mind. He was not only a personal friend, he was a devoted family man–one that would forego a political party for his son's birthday celebration. Brian remembered that his informant had warned him that Ramero's house was being watched in case someone tried to warn him.

Brian knew Ramero's phone would be bugged. Brian felt so helpless. Now the best he could hope for was that Franco was successful in getting the note sent via the neighbor's son attending the birthday party, with the message for Ramero to leave immediately with his family. He hoped desperately that Franco did not forget to tell the boy to deliver the note immediately and ask Ramero to open it right away. Hope, that is all he could do.

After an interrogation and thorough search, the soldiers permitted the Carters to proceed.

One block from home Lana could see their house in the distance. She wanted to get out and run, she was sure that she could get there faster than the car. She felt like exploding, the night had been so frightening. Now they were near she felt like celebrating.

More trouble!

A group of rebels emerged from the road side, flashing their lights at them and demanding they stop.

It seemed hours since they had left Tyne's. They went through the same search and question routine. One rebel suggested, "These might be good hostages."

"Maybe. It would give us some bargaining power," another rebel agreed.

"Let's take them to headquarters."

When Lana heard that she stopped breathing for a moment. What would the children do if they were not permitted to return home? They would be frightened now–but if they didn't return all night, the children would be terrified.

"Did I understand his Spanish correctly?" she asked Brian under her breath, hoping she was wrong, but saw he registered alarm.

"Yes, I'm afraid so. I guess I should have taken a chance and let you stay home. I never dreamed it would come to this."

Lana offered a silent prayer for the Lord to touch the rebels hearts and permit them to go home.

Brian turned to the rebels and said, in Spanish, "Our Embassy will be very upset if we don't get home so they can check on us. During this type of trouble they are good about checking to be sure we're at home safe."

There was some discussion in a low voice that was not understandable.

After more discussion and glaring looks, the Carters were handed back their papers and permitted to proceed home. Lana held her stomach and said, "This is too much. I'm nearly over the edge."

Brian pulled in front of the house in the circular driveway and they both ran for the front door. Lana offered a silent prayer of thanks. She was grateful to be home in her comfort zone and with her children.

As Lana and Brian entered the house, the frightened servants ran to meet them. They had been sitting around the kitchen table. Patrick and Tanya were terrified and sat there for a minute, then they ran to join their parents. Patrick ran to Brian and Tanya to Lana who sat down and put her in her lap with big hugs to comfort her. Tanya started to cry. Lana held her close, “Shh! It’s okay, little one.”

“Those shots are so close,” Patrick said trying to sound more mature than he felt. He was shaking inside and so glad to see his parents.

“We are safe inside the house,” Brian comforted, even though he knew they weren’t really all that safe if papers meant nothing and both sides were fighting for control.

Patrick, still standing with his arm around Brian asked, "Dad, what’s happening out there? Who are they shooting?"

"It's a revolution. We have to stay inside our own wall, better yet, inside our home until the curfew and emergency are lifted. No school or outside play until we give you the word. I see you did post the flag, Franco."

"Si, Señor, but with street lights off and all the wild gun shots it was scary. You said to do it; I did it. I was happy to get back inside the house." Franco knew the rebels meant business and wouldn’t honor the flag or papers if they decided to come into the house and search.

“What about the note?” Brian ventured a question, knowing it might be heard by the wrong people.

“I sent it,” Franco lied.

“Thanks.”

Brian sat down. Patrick let out a big rush of air as he sat on the sofa between his dad and mom. "Wow! I'm glad to see you guys. All that shooting is scary. I tried to call you at the Tyne’s to see if you were still there but the phone was dead. That was a long time ago and we didn't know where you were."

"It took ages to get home because we were stopped and searched three times on the way," Lana shared.

"Why?" Patrick asked.“What were they looking for?”

"The rebels and the soldiers both have road blocks to check to see if we're transporting people or supplies to the other side. It's a full-fledged revolution going on. Both sides are determined to win," Brian said.

Tanya stopped crying, but held tight to Lana's neck for assurance. She rested her head on Lana's shoulder, quiet, but shaking. Everything had been so strange and frightening. No lights and the shooting triggered alarm even a five year old recognized.

Patrick edged closer to his dad needing more information. "Who's shooting and why are they shooting?"

Brian rubbed his ear thoughtfully. "There are some people, the Blue Party, called the rebels, because they're rebelling against the current power of government, which is the Red Party. The Blue Party is trying to take over and put their people in power and run Paraguay the way they want. If the rebels succeed, we will then have a new president and cabinet. The rebels are trying to either kill President Stroessner, or make him leave the country."

"Who are the rebels?"

"Paraguayans that don't think the country is being run right and want to make a lot of changes. We now have two armies out there fighting for power. It's called a civil war. Let's stay out of their way. Especially out of their line of fire."

"What is a civil war, Dad?"

"When one part of the country fights another part of that same country," Brian answered.

"What will happen to us?" Patrick was interested in their well being and needed additional information. Each new statement from his father made life more frightening. Patrick wondered if either side would be hostile to the Carters. Would they enter and tear up the place as he had seen in movies and read in books. Were they in danger of being shot as friendly to the other side? He was not comfortable at all living in the middle of a war. This fear is something not experienced in the United States and being back home seemed like a good idea. Hopping a plane and leaving this war behind would be great.

"Good question. As long as we fly our United States flag out front they are supposed to honor our diplomatic immunity and not bother us. As we left Tyne's, the Ambassador made it clear we're to stay home until we've been notified otherwise," Brian said. He remembered both sides had said the papers meant nothing in the revolution.

"What's diplomatic immunity?" Patrick had not heard that term before. Maybe it was the key to their safety.

"When you're a guest in a country at their invitation, you're granted certain privileges," Lana supplied information that might ease Patrick's mind

"How will we know when we can go out? Our phone is dead," Patrick wondered.

"When the revolution is over, phones will be restored. If the Embassy needs to contact us before that, they will send word with a courier," Lana said She remembered the happenings during the rumors of the coup earlier when they had been confined for a couple of days.

"Do you think we're safe?" Patrick asked.

"Yes," Brian responded, not too convincingly.

Patrick shifted his gaze to his mother, "You knew there was going to be a revolution tonight, didn't you? Remember out by the car just before you left to go to the party you said if things got crazy, not to panic. You must have known."

Lana took a very deep breath. She realized that she must guard every word uttered now. Carters knew there was going to be trouble that evening, but Lana didn't want to put Brian deeper in harm's way. She answered Patrick, "I had heard rumors."

Brian gave Lana a long, hard look.

"I feel much safer now that we're home." Lana tried to change the subject back to safer ground. It was reassuring not to have guns waved in their face. She was realistic enough to know if their Embassy papers meant nothing during the revolution, anything could happen. The rebels or soldiers could enter their estate and cause a lot of pain. Especially if one side or the other knew of Brian's status and obviously they did or he wouldn't have received the warning.

She listened to the sporadic gunshots in the background and thought, the word "America" sounded WONDERFUL! Then out loud she ventured, "Brian, let's try and contact our parents and let them know we're safe. You know the headlines tomorrow in the newspaper will read 'Asunción under siege from rebels.' "

"You're right. Better warm up the ham set and try and get a call through. Phone patch preferably so they can hear our voice. If not at least get a message to them."

"If the phone won't work, how can you get the ham radio to work?" Patrick asked.

"The phone lines have been cut off, but the radio works on electricity.

CHAPTER SIX

Two days of solitude followed.

The phone was still dead. There were no visitors, they didn't even venture into the yard. Thank goodness for the storage room with its extra supply of food. Marcelena couldn't go to the market for fresh fruits and vegetables. However, they had their freezer with meat from Argentina, lots of canned goods, flour, sugar, dry milk, etc.

Shots could still be heard in the distance to remind them why they were confined.

The only movement on their grounds was servants going from their quarters in the back of the property to the main house. They did as little of that as possible. At times the shots sounded very close and the Carters didn't want any casualties.

Isolation was nerve-wracking. Brian paced the floor and Patrick peeked out the window to see what was going on. Patrick would yell, "There goes another big army truck full of soldiers, all holding guns. They're scary."

"It's war, son," Lana said. She wished with all her heart it would end and they could get some normalcy in their lives and get papers for Tanya.

Their home sitting high up on the hill gave them an advantage and they could see over the tall wall and watch many of the happenings in the street.

Games at first diverted their energy and feelings, but after a day of chess, Monopoly, Parchisi and ping-pong, the Carters all had frayed nerves. Then the family read. Murder mysteries couldn't take Lana's mind off what was lurking outside their wall. Two armies engaged in meaningless slaughter and struggle for power.

Which group won was not particularly important to the Carters although they thought the Blue Party was more democratic and would benefit Paraguay in the long run.

The third day, Enrique, nicknamed Rick by many of the Americans, arrived in the camioneta (van) to take Patrick and Lana to the airport.

Rick emphasized, "You must pack in a hurry. We must leave in ten minutes."

Tanya asked, "Which case shall I take?"

"Sorry Tanya, your name is not on the list. You must stay behind because you have no passport or traveling papers," Rick said.

"Tanya, Maria will take good care of you until we get back. You help Maria take care of our home," Lana requested.

"Why no me?" she demanded, with huge tears in her eyes.

"They won't let you on the plane because you don't have a passport or travel documents."

"Get 'em for me?"

"We're trying. But they weren't ready when the revolution started and we can't get them now. Be patient, little one. We're trying to be," Lana hated to have Tanya's life torn apart again. Tanya tried to be brave.

"Will Papa still be here?" Tanya asked.

"Yes for now. He'll probably go on the plane tomorrow. You can stay here in this house and you have Maria, Marcelena, Juana and Franco. They will take good care of you until we return which we hope will be soon. Be brave."

Rick told Brian, "The Fosters were held hostage overnight. So Ambassador Cassidy decided it was time to get the families out of Asunción. It will be safer in Argentina."

"Were the Fosters harmed?"

"No. The Fosters were released after the Embassy van went to deliver a special message and found them detained by the rebels."

"Thank goodness," Lana said. She had lived in constant fear some of the Americans would be victims of this crazy war.

Rick instructed, "Each one will be permitted one small suitcase. Pack separate bags. They must not exceed forty pounds."

Lana called, "Be sure and throw in a book, Patrick. It might be a day or two before we can return or go on to the United States."

Tanya, now able to understand some English was upset by the words

United States. She drew her conclusions and started to cry. "You said you'd come back. Now you say you go to United States. Without me?"

"Tanya, we don't know what's happening right now. Let's take one day at a time, okay?" With that Lana picked her up and held her close. She stroked Tanya's hair and pulled it behind her ear, "We want you with us."

Lana put Tanya down and hurriedly threw a few things in her suitcase and asked Tanya, "How about a big smile before I run for the van?"

Tanya wiped her eyes with the back of her hand and forced a weak smile. It would have to do for now. It was so painful to leave Tanya behind with those big tears in her eyes.

Brian and Maria grabbed the packed suitcases and dashed for the waiting van.

Brian hugged Patrick before he jumped in the van. He turned to Lana and pulled her close, "Take good care. I'll see you soon. I love you."

"I love you too Brian." With that she boarded the van and they were off.

Patrick and Lana waved good-bye to Brian and Tanya.

No one spoke, it was like a funeral, so quiet.

Life had been so hectic the last three days that Lana's thinking was all mixed up. Lana wanted the revolution to be over so she could proceed to get documents for Tanya. She wanted the revolution to be over so they could get their lives straightened out. Another assignment for Brian would get him out of this danger zone. They seemed locked in a time capsule and everything was out of their control.

The phones were still out of order and the radio stations were all off the air except the national radio–the one empowered by the Stroessner regime.

Brian watched as most of his family disappeared down the road in the camioneta. What now? Would he be forced to leave without Tanya? Could he somehow smuggle Tanya out during all the upheaval? This might be that golden opportunity they had been looking for. There was another problem–getting her into the States without proper papers. He stood and looked at the road where the van had hurried away. He realized he should go inside where it was safer. His heart ached for the security of the United States and comfort of being safe with his family.

Arriving at the airport Lana could see that two other Embassy vans were there. The adults grabbed their cases and ran for the terminal with their children. Rick said he would be sure the children's cases were there when they needed to board the plane.

Inside was quiet with soldiers everywhere. The airport had been virtually closed since the revolution began. The silence and emptiness made the place seem like a tomb. As a rule the airport was a very social place with happy noises and smiling people. It was where Americans gathered, sometimes even with a small band when one of the American community left or new people arrived.

This day offered no merriment, only tension. It seemed if someone yelled, or lit a match, the whole place would explode.

Each person was stopped when entering the terminal and checked by the soldiers. They checked for correct passports; then they checked to be sure that person was on their list of Americans permitted to leave.

Fear surged up in Lana's throat. She wondered if their names might be on the "don't leave" list if Brian had been discovered by the Stroessner government.

When Lana finally made it to the head of the line, she handed her passport to the soldier.

The soldier searched the list. He looked up at Lana, back at the list and the photo on the passport. Time stood still. Lana caught her breath and held it. He asked, "Señora Carter are you the only one in your family leaving?"

"No Señor, this is my son Patrick. He will be going with me." She turned to acknowledge Patrick and he wasn't there.

"Where's your son?"

"He came in with me. I'll locate him." Lana searched other lines. No Patrick. Had he been taken when she was not looking? Minutes dragged as she looked for Patrick.

Frantically she called over to Pam, "Have you seen Patrick?"

"He was with Mark a minute ago."

Patrick was over by the far window with Mark watching other children proceed to the plane.

"Patrick, you need to come and check in," Lana yelled.

Patrick ran back to Lana. The soldier checked him with the photo on the passport. Nodding, he handed Lana her papers and passport. What a relief. They had passed without difficulty.

Next they checked with Colonel Chegin, the Embassy attache, taking care of the boarding. He instructed Patrick to take his suitcase and board the plane.

The women had to wait for the lottery. Four had to stay behind for the next flight. The names were then called out of all the ladies present. Names of all except the ambassador's wife were put into a large bowl to draw to see who had to remain behind.

Fern, the Ambassador's wife objected, saying her name should also be put in the bowl.

Colonel Chegin said he had orders for her to board the plane and then he would proceed. She gave a shrug as if to say, "I won't hold things up. Let's get this settled and on the way." She picked up her small suitcase and started for the plane. Rick hurriedly relieved her of her suitcase and offered to help her board.

The contents of the bowl were mixed thoroughly, then the first name drawn. It was not Lana's. What a relief! Then the second name. She was so deep in her thoughts she didn't hear who.

Patrick was only nine years old and so young to be left alone to go to a strange country. Lana started to ask Pam whose name had been drawn. She saw Lorie start to cry and knew it was her name.

Next was Karen, an Embassy secretary. That was good, Lana thought, as she didn't have any children. Then she remembered how Karen often bragged about how she slept with different men when their wives were in the states on emergencies. Maybe leaving her here with a wide open field wasn't that great either. At least she couldn't get out and roam with confinement restrictions.

The fourth and last name was pulled. "Lana Carter"

Oh! What now? Big tears formed in her eyes and she was determined not to let them escape. Lana effectively choked them back. "Pam, please take care of Patrick until Brian and I get there."

"You know I will. He's at our house with Mark so often he seems like part of the Belt family. I'm so sorry you have to stay."

Lana picked up her bag, turned and started to the van. Then she decided she had to go say good-bye to Patrick. Lana also remembered the traveler checks that she carried in her purse for emergencies. This was an emergency. Lana set her suitcase down and turned and ran to catch Pam on her way to the plane.

"Here are some travelers checks. I'll sign a couple of hundreds. If you need to, forge our name to others to help with expenses for Patrick until we get there. I'll give Patrick a hundred dollar bill I carry in the back section of the billfold so he'll have some cash on hand. Please lend him what ever he needs. We'll reimburse you when we get there, hopefully tomorrow."

"Don't worry Lana. He's ours until you get to Buenos Aires."

Lana ran ahead to the plane boarded and found Patrick saving her a seat next to him for the evacuation. Lana put her arms around him and could no longer hold back the tears. "I'm not going to get to go with you, Patrick."

"Why not?"

"The plane will hold all but four of us and they drew to see who had to stay behind for the next flight. I was one of the four. Pam Belt assured me she would care for you until we get there. Here is what money I have on me. One hundred American dollars and some Guarani. If it isn't enough, I gave some traveler checks to Pam. I love you."

Lana could see the Atlantic ocean forming in Patrick's eyes and he was fighting valiantly to hold it back and be brave. "Mom, how will I know where to go? How will you know where to find me when you come? Buenos Aires is a big city."

"The Embassy advisor with you will direct everyone to hotels. You will be staying near, or with the Belts. The Embassy will know where you are so they can bring Dad and me to you when we get there. It should be tomorrow if all goes well."

"I don't want to go without you. I'll stay until you and Dad get on the plane too."

"No, you need to get out of this craziness. If for any reason Dad and I don't make it, you know how to get in touch with my parents and they'll make arrangements and care for you until we do get there. You're not alone. The Lord is watching over you. We'll have you in our prayers and Grandpa and Grandma are there for you if you need them."

"Mom, I don't know Argentina," Patrick protested, "I'm scared."

"I know. I know, but we both have to be brave and have faith. We'll come as soon as possible."

"Hurry!" With that he lost it and let out a big manlike sob.

"You'll be okay, Patrick, the Belts are there for you," Lana assured him. Then added, "I sure will miss you."

With that Lana tightened her arms around him, kissed his cheek and turned to get off the plane tears streaming down her cheeks.

She walked back and stood by her suitcase while the plane taxied down the runway. Lana waved in hopes Patrick could see. When the plane was airborne she turned and boarded the van.

Lorie commented, "I thought for a moment you had stowed away and gone with Patrick."

"I'd have liked that. It was so hard to leave Patrick all alone on that plane to go to a strange country and city. At least you have a teenager to help with your three. What instructions did you give them?"

"I didn't. Bob Chegin said he would take care of it and explain what had happened. I didn't want to get all messed up and crying in front of everyone again. Now I feel like a coward. They're probably scared."

Lorie Foster hid her head and Lana could hear the muffled sobs.

Lana put her arm around her. "Lorie, they'll understand. Mike is nearly fifteen and responsible. He'll be worried about you but he'll understand and take care of the others."

"I know."

"Tomorrow we should be with them. Try to hang in there and count the time till we're all together again." Lana was so worried about Patrick. How could he cope with all the adventure facing him? Would Pam realize his trauma and be there for him? Did she or Mark sit with him and let him know he had family near? Even though not blood family, they were a dear caring family. Lana knew the next twenty-four hours would be tough.

"You sound so confident."

Lana remembered the scary feeling she had coming to live in a strange country with her husband and son. Patrick was all alone, being flown off to a strange country and hotel and not knowing if and when he would be reunited with his family. Lana's stomach started to cramp big time. Her ulcer was going to flare. With the tension of the last few days it was entitled.

One nice thing about all this was Tanya would be thrilled to see her. That brought another thought. How could she think of leaving her there alone with Maria tomorrow and take off to join Patrick.

Two kilometers from the airport, twelve rebels jumped in front of the van. They waved their guns and demanded they stop, They swung open the door and asked, "Who's in the van and where are you going?"

"We have four women, their suitcases and one Embassy assistant," Rick answered.

"Open the suitcases," The leader demanded.

When the cases were opened the rebels searched the contents, throwing things hither and yon. What a mess.

Lana's ulcer revolted, she gagged.

Lana moved from the van and made her way toward the side of the road.

"Halt," commanded the rebel leader.

Lana kept walking. Her ulcer was acting up.

"Halt!" he demanded again.

Lana ignored his command. Then she started to heave everything inside. When the rebels saw what was happening they left her alone until she finished.

Cleaning herself as best she could she rejoined the others and she heard Rick tell them, "These are all American women. If America joins the Stroessner side you will be in big trouble if you take these ladies hostage. You'd better think twice before you do anything you'll regret."

"It's our call."

"The van has American Embassy on the side and will be easy to spot and cause you trouble. You know I cannot do anything to help you. I work for the Americans."

The leader paused, looked at his comrades, then nodded. "We'll take our chances. You're now our hostages."

Lana's fear escalated. She wasn't going home. Brian wouldn't know where she was. The whole earth slid right out from under her. The pressure was too much to handle. Her knees buckled; she welcomed unconsciousness.

Rick lifted her aboard. Placing her on the back bench seat and asked Karen to come help.

The rebels told Rick, "Get all the things on the ground from the suitcases and put them in the van."

"Let the women sort them." Rick suggested.

"Just put them all in and then we will worry about sorting later," The leader commanded. "Everyone board the van. Sit in front, except the sick lady."

"I'll guard the rear with the lady," one of the rebels volunteered.

"Very good. You other three come in front with the remaining prisoners."

"Free the women. Take me and the van," suggested Rick.

"Let's get moving," the leader demanded, ignoring Rick.

Lana’s worst fears were realized. She wouldn’t return to Tanya and Brian, but would be taken to an unknown place as hostage.

CHAPTER SEVEN

Brian was pleased that his son and wife were out of the chaos and he hoped to hear from someone soon that the plane had returned and he could join them. His suitcase was packed and ready to go. His big worry was Tanya, she was terrified being deserted by her new family.

"Where's my suitcase?"

"We still do not have papers for you, Sweetie. We can't take you now. We'll be back for you."

"Papa, I'm scared. What happens to me?"

"You will be safe with Maria and Franco."

"Don't leave me, por favor. Take me. I be good and we get papers there."

"It isn't that simple, Tanya. We have to have papers to get you on the plane to go."

"I never go, do I?"

"Yes, some way some time. Not today," Brian said. He held Tanya in his arms and dried some of her humongous tears. She pulled her beautiful dark curly hair behind her left ear. Tanya was shaking. She felt her newfound, secure world falling apart.

"They won't put me back in the orphanage, will they?"

"Goodness no. They will care for you," Brian assured her.

Franco appeared and asked, "Shall I go get fresh supplies?"

"No. We stay right here until the revolution is finished and it's safe to go out. No one is to leave the estate."

The rebels arrived at their headquarters in Villa Morra, jubilant that they had American hostages to barter with and another van to use in transporting leaders throughout the city.

Lana had regained consciousness and realized they had passed the Baptist Hospital. So near Brian, yet so far and so without control of her life.

What a helpless feeling.

The gunman in front waved his gun at the pile of personal effects on the floor and demanded, "Pick up your individual case and your belongings. Then proceed to the desk in front and you will be checked in."

"Take the van and let the ladies go free," Rick pleaded.

"No, I think these women have important information for us. We shall see."

When the questions were finished, Jose, the rebel leader in the compound, told the hostages they would be living in the left wing. The prisoners were put in the same wing of the headquarters but in separate rooms.

Lana was terrified. Isolation with family is grim; isolation from everyone is frightening–especially when the captors are ruthless. She feared they would demand to know about Brian's activities.

With all the turmoil of the revolution, no one missed the Embassy van until they organized to go pick up the men.

The Ambassador stayed calm knowing nothing could be done until they reached Buenos Aires and found out who was missing.

When they reached the hotel in Argentina, there was a list posted indicating the room where new arrivals could locate their families. Brian ran to the room where Patrick was staying. He noticed only Patrick's name was listed. He was shocked when Lana was not there. Brian asked, "Where's your mother?"

"She had to stay behind."

"Why?"

"They had a lottery to see who had to wait for the next flight. Her name was called. Didn't you bring her with you?" Patrick asked, his eyes wide with fright, as he realized she was not with his father.

Brian ran to Patrick putting his arm around his shoulder, trying to stay calm.

"Let's try to figure this out. Where did you last see her?"

"She was standing near her suitcase not far from Rick's van when we took off. I waved to her."

"Did she get into the van?"

"I don't know."

"One of our vans is missing. Now some of the women. Who were the other women kept behind?"

"The only other one I know was Mrs. Foster. Her son told me she never made it to the plane."

"Let's go check with them and see what the Fosters know."

Brian and Patrick left the room to go check the list to see where to find the Fosters. Ambassador Cassidy was standing near, "Robert, who is missing with the van?"

"I'm not sure yet."

"Lana isn't here, neither is Lorie Foster. Where in the world do you think they are?"

"Probably being held hostage, likely by the rebels, but possibly by Stroessner's soldiers. As soon as orientation is over I'll try to radio the Embassy and find out what I can."

All were assembled in the conference room and the Ambassador announced, "The game plan is to live in this hotel for two weeks and if the problems in Paraguay are not resolved we will continue to the United States. Pick up your envelope from Col. Chegin at the desk. It contains necessary papers and emergency money for the present. Please sign for it. A few of the women who did not get on the first plane are missing. Any questions?"

"What happens to our cars, furniture and personal belongings if we don't return?" Margo Murphy asked.

"They will be shipped to you. If they can't be found, you will be compensated for them. But let's not cross that bridge until we get to it. Remember a few months ago when there was a scare of a coup and everything was normal again within forty-eight hours? It's our hope that all will return to normal soon. If not, the backup plan of evacuation to the United States is in effect," Ambassador Cassidy replied.

"What about my wife?" Foster asked.

"We'll try to locate her."

"Is one of our choices to go on back to the States right now with our families? If so, will someone sell our personal effects?" Roger Murphy seemed ready to call it quits and leave.

"Please stay and discuss this possibility with me after the meeting."

"Is anyone protecting our property from being looted in our absence?" Walter Belt asked.

"The Marines assigned to the embassy have volunteered to stay behind and do all they can to protect your interests."

"What are we going to do about school for the children?"

"Skip it for now. This will not be for more than two weeks," Ambassador Cassidy responded.

"Okay!" shouted fifteen-year-old Mike Foster.

"Hopefully we will return before that."

"What's next?" Brian asked.

"Let's plan to meet at ten in this conference room day after tomorrow if we're still here. Please contact Col. Chegin if you have any immediate needs. I will now discuss termination of your Paraguayan tour for those desiring immediate evacuation to the United States."

Brian panicked. He had to get back and search for Lana. What could he do with Patrick while he returned to search? Brian was a pilot, but he had no plane to fly. Maybe he could charter a plane or rent one. He returned to the conference room. He waited until the ambassador finished with the Murphys, the only ones considering leaving immediately.

"I must locate Lana," Brian declared.

"How do you plan to do that?"

"I have my pilot's license to fly small aircraft. So I will rent or charter one."

"How do you think you are going to get into Paraguay? They are not letting any small planes in."

"I'll find a way. Maybe fly to a small runway in Villa Rica," Brian replied.

"No. You absolutely cannot. That would violate our agreement with Paraguay. Possibly you would be shot down in the attempt leaving Patrick with no parents."

Brian realized it was a foolish idea and asked, "What are my options?"

"There is a ham radio at the embassy here in Argentina and if one of the Marines happens to be at the one in Asunción they could possibly be of assistance."

Brian and Patrick headed for the address given them to check the ham radio set and try to locate someone to assist in Asunción, since Brian couldn't return.

The third day in captivity at the rebels headquarters was not as pleasant as the first two where they had been interrogated only. Now they were threatened with bodily torture if they did not reveal all information asked.

The huge guard they called Poco Loco was frightening in appearance with his piercing, almost black eyes, an ugly scar on his forehead and pock marks on his face. Glaring from his mouth when he sneered was a hideous large gold capped tooth in front. Even more frightening, he seemed to get pleasure out of scaring and torturing people.

Lana was determined not to divulge information about Brian being a secret agent. Before the day was over she had a few bruises to remind her of her stubbornness. She also had a promise from Poco Loco, "If you do not cooperate better, Señora Carter, next time around you will not like it at all. I can be mean, very mean."

Lana was returned to her room. It stank of mold and was not kept clean. The sheets and pillow were old and stained. They were damp from the humidity. The whole headquarters was depressing. Lana was homesick and frightened.

The headquarters was an old estate that the rebels had taken over and converted to their operation center. Lana could see through the dirt-streaked windows, which had metal bars on them, that the yard was unkept. The interior was also in need of repairs. There were large stains on the walls and a couple of places on the wall had been patched but not repainted. She longed to be in her clean bed with clean sheets and most of all Lana yearned to be with her family. Safe.

Sitting bent over on the edge of the cot, holding her head in her hands, she remembered how frightened Patrick had been when he had been sent on alone in the plane. Was he okay? She hoped Brian was with him.

Lana could not sleep at all that night, She was frightened about what lay in store for her the next day. Where was her family and why wasn't someone coming to rescue her?

Maria was furious when she came into the master suite to find Franco going through the desk of Señor Carter. "Franco, what right do you have to search?" she demanded.

"I'm looking for the keys to the locked storage in the garage. I need some supplies."

"The keys not here; they in kitchen."

"Oh, yeah."

"You been acting muy malo Franco. What you doing?"

"I'm trying to keep things up while the Carters are gone."

Tanya heard angry voices and came to check. She asked, "When I see Mama and Papa?"

"Soon, I hope."

Franco glared at Maria and Maria returned the scorching look. Tanya looked from one to the other not understanding the tension.

Franco went to get the key, but he stopped in the room with the ham radio. He turned on the set. He had practiced it other times, in the absence of Brian and knew exactly how to work it. Tanya followed and watched from the door, saying nothing.

Franco thought he could glean information from the ham radio since there was no information coming on the regular radio. He scanned the dial.

Alarmed when he heard Brian's voice calling ZP5 land. Brian called repeatedly, "CQDX, CQDX, this is Brian Carter, please anyone in ZP5 land. Please come in. C Q ZP5 land, please, if you hear me, answer."

Tanya ran to Maria. "Papa calling on radio. Come."

When they heard his plea again, Maria demanded, "Franco, answer him!"

Franco turned off the set and taking the key, dashed out the back door.

Maria called after him. "Franco, answer the Señor. He sounds troubled."

Franco went through the back hedge next door to check with Estelle.

Estelle was not only a neighbor, she was also the daughter of the former President of Paraguay–a close friend of Brian and Lana.

Estelle was jubilant, "We hope to be in complete control in a few days now. It's going better than we had imagined."

"Do you know of any special problems with the Carters?"

"No. I understand all Americans were evacuated. Oh yes, some of our group did take women hostages. Would you like to check and see who?"

"Of course. Right away."

"They are being held at headquarters."

Franco took the Carter's private car with Embassy tags and headed for Villa Morra, taking a note Estelle prepared.

When he arrived at the rebel headquarters, he recognized some of the rebels as faithful followers of the former regime when he served as gardener for the former President. They consulted together, then honored the note and showed Franco into the wing with the American prisoners.

Lana heard Franco's voice and screamed with joy. "You have located me. Thank you, Franco. I knew someone would come and rescue us. Guard, open the door and let me go please," she pleaded.

Franco and the guard turned and headed for the door without one word. Lana sat and waited for their return to liberate her. She waited all morning. No more Franco.

Fear surged through her as she realized Franco was not returning. Why had he been there if not to rescue her? Another sleepless night, long and dreary.

Franco returned home and went next door and reported, "Señora Gaston, one of the prisoners is Señora Carter. Please go and see what you can do for her. She begged me to take her home."

"Franco, I'll check soon."

"How soon?"

"Return tomorrow and we'll see what can be done. Remember she is a valuable prisoner. Her husband is somehow mixed up in intelligence work for the States. You helped us discover that."

"I'm worried. The señora had many bruises. The Carters have been very honorable with me and it pains me to see her so frightened and bruised. I feel responsible."

"I'll see what can be done."

"Hurry, please. I have given you much information on them. I have betrayed her."

"Come tomorrow, Franco."

The next morning, early, Brian and Patrick headed for the Embassy and the ham radio. First they scanned the dial to see what they could hear. Nothing.

They called for a response from ZP5 area.

No answer.

They called repeatedly. No answer. Discouraged, they left.

Franco had left the radio on so he could monitor calls. He thought he would gain information about the revolution.

Tanya heard her papa's voice again. She ran to Maria. "Come talk to Papa. He's on radio."

"I don't know how to work the radio. Get Franco."

Tanya ran to Franco, pleading, "Franco, Papa on radio. Come talk to him."

Franco didn't want Brian to know he could operate the radio. He did not want to tell the awful truth about Lana. He didn't want to be asked where she was and have to lie or incriminate himself.

Franco finally answered, "I can't right now. I'm in the middle of nailing new boards on the side of the storage area."

"Por favor, Franco."

Franco ignored Tanya and continued nailing.

Tanya returned to Maria, "Maria, come, I know how to do it. I watched Papa. He turns one switch to talk, other to listen. Come, I teach you," Tanya pleaded.

As they entered the office, they no longer heard Brian's voice. He had left the radio.

As they left, Brian reached out and put his arm around Patrick, "Someone will hear us soon son. I know they will."

"Dad, what if no one hears us? What then?"

"They will, or the coup will be finished so we can return and find her."

"This is one scary mess. I wish we were safe back in the States."

"Yes, I'm scared out of my skull, Patrick. But I'm in a no-win situation right now to rescue Mom."

"Dad, I feel ten years older than a month ago. Coming to this city by myself, then worrying about Mom. It has made me see things differently."

"Let's talk about it, Son. What's most important to you now?"

"Being together and safe as a family."

"I guess we don't appreciate all we have, until we don't have it–like American freedom."

Lana felt more comfortable realizing Franco knew she was a captive. She hoped Brian wouldn't do something foolish trying to rescue her.

Lana would gladly give up all the glamour and excitement of this assignment at the Embassy for an eight-to-five research position for Brian.

A few days ago she thought she had the tiger by the tail. Her biggest problem was papers to take Tanya to the United States. Now, freedom looked priceless. How could she attain it? What possibility did Lana have to escape?

As Lana's mind reeled a hundred miles a minute, Poco Loco entered the room by himself, leaving the other rebel to guard the door.

She gave a brave smile and said, "Buenos dias". She thought, *Being friendly surely can't hurt.*

Poco scowled at her. He came forward and commanded her, "Put your hands together. Behind your back." Then he tied them securely. Too tight. They hurt.

Lana felt helpless and terrified with her hands tied. Poco's leering smile appeared and that gold tooth glared like a warning of what was to come.

"I find you very attractive, Señora Carter. If you choose not to answer my questions I'll understand that you are not good at information–then I will see how good you are at sex."

Lana's heart froze. Under no circumstance could or would she divulge Brian's position.

Poco Loco continued his interrogation.

"What all does your husband do here in Paraguay?"

"He is supervising building a test unit at the University and he works at the Embassy."

"What does he do at the Embassy?"

"He helps in many project plans."

"What type of projects?"

"Projects to help your country. Like getting medical help increased for the masses that need help."

"What else does he do?"

"He has many important reports to make on accomplishments here in Paraguay. It keeps him very busy."

"Reports on what the government is accomplishing or the Embassy or the rebels?"

"The Embassy."

"Then how did you know there was going to be a revolution?"

“I didn’t.”

“Why did your son say you knew?”

Lana instantly remembered how Patrick had stated that she knew the night the revolution started.

She stood silently, saying nothing.

“I asked you a question, Señora.”

“I had heard rumors.”

“From whom?”

“I don’t remember. Just rumors that there was trouble brewing.”

“You don’t want to be honest with me.” Poco sneered as he came close and reached to stroke her breast. Then he grabbed her hair and yanked her head back to kiss her. He tried to put his filthy tongue into her mouth but she kept her teeth clenched tightly. No way could she let that slime bum enter her anywhere. With hands tied it was difficult to defend herself, but when he started to pull his head back giving up on his kiss, she reached over and bit Poco on the arm.

"We have a feisty one here. I like that. Would you prefer to tell me more about the rumor? Is your house wired? By whom? We could have a friendly chat."

Lana did not reply.

Poco Loco ran his hand down Lana's stomach and reached to lift her skirt. Lana's feet were free so she gave it all she could, kicking, aiming for his groin. Poco was too fast for her and caught her leg and threw her to the floor. He tore her blouse half off as he leered and laughed. "Gotcha, gotcha." His wretched smile froze Lana's heart. She felt defenseless. She didn't have a fair opportunity to fight with her hands tied. She had tried biting, then kicking. What could she do to protect herself from rape?

Poco Loco was enjoying her mental torture. "I have you right where I want you, Señora."

Lana was getting nauseated. Her ulcers were reacting.

She looked up and at the door stood Estelle. "Halt! Halt Poco!" she demanded.

Lana half screamed and half cried. A friend had come to her rescue. Lana was completely out of control and hysterical. "Estelle, Estelle. Thank goodness you're here to help me."

Lana turned, struggling to her knees as Estelle reached her. Lana laid her head on Estelle's shoulder, sobbing hysterically. A friend's arms encircled Lana.

Looking toward Poco, Estelle let go with a stream of Guarani. Lana had not learned the country language, but she recognized the body language and the tone of voice.

Lana observed the two glare at each other. If looks could kill, they would both be dead.

"Estelle, you are truly a savior. He was going to rape me!" sobbed Lana. "What happened to Franco?"

"He sent me to get you. He couldn't get you released."

Estelle still glared at Poco Loco. "Sometimes I think you are truly a bit mad, Poco."

He glared right back. It dawned on Lana that these two knew each other. What in the world?

Estelle untied Lana's hands.

Lana shook them to get the circulation going again. Would she be freed to go to Argentina?

"Estelle, can you get me out of here and home?"

"Yes, I'll take you away from here immediately."

Estelle found a blouse in Lana's suitcase to replace the torn one. She escorted Lana to the front desk.

"I want Señora Carter released in my custody."

"No, she is our most important hostage."

"You will release her now," commanded Estelle.

Lana realized that Estelle had some authority here by her tone of voice.

After a long bitter silence, he agreed. "Very well. but she is to be held hostage and not released to go home or to Argentina."

"That is agreeable."

Leaving the building they approached Estelle's chauffeur, who was patiently waiting at the curb. He opened the door and helped Estelle and Lana into the car.

"Drive us to Mother's estancia," Estelle commanded.

At Marla's estate Lana was held hostage but treated like a friend, given her private belongings from the rebel headquarters along with anything she desired in the guest suite she occupied. It was much better than the prison. The room had clean sheets, lovely surroundings and friends to talk to. No Poco Loco.

Marla, Estelle's mother, was a gracious former first lady, who spoke seven languages. She had a grand estate with orchids blooming in the courtyard. The home was built of thick adobe that kept it cool in the summer and warm in the winter.

Lana realized the only difference between being a prisoner and an honored guest was the door was kept locked when she was in her room. When she was eating or visiting in the living room or courtyard, then Jorge, the guard, was near and alert to deter any get away attempt.

Lana was a prisoner, but she was fed and treated with respect, like a houseguest.

"It is a most difficult time, Lana. The country is in need of change," Marla confided.

"What type of change?"

"To be liberated. To be freed. President Stroessner is big with his statements of democracy. But, in truth, he is a dictator. When my husband ruled they had an honest cabinet and the people had some say."

"Is that the purpose of the rebels? Give the people more control?"

"Yes," Marla answered emphatically.

"Who is financing this revolution?" Lana asked.

"Many of the businessmen who want to protect their financial base. They realize that until we are free, their business is in jeopardy."

"Do you want to be the next President, Marla?"

"No, no. I just want a trusted person elected who will return the rights to us, the people."

"Would you please liberate the other American women from headquarters? I'm concerned about them. I was treated badly and fear they are being victimized too," Lana asked sincerely.

"At this time we can do nothing more. However I will discuss this with several of the leaders and see what can be done."

"Thank you."

Lana learned more about the rebel's cause and why they felt they were rescuing the people of Paraguay.

Many of the rebel leaders visited Estelle and Marla giving Lana inside information not only on what was going on but who was in charge of making it happen.

To Lana's surprise, Estelle was one of the powerful leaders and commanded much respect from others.

Marla was also involved in planning and organizing. She had a strong influence on the rebels' actions. Most of the rebels were loyal followers of her late husband, the former President.

Lana was very interested and sympathetic to the rebels' cause and wondered why the United States was interested in keeping the present government in power if what Estelle and Marla said was true.

True democracy wasn't to happen with the Stroessner government. They had votations where the country people were loaded in trucks and busses to go and vote. But Stroessner's Red Party counted the votes. Stroessner always won, of course. He could then claim a huge victory and that the people wanted him to rule.

Lana pleaded with Marla, "Please tell Brian that I am alive and safe. He'll be so worried."

"Remember the phones are dead," Marla reminded Lana.

"You could get word to him through Estelle when she returns home in the evening. Please let him know I'm okay."

"I'm sorry, Lana, but not at this time. The revolution will soon be finished and you can return to your family."

"You don't need to tell him where I am," Lana pleaded.

"Not now," Marla stated emphatically.

Chapter Eight

At the hotel in Buenos Aires the Americans were assembled in the conference room. Ambassador Cassidy looked intent. "We have decided it is time to continue to the United States. When the political situation clears in Paraguay, we will consider your return. In the meantime many will be assigned elsewhere."

All words were falling on deaf ears as far as Brian was concerned. He would not return to the States without Lana. That was final. He made his way to the front of the group to settle this with Bob Cassidy.

As he reached the Ambassador, an aide ran in and handed Bob a note. As the ambassador read, his smile grew larger and larger. He let out a squeal of delight. "Just a minute. We won't have to go Statesside yet. We are going to return to Asunción. President Stroessner and his government are in control."

Every one shouted, clapped and hugged. Sounds of joy filled the air. Now they could get back to their possessions. Most importantly, Brian could search for Lana.

Franco heard the jubilant sounds in the street and assumed that the rebels were now in power. He was happy and felt he had supported a great cause.

Maria had the radio on full blast; many stations were available. They were announcing safety to return to the streets. President Stroessner's voice loud and clear assured the people that the government was again in complete control. The coup had been thwarted.

Franco grimaced. He was in danger. Also the rebel leaders would be hounded if identified. Corumbá! Worst of all he had put Señora Carter in a position that she would no doubt be eliminated. She knew too much and Estelle could not free her. He was filled with disappointment and fear. The Carters had been good to him. How could he have betrayed that trust and friendship? Now what could or should he do?

Franco went to his room. He sat on the bed and wondered what next for him. Franco feared for himself also. Señor Carter would no doubt realize Franco's betrayal. He alone was responsible for putting Señora Carter in this terrible mess. He had taken papers to the rebels and reported on the Carters' activities. After careful deliberation, Franco decided he must try to rescue Señora Carter.

He had even given the rebels the note meant for Ramero, warning him to escape, instead of sending it to Ramero as requested by Brian. What a fool he had been. His big problem now was how he could rescue Señora Carter.

Brian and Patrick arrived back at the Carter estate early in the afternoon. Tanya was jumping with joy. Dancing, yelling and clapping, she jumped right up into Brian's arms. "You here, Papa. You no go back to the States without me."

"We are here, Sweetie. Is Mama here?"

"No, she no with you?"

"Have you heard from the Señora, Maria?"

"Isn't she with you?"

Tanya broke in with, "Papa, I heard your voice on your radio."

Estelle was devastated when she heard the coup had failed. It seemed so well planned and certain to succeed. The rebels had many strong holds just two days ago. If Stroessner found out Estelle was one of the rebel coordinators she knew bad things would befall her whole family, especially her mother.

Her huge problem at the moment was Lana. Lana knew far too much and would have to be eliminated in a very careful way so the American embassy would think it was an accident. Estelle and Marla had both been very free with information feeling sure the rebels were going to win and rule. Now this terrible loss would cause desperate problems. Lana knew many of the rebel leaders and their future plans. She knew where headquarters was and how they functioned.

Lana realized with the rebels being defeated she was in grave danger. However, Estelle and Marla were good friends. Surely they would liberate her. She would promise to keep their secrets. She felt that promises would not be enough to liberate her. She felt completely helpless. Maybe she could open a window and escape when the guard snoozed at night. She looked up and of course there were iron bars on the windows like all good homes in Asunción–to protect them from intruders. Now they would foil an escape.

Lana thought, "what was it Mom used to say ... something like, By the yard life is hard, by the inch life's a cinch. So take it one inch at a time for now." Thoughts of her mother were overpowering, Vera was such a dear positive soul. To hear her voice and feel an embrace from her would be heaven. Tears escaped, then Lana knew she had to get control, be positive and be creative.

To be in Brian's arms would be such a comfort. Lana longed to be with her family. She wondered how Patrick was, if they had returned from Argentina and if they were searching for her.

She yearned for her dear Mom and wanted to share her children with their grandparents. She knew that Vera would be a great asset to Patrick and Tanya. Her Mom was so good with tiny children and Tanya needed a grandma to love and spoil her as only a grandma can. Vera was a positive influence in Patrick's life. He had mentioned many times how he missed their visits to Phoenix since coming to South America.

Lana was homesick. She missed her husband, she missed her children, she missed her mom and dad. She wanted to be free and return to her comfort zone.

Looking at her situation realistically, Lana knew in her heart Estelle could not free her. If Lana wanted to live, she had to escape. How?

That afternoon she was invited to tea with Marla and another guest, a Señora de Irala, a woman of pure blue blood from times past in Asunción. Lana looked for an opportunity to escape. The guard was always near.

Marla was sad but attentive. The loss of the coup had dampened the spirits of the people present and the conversation was very dreary. Their warmth toward Lana had chilled.

Lana had an idea. "El bano, por favor."

Jorge, the guard, escorted her to the bathroom.

She looked for a possible escape in the rear of the estate. She saw one through the hedge in the back of the beautiful flower garden. However, Lana knew it wouldn't help. The estancia was several kilometers from Asunción and she would be tracked down long before reaching there.

The country busses were always overloaded and she had no money to pay for passage. She had given what she had to Patrick when he left for Argentina. Maybe the bus driver would take her watch as payment. It was worth a try if she could make her way to the bus line.

With a wait and hopeful attitude Lana returned to Marla and the downbeat conversation of how the next coup would succeed.

Marla observed, "We need more support from financial leaders."

Señora de Irala agreed and added, "More important, we need more inside support of the cabinet and army leaders. After all, that's how President Stroessner gained power from your husband, Marla. We need Support from within."

"Yes, that's the answer," agreed Estelle. "It was the betrayal of the government officials and the army leaders that stole power from my father."

"We must gain information about those inside the power circle and then recruit members who still yearn for the freedom of the past," Marla decided.

"The liberal party's domain is rapidly decreasing under Stroessner's rule. He is tightening the rope. He is making it more difficult for people to think for themselves. We must free them," Señora de Irala declared.

"If we don't succeed soon it will be years before we can build a strong base to work from," Marla agreed.

Brian, Patrick and Tanya piled into the car and drove to the Embassy to ask for help from Ambassador Cassidy in locating Lana.

"Bob, if you think my wife is being held captive by the rebels how can we locate them?"

"I know where their headquarters is located. However, as a courtesy to the present President we must first notify him. He will offer assistance."

"When?" Brian was anxious to get the search started.

"Now. I'll call immediately," Bob answered.

Ambassador Cassidy called President Stroessner directly. "We would like permission to go to the rebel headquarters and see if our Americans are being held hostage."

"Yes, of course. I shall send assistance and transportation to your

Embassy immediately to accomplish this," agreed the President.

"I'll follow your convoy and greet Lana when she is released," Brian said.

President Stroessner sent a truck full of soldiers and a van to transport them in case the confiscated Embassy van was not there. Brian, Patrick and Tanya followed the convoy.

The rebels were hesitant to lead them to the prisoners. Soldiers convinced them they must. When they entered the wing where the hostages were imprisoned, they found everyone except Lana.

"When did you last see or talk to Lana, Lorie?" Brian asked.

"It has been several days. Time gets lost here."

"What was the last thing you remember?"

"She screamed. Then I think they moved her somewhere else."

"You don't remember how long ago?"

"Not exactly. But it was over a week ago, I'm sure," Lorie guessed.

"They're a cruel bunch. Poco, one of the guards was especially horrible. He took pleasure in torture. When I didn't know the answers he thought I should know, he raped me with pleasure. Tying my hands behind my back to help victimize me," Karen said.

"That's terrible, Karen. Are you handling this nightmare okay?" Brian asked.

"Not really," Karen responded tearfully. " Sex will never be the same for me again."

Brian stood near Karen and put his arm around her, "Karen, have you considered a request for a States side assignment? You should be near your family. You're alone here and you need the moral support of your friends and family."

A tear slid down Brian's cheek. More in realization of what may have happened to Lana. "When was the last time you talked to Lana?"

"I didn't. We were separated. The screams were our only communication. I'm sure it was Lana that screamed the day before I was raped."

"No telling where Lana is or what happened," Brian muttered as he was thinking the unthinkable. Had Lana been killed because of his activities?
Patrick cried with disappointment at not finding his Mother. "What do we do

now, Dad?" he sobbed.

"Question the former rebel that was in charge. He's being held prisoner by President Stroessner. I think his name is Jose. He must know something about where Lana is. I'll ask Ambassador Cassidy for some official assistance."

Jose was not helpful. He said he had no information on Señora Carter. It was possible she had escaped and was hiding out.

Brian spoke to Ambassador Cassidy. "It's doubtful that she's hiding. Lana would have heard by now that the coup had ended and she would come home if she could. If she's alive they have her. But where?"

"I don't know. But we'll follow each lead and find her," Bob assured Brian.

"She may be dead," Brian whispered as tears again escaped. He wouldn't say it in front of the children. He didn't want to frighten them. His stomach was boiling with fear. He had to do everything possible to locate her. Soon.

Rick drove to the Carter's to try and find out more about Lana since she was not one of the hostages released when he was. Franco answered his ring of the bell at the gate.

"Have you heard anything more about Señora Carter?" Rick asked.

"No. I'm worried. I have a feeling I know where she might be. Would you lend me the van so I can go check?"

"That is forbidden. I am not permitted to let you drive an Embassy vehicle. But I could take you," suggested Rick.

"I have information I can't tell you."

"I can keep a secret," Rick promised.

"That will be very important. I have a feeling she is being held in the country."

"Let's get a back up of some soldiers?"

"I think it best we go alone."

"Soldiers could help in an emergency."

"I feel alone and in secret best."

"Okay. Where in the country?"

"Rick, you must keep this confidential if you go. It is very important to me and to many people. Promise?"

"Yes, of course. If we can rescue Señora Carter, that is the important thing. You don't have to explain anything. My lips are sealed."

"Start driving out toward Lake San Bernardino. I will tell you when and where to turn," Franco requested as he climbed into the van.

When near Marla's estancia Franco said, "We need to find a hiding place for the van near here. I will go on foot and get the Señora. It might take a lot of time. Be patient."

"Let me come with you? There is safety in numbers."

"In this case maybe not. I'm known there and won't look so suspicious if I'm caught," Franco said.

"As you wish."

"Speaking of getting caught. If I don't return by dark go tell Señor Carter I'm looking for the Señora and will return as soon as possible. Please return to this exact spot tomorrow and wait again."

"This sounds very risky. Are you sure you don't want some military backup?"

"Definitely not. Do as agreed. If I don't come tomorrow then alert the police and the Carters and come rescue us if you can. We will be in the estancia to the east."

Franco sneaked up to the corner of the garden of the estancia. His thoughts were on how to signal the Señora. She must be notified he was there waiting and find an opportunity to sneak away.

Lana, Marla and Estelle were having tea in the courtyard–their usual afternoon activity. The guard, Jorge was posted near the garden gate watchful of all movement.

Once Franco thought Jorge looked his way and even though Franco was hidden among the shrubs and could not be seen, it made him uneasy.

If the guard found him hiding instead of coming directly to the door, he would probably be eliminated along with the Señora.

Lana excused herself and returned to her room. The guard followed and locked the door. He returned to have a jovial time teasing the maid.

Franco thought maybe the chance would present itself when the guard was distracted by activities with the maid. Hopefully. That seemed the only possibility at the moment. Franco continued to hide and tried to hear what Marla was saying. "I don't approve of killing Lana."

"She knows too much," Estelle said.

"Maybe we could pull some strings and have the Carters deported. If Stroessner knew Brian was working as a double agent he would ship him out immediately."

"How do we accomplish that, Mother?"

"I don't know. Let me think on it. If we kill her and we are found out, it will be worse than all the rest of our problems."

"True. We have to make it look like an accident somehow."

"Jorge could devise a way. But I hope we can find another solution. I like Lana."

"I do also, however, I think the sooner the better. If it is accomplished quickly it is over and we don't have to worry about being discovered."

"Yes, that's true," answered Marla. They sat and looked into space for a minute. "Let's talk to Jorge and see what he advises."

Franco watched and waited from his hiding place beyond the shrubs.

Lana rang her bell to be released to use the bathroom. The guard did not like being interrupted in his fun with the maid. Jorge slowly went and unlocked the door. He followed Lana to the bath and waited by the door. The maid came by and giggled and signaled Jorge to follow her.

When they were alone the maid smiled, held out her arms and Jorge gladly accepted the invitation. The embrace was more than casual. She tugged at him to follow her to the rear to the servants' quarters. He did, forgetting for the moment his charge of locking Lana's door again.

Franco was delighted. Now was the time. He watched and when Lana came out of the bath she looked for Jorge. Not seeing him, she turned and started to her room.

Franco came out of hiding and motioned to Lana to come to him.

But Lana didn't see Franco. She headed for her room.

Franco couldn't catch Lana's attention. He hurriedly secured himself in the shrubbery again.

Lana started for a word with Marla, then reconsidered. Her heart sang with hope of a good ending to this horrible nightmare. If Jorge did not come to lock the door, she could leave after dark. Probably her only opportunity to return to her husband and family. Brian would never suspect she was being held prisoner at Marla's, unless Franco told him. She now suspected that Franco was involved. He was the only answer to how the rebels had her note from Brian about the house being wired. He wouldn't dare say a word. It would be a dead giveaway of his involvement. Lana knew her time was limited if she didn't escape soon.

Hours passed and Franco knew if he approached the house in daylight he was a goner. He had to wait for another opportunity or dark, which was not far off Then he could sneak up to Lana's window and have her come out and join him for a fast flight to the van. He had not seen Jorge return to the house. That gave him hope. It probably meant Lana's door was still unlocked. Maybe he was being given a second chance after all. Patience.

Jorge, remembering his charge of watching Lana, emerged, entered the house, then returned.

Franco watched and realized Jorge had probably gone to lock Lana's door. Another opportunity foiled.

Lana heard the key turn. Why hadn't she escaped to the shrubs in back before he locked the door? Now it was too late. That hope was down the drain. Darkness was approaching, and she had to think of some way to escape. Time was of the essence. Marla's coolness indicated all was not well. They had been very close friends. She knew Marla was withdrawing that warm friendship to justify Lana's death. How sickening.

When it became dark and Franco didn't return, Rick decided he must go tell the Carters what was happening.

Brian was delighted to have some information giving him hope because the commander of the rebels had refused to give any information. "Where is Franco?"

"I promised not to tell," Rick responded.

"Please tell me and maybe we can help in rescuing Lana," pleaded Brian.

"Señor, a promise is a promise and I cannot do that. But he did want you to know what he was trying to do. I think he knows where Lana is and has a good chance of getting her. I'm to go back tomorrow and wait for him."

"Please go and wait. What if he doesn't come tomorrow?"

"Then I'm to tell you and the police where he is. Then you must try and rescue Franco and Lana."

Brian paced the floor most of the night. Maybe Lana was still alive. Where? Why couldn't Rick tell them? He was frantic to know more. Brian was desperate to find Lana. He felt completely helpless. Maybe he could follow Rick tomorrow and see where he went. On the other hand that might foil the escape.

"Can't you sleep either, Dad?" Patrick asked, appearing at the door.

"No, Son, I'm too worried about your mother."

"I heard what Rick told you, Dad. Franco seems to have some information. I hope he isn't too late."

"Me, too. I'll not rest until I hold Lana in my arms," Brian felt at the moment his need was to comfort his son, "Come, let's read awhile and maybe that will helps us relax. Your choice, what shall we read?"

Read they did, for over an hour.

Patrick curled up on the chaise and succumbed to sleep. Brian wasn't able to do the same. Every muscle in his body seemed to be tied in knots.

Franco waited until dark, then seeing the light on and supposing Lana to be in the large guest room, he approached and tapped on the window lightly.

No response.

Franco tapped again, a little louder.

Lana came to look out, she opened the window and looking through the bars, seeing Franco, asked, "What goes?"

"I'll be waiting in the bushes near the corner of the orchid garden through tomorrow. Any time you can get free, please come. I have Rick and the van waiting near. I fear for your safety here," Franco whispered.

"I know. Me too. I'll come if possible." She closed the window in case Jorge had heard her talking.

Franco spent a long sleepless night in the bushes and hoped tomorrow would again present an opportunity for escape.

Not long after light dawned a tray was delivered to Lana. She was not invited to the table for breakfast. That seemed bad news to Franco. He watched closely for Lana to emerge for the bathroom and her morning shower.

Jorge agreed with Marla, that to get rid of Lana and leave no clue would be easier if the small auto was wired with a bomb, then offered to Lana as a means to go and check on her family. She would be blown to bits and leave no evidence of the whole mess.

Jorge promised to take care of it.

Franco saw Jorge working on the car and he put the puzzle together and groped for a way to warn Lana.

The car had been driven out of the usual parking space and parked beyond, far enough not to harm the other cars when it blew. Franco panicked.

Lana rang the bell to have the door unlocked to use the bathroom. No one answered. She rang again. No response. Finally, very late, Jorge came to unlock Lana's door. It was mid morning and Lana's bladder was killing her.

As she hurried to the bathroom. Jorge was trying to tell her something but she couldn't wait and talk right then. When she had emptied her bladder she came out of the bathroom and asked, "Jorge, what were you saying?"

"I have good news for you, Señora. You are free to take the blue car out beyond the parking area and go check on your family."

Lana was ecstatic. Freedom.

Singing in the shower was a way to celebrate her newfound hope of freedom. She stopped singing in the middle of a sentence, as a new thought struck her speechless. Why hadn't Marla delivered the good news? Why had she not been allowed in the breakfast room this morning but instead sent a tray? It was strange, unusual and cold.

If Lana was being offered freedom why not celebrate with her and wish her well? What game were they playing?

She dried off and dressed then returned to her room to pack her personal belongings. She decided she would go to Marla and thank her for her gracious hospitality.

Jorge was at the door of her room. "Where are you going, Señora?"

"To thank Marla and say good-bye."

"I'm sorry, that's not possible. Marla left early for Estelle's and will not return until evening. I would suggest you thank her later," Jorge said and he again headed back to his love in the rear of the property.

Maybe that's why all the changes--tray in her room, no one answering the bell to unlock the door to go to the bath. Lana was crazy with suspicion.

Maybe she should go to Franco in back and escape with him. But Jorge went to the back with the maid. He would see her. She could not go that direction. She must leave in the car.

With a car waiting and the opportunity to get away, she took the keys left by Jorge, picked up her small suitcase and headed for the blue car.

Another weird thing. Jorge did not offer to help her. He wasn't carrying her suitcase, he was not going to the car with her to help her in–most servants and guards would do that. Instead he returned to the maid, Trina.

A tug of fear sprouted in Lana.

As she reached the car and started to open the door she heard Franco from the bushes, "Señora, stop! Don't start that car! Don't start that car!" he commanded in a very strong, but quiet voice. "Come with me."

She looked toward the edge of the orchid garden and there was Franco hidden from the house in the shrubs.

"Come with me. NOW!" he repeated.

His tone of voice turned Lana's fear into panic and she left the car door open, dropped her small case and ran to join Franco who was now at the side of the yard behind some shrubs, out of sight of Jorge and the maid. Franco took her arm. "Follow me–Rick is waiting for us." They ran toward the hidden van, jumped in and sped toward the city.

Jorge was occupied with Trina, the maid, but subconsciously waited for several minutes to hear the big explosion. Nothing happened. He finally walked to the door to see if he could see the car. It was around the corner so he couldn't get a good look. He waited longer, not wanting to be near when it exploded. He went back to Trina to wait for the bang.

"I'm so glad you trusted me and didn't start the car, Señora. It had been wired with a bomb to get rid of you in a very quiet way."

"That would not be too quiet."

"I meant in not an obvious way. The rebels are very good at those things. It's an easy way to get rid of an enemy and leave little evidence of what happened or even who was in the car if the bomb is large enough."

"Wow! That was close. I'm so glad you were there, Franco. This is the second time you have rescued me. I'm much in your debt. Did Señor Carter send you?"

"No, I had a hunch this is where you were hidden and Rick agreed to help me find out."

"How long have you been hiding and waiting, Franco?"

"Since yesterday. When your guard went with the maid last night I hoped to get your attention but failed."

"You were there and watching?"

"Yes. After I asked you through the window to come if you had a chance, I slept all night in the bushes."

"Thanks."

"Thanks for coming back this morning, Rick. If you hadn't been there I would be dead by now."

"My pleasure. Señora, your husband will be thrilled to see you. He has been very worried."

"Is Patrick back too?" Lana inquired.

"Si, they are waiting our arrival," Rick announced.

Lana was very quiet as she contemplated the events of the last few weeks.

Would Estelle and Marla also be awaiting their arrival? They lived in the estate next to the Carters and if Jorge got word to them that Lana escaped, would they find another way to keep her from reaching safety? Lana had butterflies in her stomach anticipating some unforeseen accident. She didn't feel she could count on anything or anyone.

When the front gates of the estate were opened and Rick started the drive up the hill to the house, four people ran toward the van. When the van stopped, Brian swung open the door first and seeing Lana in one piece he burst into tears of joy. Lana was overcome with joy at seeing her whole wonderful family, and the tears streamed down her cheeks. Maria and Marcelena soon joined them with joyful exuberance and lots of questions. Where had she been? Who had kept her captive? How did she escape?

Lana answered nothing. She thought sealed lips for now the best policy. Lana kept staring at each of her family as her heart swelled with joy. She had feared she would never see–and be together as a family again.. The escape was what she had hoped for–but feared it was not possible. She would never take her freedom for granted, it was too precious.

"Brian, Franco actually rescued me twice during this whole mess. We must show our appreciation and give him a raise. It's time we showed appreciation to all the servants for their commitment and help during the coup as well as for daily responsibilities," Lana said.

"I agree a raise is in store for all."

"Nothing can spoil the great feeling I have at this moment, being together again as a family." Lana was thrilled to be safely home.

Brian was dying to know some details, but since the house was bugged he didn't dare ask any questions. He slipped a note to Lana. It read, "I want to know details when we are where we can talk. I need to know everything that happened."

Lana nodded, smiled and reached around Brian's neck for another embrace. She was so excited to be free and with her family.

"We were so worried, Mom. We tried and tried to talk to you or someone when we were in Argentina. But got no answer."

"Thanks for trying Patrick. I knew you would. I'm glad that you two weren't harmed trying to rescue me. I worried about that–knowing you would do everything you could when you realized I was missing."

"I not know you missing, Mama, until Papa came home. Then I scared too," Tanya added.

"It was scary when you weren't with the others at the rebel headquarters," added Patrick. "Dad and I cried."

Lana's heart was touched by the thought of her two big strong men crying for her. Patrick, being raised mostly with adults, was very mature for his age.

Brian's arms were a protective shield for Lana. She was anxious to be alone with him, away from the microphones and talk openly. "Maybe we should celebrate and have dinner at one of our favorite restaurant tonight. Do you think the children would mind terribly?"

"No. Which of our favorite restaurants would you recommend?" Brian asked.

"We'll decide on the way."

Lana glanced around the restaurant to see if Jorge, Marla, or Estelle were present to spoil her newfound freedom.

"What are you looking for?" Brian asked.

"My enemies. I have a lot of them now. You see I was held captive at one of the leaders' home and was privy to a lot of information. I know many of the power figures involved and what they are planning next."

"You know that puts you in great danger, Lana. We've got to get out of Paraguay as fast as possible."

"Was Estelle the neighbor you discovered involved with the coup?"

"Yes, how did you know?" Brian asked.

"I had a hunch," Lana replied.

"I understand she is one of the leaders," Brian said.

"She was kind enough to rescue me from the guard who was about to rape me."

"Rape you?" Brian was horrified.

"Yes, it was terrible. She rescued me and took me to Marla's home where I was kept as a prisoner for the rest of the time."

"Rape you?" Brian repeated with rage in his eyes.

"Yes. Poco Loco, one of the big ugly guards at the compound didn't like it that I wouldn't answer all his questions. He tied my hands, tried to kiss me, then tore my blouse nearly off and when I tried to kick him, he caught my foot and threw me to the floor and was about to rip off my skirt when Estelle showed up."

"How did she know you were there?"

"I think Franco told her and asked her to help get me out of there. He showed up the day before."

"What a brave thing for her to do. How can we repay her?"

"I'm not sure repayment is necessary. You see, they offered me a car rigged with a bomb to come and check on my family. Franco watched from the bushes as Jorge, the guard, wired it to blow up. Franco stayed nearby and when I came to drive the car home, he quickly warned me before I tried to start the car and brought me to safety. He is the one we should give the reward to. What a loyal servant."

"Indeed," Brian agreed.

"What is our next move?" Lana asked.

"Get a message to Washington and have them get us out of Paraguay as soon as possible. I'll send that message first thing in the morning. Better yet we can go by the ham station on the way home and I can send the code tonight."

"Wonderful," Lana was anxious to get out of the danger zone.

"Lana, we must be ready to leave on short notice."

"We still have not resolved the giant problem of getting papers for Tanya. I can't bear to put her back in that orphanage–even if I have to pack her in a large trunk and put ventilation in so she can survive."

"You know that wouldn't work, Lana."

"We have to do something and quick."

New idea! New day and new hope. The revolution was over and Lana had thought of another plan that might work for Tanya. She needed to check it out right away.

The phone was working. Lana called Bob Cassidy, "I have an idea for getting Tanya to the States."

"Good, what is it?"

"We could ask another American family to keep her until the spots could be proven inactive. They could then bring her to us or we could return and get her," Lana explained excitedly.

"That sounds plausible."

"Could you please check on it right away? This is so important to us. I cannot put Tanya back in that orphanage."

"Of course," Bob answered.

Two hours later the phone rang, Bob Cassidy was pleased to report,"We can do it!"

"Hurray!" Lana shouted.

Lana rang Brian immediately to tell him the good news.

Next came a search for a family to take Tanya for the nine and a half months. Lana checked every name on the Embassy roster before deciding that the Arnolds would be perfect. They had no children of their own and had often played with Tanya when they had come to visit. They would be in Paraguay for ten months.

Caroline Arnold spoke fluent Spanish; Lana knew she could depend on her. She was older than Lana, small in stature, but big in heart. She was always there when needed. Bernie, her husband, was long and lanky, good natured and one they could count on. Tanya would be well cared for in their home.

Lana rang Brian to tell him she voted for Arnolds.

He concurred they were a great choice.

Lana rang Caroline, "We need a family to take care of Tanya while the doctor proves her TB's not active. Please, would you and Bernie help us?"

"What a wonderful solution. Why didn't I think of it?"

"Bob Cassidy said he could then issue entry papers for immigration. It would be ten months of changes in your life. But we would be so grateful."

Caroline agreed, "Of course, we'd love to help. The only problem I can see is if we still can't get the papers. What then?"

"Let's cross that bridge when we get to it. The doctor said he felt sure they were old scars. He didn't see any symptoms of active TB. But he couldn't prove it yet. He needed time and tests to prove his evaluation."

That night Lana had her first good night's sleep in ages. It seemed they had a fair solution and even though it would take some new adjusting on her part and Tanya, they would soon be together.

Lana could leave Tanya with a family that she knew would love her and care for her. She could never, never put her back in that horrible orphanage.

At five in the morning, Maria called at Lana's bedroom door. "Señora, your father is on the phone."

"Possibly I have good news for you. I will try to attach a special rider to a bill now in Congress that will give you permission to bring your new daughter into the States. She will have to be in isolation until her scars can be proven to be inactive."

"For real, Dad? How soon?"

"Right away. I would attach it to a bill now ready for a vote. I need a lot of information . . ."

By the time Lana had finished giving him all the pertinent information all the family had been awakened and they were waiting anxiously to hear what her squeals of delight were about.

With the family gathered around she announced to her dear husband and children that they still had hopes that they could return together. Via plane, in isolation, but together.

Patrick caught both of Tanya's hands and whirled her around and around. Tanya not only smiled, she giggled. Lana was thrilled to hear her first honest to goodness out loud joyful laugh. Brian broke into their circle, then Lana. They all caught hands and joined in the happiness.

Twenty-four hours later Lana's father called again.

"Hello, Lana."

"Dad, good to hear from you so soon."

"No, not good at all. I was unable to get approval to tack the rider on the bill. You're not given permission to bring Tanya in under quarantine."

"Why?" gasped Lana, trying not to cry,

"They refused."

"Any other ideas, Dad?" sobbed Lana.

"Not really. What did you have in mind?

Lana got control of her emotions. "We have cleared it with the Embassy to have friends keep Tanya, then when the scars are proven inactive they could bring her to the United States to us."

"Lana, I think that's your best bet. If I think of any other possibility, I'll call back."

Lana felt defeated and her heart sank to the bottom of her toes. How could she possibly tell Tanya the disappointing news?

Brian was first to want to know why she looked so down. Lana realized they still had the Arnolds as a backup, but they would have to leave Tanya for several months. Lana told Brian the sad news. After having their hopes so high then smashed, it seemed more than they could take. Again she got tears in her eyes, then his misted and his tears began to flow. They cried together.

Tanya entered the room and asked, "¿Que paso?" (What happened?)

"We can't take you with us after all. We're so disappointed."

Disappointed was not strong enough to describe Tanya's feelings. She burst into tears and ran to her room sobbing. Lana and Brian followed. Kneeling they put their arms around her; they held her and silently suffered with Tanya. They couldn't think of anything to say at the moment to make it better.

"I go back to the orphanage?" she wailed as she reached around Lana's neck.

"No. Señora Arnold has invited you to live with them until they come home. Then they will bring you to us."

"How?" Tanya inquired.

"Either on plane or ship. I don't know yet how. But they will get you safely to us. Have no fear, little one. We're not putting you back in that orphanage. Never!"

"Will you and Patrick go?"

"Yes. Your Papa has work waiting for him in the States and we must return now."

"Can't you stay with me, Mama?" Tanya pleaded as she leaned back and looked into Lana's eyes. Then she tightened her grip on Lana's neck and snuggled her head on her shoulder.

"I hate to leave you, Tanya. But I must. You'll understand when you're older. We'll all be together always," Lana said.

"When?"

"Soon. We love you dearly, little one. Thank goodness we found you."

She sobbed into Lana's shoulder and kept a firm grip on her neck as if to say, "I'll not let you go without me."

Lana kept her arms around Tanya and held tightly, while rocking her back and forth. Maybe that oneness would dissolve some of their problems.

It was a long, difficult, emotional day.

"Brian, it is time we finalized the discussion on taking Ignacia and Juan. How do you feel about the extra two in our family?"

"That is a lot more to add and we are having enough difficulty resolving Tanya's situation. How do you feel?"

"I'm concerned about the compact threesome being more than I can handle at the moment. I fear they would gang up on me and on Patrick and stand together. I don't think it's wise. I hate leaving them behind because I see no opportunity for them here."

"My sentiments exactly. I feel terrible about saying no, but I do think it's the right decision," Brian agreed.

The revolution had been over for several days and most things were back to normal, except for the sadness in their hearts at not finding a way to take Tanya with them. At times her little eyes reflected the same sadness seen when they first met. It twisted Lana's heart. Tanya seemed unsure. Lana realized Tanya's life had been so crazy she didn't have much confidence in the future–especially a future without the Carters. How could she reassure her and help her catch that beam of happiness in her eyes again? Tanya would sit and look longingly at them. Then burst out crying over nothing. Her nerves seemed strung tight, Lana was concerned.

Brian decided it was time to check on his messages from Washington to see what progress had been made to get the Carters out of Paraguay. He wondered if they had received the coded message. There had been no response. Both he and Lana were in great danger.

He slipped Lana a note it read, "Going to office. Don't wait dinner."

Lana knew that even though he had said he was going to the office, he probably meant to the MARS station to contact the home office in the States.

Poco Loco, the demon at the rebel hostage center, left headquarters immediately when the revolution collapsed and escaped being caught.

Poco resented Estelle rescuing Lana from his clutches. To have Lana escape from Marla's compounded his rage. He decided he would get revenge against the Carters some way. In the mean time he would stake out the Carters estate and get a pattern on what they did and when. He would not be made a fool of and let it go unpunished.

He watched as Brian left the house. He had to decide to either watch the home or follow Brian. He decided to watch the home and Lana. He might have an opportunity for his revenge.

Dinnertime came and no Brian. Lana began to worry. What if the rebels were waiting for Brian to make a move and they caught him in the act of receiving the message? When held hostage, Lana learned rebels were the ones listening to all their conversations. They knew what was going on in the Carter home.

Lana paced the floor, anxious to hear from Brian. She decided to call his office. No answer. She walked to the door, looked down the hill. No headlights were coming up their driveway. Sit and wait, that was all she could do. This would no doubt mean they would leave even sooner than the scheduled time. The big question was how soon?

It would take several weeks to sell their furniture, car and personal belongings. In the meantime they would walk each step in fear. They would need to get Tanya used to Caroline and Bernie so the transition would not be too rough on her.

Lana needed to make arrangements with the doctor and clinic to care for Tanya's needs in their absence. Doctor MacClanahan was a friend as well as their doctor. He lived in a nearby neighborhood and Patrick played with his sons. Lana felt he would be happy to extend the services needed for Tanya, then send them a bill knowing they would pay.

After dinner Lana invited Patrick and Tanya into the living room, "Would you like to go to Arnold's and see Tanya's room?"

"No," Patrick answered.

"Not tonight," Tanya agreed.

"What would you like to do?" Lana asked.

Brian soon returned. He looked pale, tense and very tired. The whole situation had gotten to him. Leaving Tanya was tough. Also the uncertainty of what was happening with his work was stressful. He worried Lana would be hunted after her escape–knowing so much about the rebels and their plans. Brian was a nervous wreck and wanted an end to this stressful situation.

He slipped Lana a note. "No answer to my message but I'm certain that we'll be leaving soon."

"How soon?" She wrote back.

He shrugged and they continued to decide with the children what activity they would pursue for that evening. They loved to swim so they phoned Patty and Mike. "Want to join us in the pool for a swim and have some dessert?"

"Sounds great," Patty said.

Brian wrote Lana another note. "Called Ramero. No answer. Not even the servants answered the phone. I'm worried!"

Lana wrote back, "What can we do? Shall we drive over there before the Rogers' come?"

"No, that would tip our hand. We have to wait."

The Carters relaxed a little with the Rogers and had some fun. After they left, the Carters tried to get some sleep but without success. Their future seemed to hang by a thread and out of their control. They were stressed to the limit–wondering what was next.

As the next day dawned, they decided to continue living as normally as possible. When the school bus came, Patrick boarded for school like any other day. Brian got ready to go to the office as usual.

Brian picked up the phone, glad that isolation was finished. He started to call the office to see if there was any special messages for him. Then he realized that would be suspicious and possibly alert his uninvited listeners that something was happening. He put the phone back in its cradle, "Lana, why don't you pass up Ladies Day golf today? There is a special meeting this afternoon and I'd appreciate it if you would attend. Could you come to the embassy around two?"

"Sure. What kind of meeting?"

"It's dealing with underprivileged children in Chaco Land. You've done a lot of research on children and their living conditions. I think you could contribute a lot of information to the committee."

"Glad to help. Shall I bring some of the files from the Wives Club with stats, etc.?"

"That's a good idea. Why don't you come early and we can go to lunch together?"

"I'd love to. When and where shall we meet?"

"Our favorite restaurant near the Embassy would be nice. One of Mikas' great steaks with sizzled potatoes sounds delicious."

"Will twelve noon give us enough time?"

"Perfect. There comes my chauffeur so I'll see you at twelve. Do you want me to send for you?"

"No, I'll drive myself. I have a couple of errands I'll need to do on the way home."

After getting settled into his office Brian wanted to call Ramero again but decided to wait until later and then call his office and see what he could find out.

Juan Lopez came by to say hello. He was the one who had first alerted Brian about Ramero's danger. "Juan, Ramero has not been by the office since the revolution finished. Have you seen him?"

"No. Come to think of it I haven't heard from him lately either." He answered with a scowl on his face indicating he didn't want to pursue the subject further.

Right, Brian thought, who was listening? Best not say anything more. He switched topics.

A new day and still no word from Washington. Brian wondered if the people in Washington got the messages. Waiting was such a weary game. He had no choice; he would wait. Each day he feared for himself and for Lana. If they would let him know what to expect it would help. How soon would Washington get them out of Paraguay?

Patrick was still hesitant to leave home alone. The coup attempt had taken its toll on his emotions, but he bravely boarded the school bus.

Brian got ready for work and waited to be driven to the Embassy. It was ten minutes past the time his chauffeur usually came for him. He was concerned.

Enrique (Rick) the driver of the van, pulled up to the gate. Brian ran and opened the gate, not waiting for Franco, wondering why Rick had come instead of the usual chauffeur.

Rick was excited. Waving an official paper at Brian he exclaimed, "The official word came and you need to be on the ten-thirty flight out of here. That is only two hours from now. How fast can you pack?"

Brian ran back into the house and turned to Lana jubilant with the news. "Ring the bell for Franco. He needs to run to school and pick up Patrick immediately. Then let's throw some things in the suitcases and head for the airport."

"What in the world are you talking about?" Lana asked, completely bewildered.

"You're going home to see Dr. Lewis."

"Now?" Lana asked.

"We leave on the next flight to the States."

"We can't! What about the furniture, the car and all our personal things. Our treasures we've collected from South America?"

"I've written a note to Bob to take care of all of it for us. I thought we might have to leave in a hurry, so I'm prepared." Brian realized he had been talking, not writing notes. Who might have heard?

Lana was not ready. She balked at leaving all her treasures behind. "Let's make it next week. We'll have a chance to get Tanya situated, talk to her doctor and all that."

"No! It must be now." Brian insisted as Franco came in answer to the bell. "Franco, please drive over to school and pick up Patrick. We're going to be leaving on the next flight. So please hurry." Brian tossed the car keys to Franco and turned to start packing.

Lana realized the principal at school needed a note to let Patrick leave school with anyone except his parents.

She quickly scribbled a note and ran to the back door to catch Franco as he passed the back patio. The garage sat on the back of the property next to the servants' quarters. As she stepped out onto the patio she was met with a powerful explosion. The whole garage seemed to disintegrate, knocking Lana down as splinters of glass, wood and metal flew everywhere.

Maria came on a run to see what happened.

Brian burst through the back door looking stunned. Seeing Lana bleeding and on the patio floor he panicked.

"Are you all right?"

"NO!" Lana declared in a state of shock.

Brian sat down beside her and Lana flung her arms around his neck squeezing harder, as she realized the Carters should have been in that car. Lana suddenly burst into a real panic. "We should have been killed. It was set for us Brian!"

"I know. I know."

"Let's get out of here. Now!"

"Rick, please go collect Patrick in the van," Brian requested.

"Let's put what we have packed in the van and go get Patrick on the way to the airport," Lana requested.

"Let's finish packing while Rick gets Patrick," Brian said.

"Okay. Here is the note for the principal to let Patrick come with you," Lana said as she handed the note to Rick.

If Rick had not delivered the note and come to take them to the airport in the van, they would have been in that car. If the office had called and said they would meet them at the airport with tickets and documents, it would have been the end of the Carters. As it was, they lost a faithful friend and gardener.

"My heavens! Who in the world would do that?" Lana shuddered and asked in between sobs. How horrible to think someone wanted them dead. She remembered the blue car at Marla's and realized the same people were still around.

"Lana, I won't tell you. If you knew, it would put you in danger too."

"Maybe I should know so I can be prepared."

"No way. It would be too dangerous." Now Brian realized in their frenzy they had been talking out loud again and not writing notes. The word was out. The gardener was killed not the Carters. Lana was shaking, crying and totally out of control.

Standing up she tried to collect herself so she could finish grabbing some precious things to take along. She brushed her dress off and headed for the bathroom to get rid of the blood and get a quick change of clothes.

Brian followed to help.

When Rick arrived with Patrick, Brian and Lana were waiting with cases packed. Turning to Maria, Brian handed her a huge roll of bills mostly Guarani, with some American dollars. "Please get Tanya to Señora Arnold's with her clothes and explain that we had to leave early. This money is for you, Juana and Marcelena. Pay bills that come here, then split the rest to help you until you find other work."

He added, "About other work, Señor Ball promised to find you employment in the American community. We'll get in touch with you through him or Caroline for the time being. Please tell Caroline that we'll send money for Tanya's care soon."

Tanya clung to Brian's leg, "Please don't leave me...please please."

Brian scooped Tanya up in his arms, She hung onto his neck tightly, crying now. "Tanya, we can't take you. But we will look forward to seeing you soon. Señora Arnold will take care of you and get the reports we need to bring you to the States. Keep smiling. That will brighten each day. We will see you soon." Brian gave her a final huge hug, kissed her cheek, and pulled her tight arms from his neck, then handed her to Lana.

She hurriedly threw her arms around Lana's neck. "If you leave, now I no see you again, ever."

"Yes," assured Lana, "you will join us in a few months. We are sad." With that Lana lost it and the tears flowed.

Rick interrupted, "We have to leave right now to make that flight."

Rick helped with the luggage and check-in at the airport. Then he gave each of the Carters a huge abrazo (hug) and handed Brian an envelope saying, "Juan gave this to me as I left to pick you up. He told me to give it to you before you got on the plane. Don't open it until you're in the sky and on your way."

With a firm handshake, Brian said, "Bye, Rick and thanks for all the help you have been to our family while we were here."

"It is nothing, Señor. May God go with you always."

"Thanks," Lana said as she held out her arms for a final hug.

As they settled into their seats on the plane, Lana felt relieved. She was on her way out of Paraguay. Many times that seemed the impossible dream.

As they became airborne Brian opened the letter from Juan. Lana saw the stricken look on Brian's face as he read the note. "What's the matter?"

"Ramero and his family were slaughtered during the coup attempt. That really tears me up. I don't know how to handle this." He couldn't for a minute and sobbed. His chest heaved in revolt. Collecting himself he dried his eyes. Turning to Lana and Patrick he stated, "Don't ever take your American freedom for granted. Cherish it and protect it."

"How terrible," Lana whispered as she slipped her arm around Brian.

After a time Patrick let out a big sigh and said, "I'm glad we're going home."

"Me too!" agreed Lana.

Lana bowed her head and said a prayer of thanks for the safe getaway. The explosion of the car and garage had been very frightening–but now they were on their way back to the wonderful United States of America, but without their beloved daughter Tanya. Lana's emotions were mixed–joy mixed with pain.

Brian struggled to keep control of his emotions and sighed heavily. He would never forget the last few weeks. His good friend had been killed; and they had to leave Tanya after trying so hard to get her documents; the revolution and Lana being held as hostage and brutalized. All the traumatic events made it seem like years instead of weeks.

Brian was thankful that he and his family were safe on the plane–but were they? Someone could have followed him onto the plane and could take him or Lana out when they landed, or quietly as they flew.

It was spooky and he wondered if he would ever walk carefree again and not look over his shoulder checking doors to see if they were rigged, or phones to see if they were bugged.

Brian knew for sure he was leaving this risky style of life and returning to research. After all, what did he go to graduate school for? Not to jeopardize his whole family and live in constant terror.

He remembered the excitement he felt when Todd Martin from Washington had offered him the assignment in Paraguay. He thought it was going to be the adventure of his lifetime and so desirable. It had been an adventure. However, the last few weeks had been anything but desirable.

"Lana, How do you feel about my going back to research? Dr. Donnert said they needed a good scientist at NDL in Maryland."

"That's a great idea. I'm ready for the calm of an eight-to-five job again. We'll be with the children more."

"I thought you might resent leaving the glamour of a foreign assignment. Giving you the opportunity to associate with powerful people at great parties."

"No way. I'll miss many aspects of that life. I'll treasure many of the good times and the glamour as you call it. It was special in many ways. I think I'm glad we did it. I wouldn't want to live that way for the rest of my life. It's too artificial. The children need a more realistic view of what life is all about. Besides, I never want to live through another revolution or car bombing."

Lana had been homesick for her parents. But her yearning for Tanya was deep and painful. She couldn't get Tanya's voice out of her head. She vividly remembered their conversation as they waited for Rick to return with Patrick and take them to the airport. Tanya had pleaded in Spanish, "You no forget me will you?"

"No! Never! We will call and write often. Even though you can't read, Caroline will read our letter to you and you can tell her what you want to say to us and she can write back and tell us how you are doing and what the medical results are. We'll call often so you can hear our voices and we'll want to hear your voice. You can tell us all you're doing and keep us up to date on what's new in your life."

"How long 'till I see you?" Tanya asked.

"That's a fair question. If all goes well, in nine months, three weeks and four days," Brian assured her. "It'll be here before you know it. It will seem like a long, long time. Every day will be long without you, Tanya. We'll be so happy to see you when you walk off that plane and we're together again."

"I like the Arnolds, but I like you more."

"Thanks! We'll be anxiously waiting for you to return to us. Keep smiling, Tanya, it keeps the sunshine in your life," Brian said.

"I'll try. I'll be a big girl, Papa." Her eyes misted and Lana did all she could to hold back her tears. Not succeeding she sat down and pulled Tanya onto her lap and held her close.

"Don't cry Mama. I'll be all right."

"I know Tanya, but I'll miss you so much."

Will and Vera Brahn, Lana's parents, were waiting for the Carters' plane to land. A joyous reunion followed. The Brahns had counted the days until Lana would be back in the States. Since Lana was their only child it was especially frightening to know she was in danger during the revolution. They were anxious to hear the details.

As Lana descended the stairs of the plane in Phoenix, she saw the Brahns waiting. She ran with outstretched arms, Patrick and Brian right behind her. It was a big family hug together with much crying and laughing. They were relieved to be on freedom's soil once more. Lana couldn't contain her emotions. Then Lana knelt down, bent over and kissed the ground.

"What in the world are you doing, Lana?" Will asked.

"Mom, for heavens sake, get up. You look ridiculous," Patrick added.

"I'm kissing freedom's soil. When I was being held hostage, I promised myself if I ever returned to the States I would kiss the ground of this wonderful free country."

Vera extended her hand to help Lana up.

Lana's mascara had smudged from tears. They saw the next grand surprise waiting. Brian's parents, the Carters had come to welcome them home. They had stood to one side until the welcome with the Brahns was complete. Brian was unashamedly emotional. Seeing them so soon after arrival was an unexpected treat.

When they were securely in the palatial home of Lana's parents, Vera asked what it was like during the revolution.

Lana shared tales of many of their challenges, then hesitated.

Vera anticipated her silence, "Please tell us all. We need to know. It was so frightening to read the news and with the phones dead we felt so isolated. We tried the ham set, but could get no answer."

"That was a terrifying time for all of us. Being held prisoner by the enemy was not enjoyable. . . It was horrible! If my neighbor had not come to rescue me, I would have been raped by a big ugly angry guard named Poco Loco."

Vera gasped, "Raped? Why?"

"I wouldn't tell them what they wanted to know about Brian's assignment. Really I think Poco Loco was looking for some excuse. He leered at me from the time they took me prisoner and I knew it was going to be tough."

Everyone was silent for a moment then Will asked, "Did Poco get killed in the revolution?"

"No, I don't think so. Someone wired our car to blow up. Yesterday when our gardener got in the car to go pick up Patrick at school, he tried to start the car and the bomb blew. The garage, Franco and the car are history. I think Poco was responsible."

"Could you prove it?" Will asked.

"No. Just a suspicion," Lana replied.

Brian interceded, "We're in one piece, we're all together and should rejoice and not lament. What was, is past. We're okay. But I have to admit that it took a lot of willpower not to look up Poco and blow his brains out after Lana told me about his abuse when she was hostage."

"Better we bring you home than leave you in jail down there in no mans land. I'm glad you didn't," Lana declared.

After visiting dear family friends started arriving. Vera, being her usual social self had invited a crowd to celebrate the home coming of their daughter and her family.

It was an elaborate, wonderful evening.

Although after all the partying in Asunción, Lana would have preferred a quiet evening with their parents. Having all four parents there to share this marvelous homecoming was so rewarding.

After vacationing for a month the Carters arrived in Maryland, located a home, and settled into their new community in Bel Air. Brian was thrilled to be welcomed back to Nuclear Defense Lab.

Lana's top priority was to write to Caroline and Tanya, send money, their new address and let Tanya know they had not forgotten her.

Dearest Tanya,

The trip home was safe, but so lonesome without you. You'll love riding on the big airplane. It's a big adventure. Remember how we used to watch the planes take off at the airport? That was fun, but it is even more fun to ride.

Have you learned to swim yet? Does Aunt Caroline still take you to the club for lessons?

Did you get out to see Ignacia and Juan this month? I'm sure they are going to miss you a lot when you come to the States. Then you can write back to them like I'm writing to you.

When your adoption is complete your name will not have to be changed; we will add Carter. Tanya Bernarda Carter, sounds good doesn't it. I think the middle name of Bernarda will be nice. Nice to be named after your Uncle Bernie. They are such dear friends and it will always be a reminder of their goodness to you when we had to leave so abruptly.

Is Dr. MacClanahan encouraging about the tests? Be sure you get there every eight weeks so he can show there is no change in those spots and prove they are only scars. That will help Señora Arnold get proper documents to bring you to us. We would be brokenhearted if you didn't come with them. We count the days until we see you again. Keep smiling.

Our love and lots of hugs and kisses,

Mama, Papa and Patrick

Dear Caroline and Bernie,

Thank you for making a home for Tanya. Enclosed is the check for her care. If there are extra expenses, please let us know. Also if you are successful in starting her in the Embassy school for this year let us know how much the tuition is. I understand it has increased.

We are anxious to get a letter and know how she is adjusting to her new surroundings.

I'm afraid we left so abruptly that she might feel deserted. She was so emotional. So was I. Then I found great comfort in knowing she would be with treasured friends who would make her feel at home and care for her. Thank you Caroline and Bernie.

Is Tanya making friends at the Club with the American children? Has her English improved? It's great that you're so proficient in Spanish, Caroline.

Have you heard where Maria, Marcelena and Juana found work? Bob said he would be sure to get good employment for them. I'm enclosing an envelope for each could you please find out where they are employed and give them these letters? It would be appreciated.

We are indebted to you for taking Tanya and providing a loving home for her until you come to the States. We'll be grateful always for your generosity and love. You are such dear friends.

We have always treasured your friendship. It seemed you were our family when we were away from our own biological family. Your willingness to help us in this crisis deepens that feeling of appreciation.

Does Tanya still have nightmares? I found if I put her on my lap and talked softly to her it usually soothed her and she was able to go back to sleep.

Do you know where your next assignment will be?

With much love and appreciation,
Brian, Lana and Patrick

At first, letters from Caroline were frequent and full of news and cheer. Calls were most difficult as the Carters often became emotional when talking to Tanya. Brian always ended each call with, "Keep smiling. That's what puts the sunshine in your heart and ours. We love you!"

The long-awaited letter came. It was a short note from Caroline.

Dear Lana and Brian,
Dr. MacClanahan has given Tanya a clean bill of health
and the papers are being prepared for Tanya's exit from
Paraguay.
Love, Caroline

No information on when the Arnolds would arrive or where. Still it was great news. So Brian, Lana and Patrick celebrated by calling to talk to Tanya and let her know how excited they were that she would soon be coming home.

Marcy, Caroline's maid, answered the phone, "Buenas dias."

"Marcy, this is Lana Carter. Could I please speak to Señora Arnold?"

"Lo siento, no hay nada ahora."

"When do you expect them to return?"

"No se."

"We received the letter. We are so excited. We'll call back later."

"Bien. Adios."

A few hours later the Carters called again, "Could we please talk to Señora or Señor Arnold."

"Lo siento, todavia, no estan."

"Please, then let us talk to Tanya."

"No esta tambien."

The next day, a third call was made, with the same response. No one was at home. Lana asked Marcy to have the Arnolds please call so the Carters could make arrangements on when and where to pick up Tanya.

The Arnolds did not call.

The Carters called again. Marcy assured Lana that Tanya and the Arnolds were not available.

Again the Carters requested the Arnolds return their call.

No call.

The Carters sent letters requesting information and made many calls received no letters or call from Asunción.

Finally when Lana called, Caroline answered, "Is Tanya all right, Caroline?"

"Yes, she's okay."

"We were worried when we didn't hear from you. It has been ages since we got your note. Great news about Tanya. Did you get the messages we left with Marcy?"

"Yes, but this has been a terrible time in my life, Lana. You should receive my letter any day. Sorry I haven't kept in touch. The letter will explain."

"Are you okay?"

"No, not really. The letter will explain."

"What's the matter, Caroline?"

"I don't want to talk about it. As I said, the letter will explain."

"Does Bernie know where he is going next?"

"We think Washington D. C., but it isn't definite."

"You're still coming home soon aren't you? We're so excited. We can hardly wait to see Tanya and you again."

With that, Caroline broke down and started to cry. "I've got to run now. Talk to you soon." She hung up without saying good-bye, or giving the Carters an opportunity to talk to Tanya.

Now Lana was worried. What in the world was wrong? Caroline's tone of voice and actions definitely indicated serious trouble.

The shocking letter arrived.

> Dear Brian and Lana,
>
> We would like you to consider letting us keep Tanya permanently. We have fallen in love with her and she is now very much at ease in our home. You have been blessed with one son and we have no children. We are older and find it impossible to adopt in the States, but could get custody of a child to bring with us then adopt her there. You can still adopt

other children. Please give this consideration as it would mean so much to us.

We realize this will be a big disappointment for you. But she is so much a part of us and our lives now.

Tanya has brought a new dimension of love and happiness into our home and we can't bear the thought of losing her in less than two weeks. She has lived with us much longer than she lived with you. We are bonded so tightly we can't bear the thought of never having her joyous laugh resounding through our home. Please try to understand how important this is to us.

We promise we would care for her and bring her up Catholic as requested. Please consider our feelings and Tanya's. We are also considering bringing Tanya's older sister with her so we can keep part of the family together.

This is so difficult to write. You know how dearly we love you and how valuable your friendship is, but we are so desperate and determined to have this family unit continue that we must face reality."

Love,
Bernie and Caroline

Shock was not a strong enough word to describe Lana's feelings. She jumped up from her chair and threw the letter in the air and shouted. "How could they even consider stealing Tanya? That's what it would be. Stealing!" Lana felt like she was split in half. One part of her was grateful for Caroline's willingness to keep Tanya, the other part of her was furious that she would consider stealing their daughter.

"Lana, what are you talking about?"

"Read this. It'll explain." She gathered up the letter and handed it to Brian and sank into the chair, devastated.

"My heavens, they treat our daughter like she is a piece of furniture, easy to replace."

"Can you believe it? Let's call Caroline and get this straightened out."

"Sounds good to me."

They called the Arnolds, "You can't be serious," Lana pleaded.

"We were never more serious about anything in our lives. Lana, you can adopt another child there."

"Caroline, this is not a car or piece of furniture we are talking about. It's our family. A human being. Our daughter. As much as we love you, we can't give you our daughter."

"Please try to understand our side, Lana. We are so attached to Tanya now we cannot part with her. The thought of letting her go depresses me for days. This has been a tough decision to make. I know you must feel betrayed."

"Betrayed! That's the understatement of the year. You're trying to steal our daughter."

"It must seem that way to you now. But think of the big adjustment if Tanya has to change homes again. She is happy here with us. She knows we adore her. We'll care for her and give her a good life. Be reasonable."

"Be reasonable! You want to take our daughter, then advise us to be reasonable! How can you possibly think we could sign her away?"

"She has lived with us longer than with you. We know her better. It is for the best for the whole family. Lana, try to think about this logically."

Lana knew that their willingness to bring Ignacia with them would also give another small girl a chance at a decent life. But logic was suspended for the moment.

Deep in thought, both were quiet for many seconds then Caroline hung up.

Lana and Brian were desperate. They were heartsick thinking of losing their adorable daughter permanently.

The Carters refused to sign Tanya over to the Arnolds. The Arnolds filed suit to keep her. It was horrible to have dear, wonderful friends turn into bitter enemies.

Chapter Nine

The Carters seemed to be fighting a losing battle. So much was on the side of the Arnolds. They were in Asunción long enough to have medical proof for Tanya to come to the United States. They were willing to bring her sister with her and keep two of the family together. That was a big plus in their favor. They still had Tanya living with them.

The first court hearing proved nothing. Its only result was the destruction of the close bond shared by the Carters and Arnolds over the years. The Arnolds still had Tanya.

Many ugly legal battles followed. Each family claimed the right to have Tanya as their child. The disintegrated friendship got more bitter with each court appearance.

Instead of trust, love and understanding, there were many nasty exchanges of hard words. "When you had to leave Asunción, what would have happened to Tanya if we hadn't made a home for her?" Caroline asked.

"Someone else would have kept her. Someone who wouldn't try to steal Tanya," Lana countered.

"You were offered an opportunity to bring Ignacia, but refused."

"That is not part of this problem. This is about your betrayal," Brian said.

"We want what is best for Tanya and her family," Caroline advised.

The whole mess was a fierce fight with Tanya in the middle.

Patrick waited patiently for a final solution. Knowing how desperate his parents felt, he seldom voiced his own concerns. He felt he was taking the back seat and being ignored. He felt unimportant.

Tanya was the one they were worried about. No one seemed concerned about his feelings of loss of his only sibling, his sister. He became depressed at times in the shadows.

Being barely ten years old he was having difficulty dealing with his many frustrations. For the first time he needed attention desperately and a statement from his parents that he was important to them. Even negative attention would let him know they still knew he was around.

Patrick plotted to steal from his mother' purse to see how she dealt with that. Patrick took $20.00 and laid it on his chest of drawers, conspicuous so it would be noticed. Lana didn't even miss the money. "Mom probably wouldn't miss me either if I disappeared," Patrick thought. Maybe I'll do that.

The Carters were consumed with the legal battles and the disintegration of what had been a close and loving friendship. Their whole world changed.

The Arnolds further complicated matters and strengthened their position as they agreed to take Tanya's brother, Juan, to live with them also keeping three of the original orphaned family intact.

The legal fights had been vicious. The Carters claimed they had the right to have Tanya. After all, they had discovered her, taken her home, loved and cared for her until they had to exit Paraguay hurriedly.

The Arnolds countered that if they had not taken Tanya into their home, she would have been returned to that awful orphanage. They were, after all, the ones who really rescued Tanya and made a home for her and others of her family.

The Carters were sitting in court for the last battle. As Caroline and Bernie entered, Lana looked away. She couldn't smile and didn't want to acknowledge that they even existed. Lana had knots in her stomach.

Lana admitted to herself that she admired Caroline for her courage to rescue more of Tanya's family, giving her sister and brother a chance at a better life. She loved Caroline, her sister of the past–the only true sister she had ever known.

However, right now Lana's anger made her sit tall and her blood pressure shot up. She was angry with Caroline for her betrayal, mad at Caroline and Bernie for wanting to steal their daughter. Why did they think they deserved Tanya?

Lana was full of mixed feelings, love and hate.

She had dammed tears in her eyes. Dammed because she was

determined to look in control and not weepy.

Judge Marren arrived and they stood, then were seated again. Judge Marren stroked his beard, rubbed his forehead and looked absolutely perplexed. Then said, "This is a most unusual case. Both the Arnolds and the Carters have rights. It's beyond me to decide. After all the testimony I can only say you both care, you both have the best intentions as far as this young lady is concerned. Flipping a coin certainly is not justice. So I'm going to put Tanya on the stand. Please come forward, Tanya and sit in the big chair, where all the witnesses have been sitting."

Brave five year old Tanya slowly approached the chair.

"Now you will be sworn in and you must answer with all honesty. Take your time. This is very important."

Tanya raised her right hand. She was sworn in and the Judge proceeded.

"You lived first with the Carters. Is that correct?"

"Yes sir." Lana recognized Caroline had taught Tanya the respectful way to address adults; the southern way, sir and mam. Caroline had lovingly instilled many admirable traits in Tanya. In Lana's heart she knew Caroline sincerely cared for and loved this tiny girl. For a minute Lana understood her pain and actions of betrayal when faced with losing this charming girl. Then the knowledge of losing their daughter jumped into her immediate thought and the anger returned full blast.

"How did you like living with them?" Judge Marren asked.

After a small hesitation she answered, "It was nice."

"I believe you have lived with Arnolds ever since. Is that correct?"

"Yes sir."

"You have your sister with you now, is that correct?"

"Yes sir."

"I understand your brother will also be with you. Are you excited about that?"

"Yes sir. I love my family."

"You have a brother waiting at the Carters also, don't you?"

"Yes sir, Patrick." After a long hesitation she added, "I love him too."

Lana wondered where this was going. Was the Judge going to have

Tanya make a statement that he could base his decision on? Surely not. She was so young and a lot of time had passed since she was living with the Carters. It didn't seem fair.

"If you could choose which family you wanted to spend the rest of your life with, which family would you choose?"

There it was. Bold. Unfair. Lana wanted to object. She wanted to scream, you can't have a child make this important decision! She was stricken mute by surprise and fear of what Tanya would say.

Tanya looked at the Carters longingly, then she looked behind them at her sister and brother. She didn't answer.

"Tanya, please tell us where you would prefer to live. With the Arnolds or the Carters?"

Slowly Tanya lowered her eyes as she bowed her head, then answered, "With the Arnolds."

How could she? Lana jumped up and screamed, "No! You can't!" She started down the aisle to Tanya, tears streaming down her cheeks. The guard grabbed Lana, restraining her. She beat his chest with her fists. She lost it completely and looking directly at Caroline and Bernie she screamed, "You can't steal our daughter!"

Judge Marren banged his gavel and demanded, "Order in the court, or I'll have you removed."

Brian quickly came to Lana's side and held her in his arms. Lana's heart was broken. Lana looked at Tanya and realized she was sobbing.

Lana broke loose and scooted around the guard and started to run to Tanya. The guard quickly ran after Lana and physically picked her up restraining her and headed for the door to remove her from court. She started to fight him, then calmed down and sobbed as only a broken heart can sob.

Lana turned to the guard and in between sobs pleaded, "Let me stay. I'll be quiet." The guard looked at the judge and he nodded. The guard set Lana down and she sunk into the nearest vacant chair. Brian sat beside her with his arm tenderly around her shoulders.

In a slow deliberate voice the judge said, "There was no reasonable way to decide what was right. Tanya has made that decision for us. It will keep part of her family together. Bernie and Caroline Arnold you are given complete custody of Tanya. Please live up to her and our expectations and enjoy her and her family always." Then Judge Marren banged his gavel and said. "Court is adjourned."

Lana had discovered Tanya and brought her out of the Orphanage and made all of this possible. That knowledge didn't soothe the painful void of knowing she wasn't waiting any longer to be reunited with that charming little girl who was so much a part of her. She had to adjust to not having a daughter again.

Brian cried; Patrick cried, and Lana cried. The last petition was gone and they lost. Lana felt intense pain. Losing her daughter and her beloved sister, Caroline. Both incredibly soul depleting, leaving such an empty hole within.

Several days after the court decision Lana called Caroline saying, "I think you are wonderful to take Ignacia and Juan and keep part of the family together."

"The courts decision is final, Lana. I wish you would not call again. It's finished. Our friendship will never be the same. Let's go on with our lives."

"Caroline, we lost the court battle, but we still want to be part of Tanya's life and share in her progress."

"No way! It would only frustrate her and her loyalties. Leave us alone." With that, Caroline hung up without saying good-bye.

The Arnolds obtained a restraining order and the Carters were told to stay out of Tanya's life and not make any contact.

Insult to injury. Lana found courts to be merciless. So impersonal. So definite. So cruel! The next few days were just survival. Lana was foggy and distraught. She struggled with Caroline and Bernie's unreal demands to keep Tanya and to cut the Carters out of Tanya's life completely. She couldn't understand how a friend who was dearer than a blood sister, who had been by her side through thick and thin, could do this. She had not only lost a daughter, she had lost a dear sister. Lana’s world was shattered.

Lana paced the floor for over an hour. She called Brian. "Patrick isn't home from school. He's an hour late. I'm worried."

"Call the school and see if he was involved in a special project or activity and forgot to tell us."

"I did. They said no. I'll call the police and see if there was an accident."

"Please call if you find out anything," Brian replied.

"Sure."

Lana called the school again and they verified that Patrick had left on the correct bus right after school. The police had no accident reports that involved Patrick Carter. The hospital did not have a Patrick Carter in the ER.

She dialed Brian, "No trace of Patrick, Brian. I'm desperate. He is eighty-seven minutes late. He always calls if he goes to a friend's."

"Maybe he forgot this once," Brian said.

"Possibly. I'll call his best friends and see if I can locate him."

"I'm on my way. I'll come help you search."

"Yes, please," Lana pleaded.

"Patrick is always dependable. This is not at all like him."

"That's why I think it's scary. Do you think he has been kidnaped?"

"We aren't rich enough for kidnaping."

"No. But my father is. Maybe someone knows."

"That's possible. Hang on, I'll be right home."

Lana called Robin Strand, one of Patrick's best friends. "Is Patrick with you, Robby?"

"No, I haven't seen him since school. Why?"

"He didn't come home from school today."

"He has seemed a bit down lately. Different."

This concerned Lana. Why hadn't she noticed?

Next Lana called Jeff Landers, "Jeff, have you seen Patrick since school today?"

"No."

"Did he get on the bus with you after school?"

"Yes. Why?"

"He still isn't home."

"Mrs. Carter, Patrick has seemed different lately. Even when he comes over to shoot baskets or play, he isn't the same."

Another testimony of Patrick's changes. Lana ran to Brian as he came up the drive and told him what the comments were.

"You know I have noticed a difference too, but I thought it was normal growing pains. What do you think Lana? Should we call the police and report him missing?"

"Yes."

They called the police only to learn a person had to be missing for at least twenty-four hours to be considered a missing person. However Chief O'Brien agreed to put out a bulletin for officers policing the street to keep an eye out for Patrick.

"I'll go west in the neighborhood , Lana and you drive through the eastern part of our area and we'll see if we can locate him."

"I hate to leave the phone in case he calls and needs us."

"You're right. I'll drive and you watch here. Why don't you call more of his friends?" Brian suggested.

"Please check back often. It's nearly three hours now and will soon be dark. I'm frantic."

"Me too," Brian called as he ran to his car and drove away.

Lana phoned her father, "Dad, Patrick didn't come home from school today and we are worried sick."

"You sound terrified. Where have you checked?"

"With police, his close friends, the hospital and school."

"What time does he usually get home?"

"He is home by five minutes after four and it is after seven in the evening. His friends haven't seen him but say he has been acting different lately."

"Lana, I'm going to come immediately. This sounds like foul play."

"You haven't heard anything then?"

"No, why would I?"

"If he was kidnaped, it would be to tap your money. We don't have enough to make it worth while."

"No. Not a word. That's good."

"I'll keep checking friends. Maybe he's somewhere and forgot to call."

"Keep looking and I'll get there as fast as my plane will bring me."

Hanging up the phone, Lana searched for phone numbers of other friends of Patrick. Lana hated to tie up the phone in case Patrick tried to call. She decided to stop calling and leave the line open.

She was a nervous wreck.

Brian drove up, "Have you heard anything, Lana?"

"No. I'm getting desperate. It's getting dark. He'll be starved, Patrick always has a big snack after school. It's dinner time."

"Besides it is getting chilly out here. Where would you suggest we look now?" Brian asked. His head ached with fright. He was scared of where and how Patrick was.

"Have you tried the parks?"

"No. I'll try the one east of school. See you soon."

Lana wandered out in the yard and down the driveway to the side walk, looking both ways for some sign of her son. There was no tall red head in sight.

Patrick slowly walked through the park and realized night was near. It was getting dark and he was hungry and scared. Where was he going to sleep? It was a scary situation for a ten year old.

He saw someone on the park bench, bent over. Patrick heard his stifled sobs. When the lad looked up, Patrick saw bruises on his face and a swollen eye that was turning black and blue. Patrick approached him and asked, "Don't you have a home to go to?"

"Not really. Since Mom remarried, our home is a battleground. When my stepdad has been drinking he yells and then beats us up. I hurt, but I can't stand to see him punch Mom out any longer. I left today for good."

"Can't you get some help?"

"Who would help us? I tried to get Mom to come with me but she said it was her house and Max should leave. But he doesn't."

"Call the police when he's mean," Patrick advised.

"Max sobers up, promises to never do it again and Mom drops charges. Then when he drinks again he is meaner than ever. I had to leave."

"Where are you going to sleep tonight?"asked Patrick.

"Probably here."

"Have you had anything to eat?"

"I'm not hungry."

Patrick's heart went out to this young man from a terrible home. What a jerk his stepfather must be. Patrick wandered on through the park wondering where he was going to sleep and what he would eat. He felt desperate.

He was approached by a nicely dressed man who asked, "Do you need a good meal and a roof over your head tonight?"

"Yeah, I guess so. Why?" responded Patrick.

"Come with me. Have a good hot meal and a nice warm bed. We will discuss other possibilities for survival tomorrow."

Although there was something about this man that Patrick didn't trust, he got up to follow the man. "I have very little money with me to pay for room or food."

"That doesn't matter. There is no charge for tonight and I'll show you how you can make money to pay in the future."

"Like what?"

"Don't be concerned tonight. Let's get you some dinner and we'll discuss the rest later."

The man started forward and Patrick followed. Patrick thought about his home and food and love. He wished he hadn't run away. If he went with this man and his folks were searching for him, they wouldn't know where to find him.

Patrick stopped and said confidently,"No thanks. I'll stay in the park. My dad will be coming soon."

The man grabbed Patrick's arm and said, "Better come with me, sonny. I will make it worth your while." Patrick jerked away from the man's grasp and emphatically replied, "No. I'm staying here."

Patrick hurried back to the huge rock. He sat down to contemplate his position. He could go home and apologize. He didn't have a mean stepfather to return to. He had a nice dad who ignored him.

Patrick longed to know he was important to his parents, important like Tanya was. They had spent months fighting for her and cried over her a lot.

His parents had never mistreated him. They didn't seem to know he existed. Patrick bent over, head in hands. Thinking deep and hard thoughts about how frightened he was when he went to Argentina. Worried that he would never see his mother or father again. Then when his dad had come without his mother, that was horrible not knowing where or how she was. He remembered the joy he had felt when his mother had escaped. To be a family again was comforting. Patrick felt more mature than most youth after experiencing the fear of the revolution and the separation from his family.

He was making his life scary again. Why hadn't he talked to his parents? Was it because it wouldn't be the same as their searching for him? He was confused. He knew in his heart his parents would be frantic, but he wanted to be convinced by their actions. Crazy world. How should he cope?

He shuddered as the dark crowded out light and the park became eerie. The park lights were very subdued. People still in the park were quietly talking like it was not okay to shout. Gradually most people left.

Patrick thought about the other young man with a bruised face. He didn't have a decent family to be with. Patrick knew he always felt loved and cared for. How silly he had been to start feeling sorry for himself. Maybe he should head home, apologize and sleep in his own bed. And food sounded great. His mom always had good snacks and meals. He had great parents. They were fun to be with, always showed him love. He felt foolish for being so self-centered.

Patrick was homesick. He was feeling depressing pangs of "Wish I was home" when a blinding spot light came on. The police! He knew it was against the rules to stay in the park after dark. He decided to run and hide.

Brian returned again with no luck in locating Patrick. They sat at the table. They were empty, but no one had even thought about food except to worry about Patrick not having any.

"It's a bare table, so are my thoughts bare. I don't know where to look or check next. I'm desperate," Brian admitted.

"Me too. I'm going to call Chief O'Brien again and see if they've found him."

The police had not seen or heard anything that might be connected with Patrick Carter.

"You know that park over on St. Petersburg? I hear it is a hangout for runaways. It's farther away, but I should have checked it sooner. If Patrick left on purpose maybe he's there. I'm going to check it out." Brian was revived somewhat thinking of another place to search.

"I'll stay by the phone and see if he calls. I called Dad and he's on the way," Lana responded. Her nerves were completely frayed. Patrick never gave them a minute's concern. How could he just disappear so quickly?

Brian took the spotlight and drove to the east side of the park and started walking. He didn't want to flash the light unless he saw something suspicious. The lighting of the park was dim, but he could see the park benches, play areas, and around most of the shrubs. He walked through the park one way then started to crisscross when he saw something curled on the park bench.

He flashed the light on the person. It was only a bum, finding some refuge from the elements, all snuggled up under some newspapers and an old army blanket.

Brian was ready to give up when he saw a figure hunched over, sitting on a large rock, near the pond. It didn't seem the right size for Patrick, but he directed his light on the figure and turned it on. The figure unfolded and straightened up and started to collect his books and run. Brian recognized him. "Son!" he called.

"Patrick, Son!" he called again.

Patrick turned. He could only see the bright light in his eyes but he recognized the voice. He headed toward the light and ran into the outstretched arms. Patrick cried, "I thought you were the police."

"I'm so glad you're all right. We've been worried sick."

"I didn't think you would miss me," Patrick admitted. He was so thrilled to see his dad. He threw his arms around his neck and hugged him. Man to man he didn't care whether he should hug or not. He was so thrilled to see his father it was his only way to respond.

Brian returned the hug and saw the love radiated in Patrick's eyes.

"We have been desperately looking for you for hours. Your mother called me at work when you didn't come home from school."

"I'm sorry."

"You're safe, thank goodness. Let's go tell your mother you're okay."

"I didn't think I was important to you. You fought for Tanya but ignored me for months."

"It must have seemed that way. You're very important to us–the most important thing in this world. We would fight even harder for you, Patrick. Luckily we haven't had to. You're always so dependable and when you didn't come home as usual we were frightened. No, scared out of our minds is better explanation. What happened?"

"I needed to think."

"Please call next time. I was just going into a meeting when your mom called. But you are more important than any meeting."

"Sorry I fouled up your meeting, Dad."

"Don't be. I'm so happy you're okay."

"Thanks."

"Come on and let's jog to the car."

"It was getting cold and I'm starved. Some man came and said he had food if I wanted to go with him. I was tempted, but I really wanted to go home."

Brian flinched at the thought of such a person and what he might want in repayment. Also how would they have known where to search for their son?

Patrick continued, "I didn't like the guy's looks. Actually he was dressed okay, but there was something about him I didn't trust or like. So I told him no thanks, I'd stay here until my Dad came to pick me up."

"Good thinking."

"I was hoping."

"It's good that you didn't go with a stranger. That could have been terrible. We might not have found you for a long time."

"I was hungry. But not that hungry. I wanted to talk to you and Mom."

"We want you to share your feelings with us. I'm sorry we have been so caught up in Tanya's life that we have neglected you. You're a wonderful son and I want you to know how much I appreciate you. You're always so willing to help me in the yard or pitch in and do anything we ask. I've seen you anticipate what your Mom needs and lend a helping hand there."

"I like helping; it's fun."

"Patrick, I love you!"

"Dad, there's a young man with bruises on his face and says his stepdad is mean, especially if he's been drinking. Could we take him home and feed him and let him spend the night?"

"Sure. Where is he?"

"Over on the south side of the park. He said he was going to sleep on the bench there."

They changed directions and when they approached the bench he was not there. "He must have decided to go home after all. He was worried about his Mom."

"I'll beat you to the car. It's halfway down the block on the east side. Get set, go."

They took off running together like old times. Both laughing as Brian accidently stumbled, but caught his balance and they were off again in high spirits.

As they got near the car, they saw a police car with lights flashing, two cars up from theirs.

"Hey, Dad, that's the man I told you about. The one the police have in handcuffs. He's the one who offered me dinner and a bed. I wonder why the police have him."

"Maybe I should find out."

"Dad, the boy that was hungry and beaten is sitting in the police car."

Brian approached the police and inquired, "This man offered dinner and a bed to my son earlier. Why is he in custody?"

"He is one of our nightmares in town. He approaches hungry scared kids, often runaways. Offers them food and bed then uses them for illegal purposes. Pushing drugs, prostitution, or whatever he can make money from. Once he gets the youth he doesn't let go and imprisons them to do his bidding. We have been wanting to catch him for a long time in the process of soliciting someone. Tonight we got lucky when he tried to get the young man in the car to come with him."

"What will happen to the young man?"

"We'll put him in a shelter, use him for a witness, and see what we can do for his mother."

"Could we take him home and feed him?"

"Yes, but I would prefer to put him in a shelter and work with him and his mom. From what he tells us, his mother needs help. We'll go by their house and check now."

Brian returned to Patrick, "They're going to try and help the boy and his Mom. Let's go home to your mother before she dies from worry."

Watching from the window Lana saw Brian drive up. Two people emerged from the car. Lana opened the door and ran full speed. She wrapped her arms around Patrick and held him close. "Thank goodness you're safe and home. We've been out of our minds with worry."

CHAPTER TEN

Will emerged from his private plane, and instructed Vern, the pilot, "Please put the plane in the hanger. I'll call you tomorrow with more information about what's happening."

"I'm staying at the Marriott as usual?"

"Of course, Vern. I'm so worried about my grandson, I forgot."

Vern knew he always had his room reserved at the Marriott when they were here visiting the Carters and Will picked up the tab for food too. Working for Will Brahns was a year-round vacation.

Mr. Brahns proceeded to the storage garage to get his private auto that he kept there for when he visited Lana. He then drove to Carter's.

When Will arrived the house was dark. He wondered if that was a good sign or a bad one. Will rang the bell. A sleepy voice responded, "Who is it?"

"Lana, your father. What's new on Patrick?"

"Oh, my heavens. In my relief to have him home I forgot to call you and tell you we found him. I'll be right down."

After a huge hug Will asked, "He's okay?"

"Yes."

"I would've been on my way by the time you found him. We do need to call your Mom. She is in Palm Springs with an old college friend. She was planning to catch a flight here tomorrow if we didn't have news by then."

"You're okay parents, Dad. I love you."

"Lana, you manage to keep our life exciting."

"Patrick told us about a young man all bruised with a swollen eye in the park. He had run away from an abusive stepfather. How lucky I am to have grown up in a house of love."

The next morning the headline in the newspaper announced, "Caught Buck Wright, Alleged Predator of Runaway Kids." The story told of Buck finding many runaway kids, feeding and sheltering them and turning them into drug pushers and prostitutes to support themselves and make Buck rich.

The article continued, "Remember the young girl found beaten to death last month? One of the teens held by Buck Wright said it was because she tried to call police for help. She didn't want to prostitute any longer and Buck insisted. She had tried to escape, was caught and beaten."

Another big story was about a woman taken to the hospital in critical condition after being beaten by her husband. She was discovered by her son and the police. Max Harper, her husband, was taken into custody. Jay, his stepson, had also been abused and has an eye swollen shut and many bruises which he stated Max inflicted on him."

"Mom, that is the man in the park, that Buck Wright and that other story is about the boy and his mother. My gosh! I saw news in the making."

"What do you know about all this, Patrick?" Will asked.

"Jay was in the park and looked terrible last night. When I found him he was sobbing. His eye was swollen nearly shut and he had bruises on his face. He looked terrible, however, he said the worse thing for him was to see his mother beaten."

"Shall we go visit them in the hospital and see what we can do?"

"Yes, please, Grandad."

Will and Patrick found Jay by his mother's bed. Patrick walked up and laid his hand on Jay's shoulder. Jay looked up, recognized Patrick and smiled. "Did you find a place to sleep last night?"

"Yes, Jay, I'm Patrick Carter. This is my granddad, Senator Brahns."

They shook hands around.

"My dad came for me and I went home to sleep. Dad and I tried to find you to take you home and feed you and give you a place to sleep. The police had you in the car and wanted to go check on your mother," answered Patrick.

"Thanks for looking for me. I was miserable."

"I knew you were hungry too."

They all stood there silent for a few minutes. Then Will asked, "How is your mother doing?"

"She seems better. I'm waiting for the doctor."

"Mind if we wait with you?"

Before Jay could answer, the doctor arrived.

Will asked, "What is Mrs. Harper's condition, Doctor?"

"Not great. But she'll survive. She'll need some patching up. Her jaw bone is broken. Other than that and two broken ribs it's mostly bruises and will take time to heal."

"Can she go to work?" Jay wanted to know.

"It will be sometime before she returns to work. She needs to have surgery and recuperate."

"She'll get fired then. That means no insurance. Last time Max beat her so bad she missed a week of work they warned her if it happened again she was out the door."

"Where does she work, Jay?"

"At a shoe factory. It doesn't pay much. But it keeps food on our table."

"Do you have family that could help? Maybe grandparents."

"No. Grandpa is dead and Grandma lives in California and she told Mom if she married Max, not to come running to her."

"Don't worry, son. We'll figure something out," Will assured Jay.

When they left the hospital Patrick asked, "Grandad, how are they going to get along? No job, no insurance and a mean man in the house."

"Maybe your mother could use a maid for a year?"

"I don't think so. We have a cleaning lady once a week and that's it."

"We could give her the maid as a present."

"I don't think Dad would like that."

"You're probably right. It's too near Max here anyway. Better to get her away."

"How can you do that?"

"Let's talk to Grandma on the phone when we get home and we'll see."

"You're going to help them?" asked Partrick.

"I don't know how. But the answer is, yes."

"Are you going to get rid of Max?"

"Max belongs in jail. A move to Arizona would be a good idea for Jay and his mother," said Will.

"You mean take them home with you?"

"Possibly Mrs. Harper is going to take a long time to heal and she'll need some medical attention. I know some good doctors who could patch her up."

Vera was receptive to having another maid and assistant. Someone who would be partly house maintenance and partly personal administrative assistant. They would try her out. If it worked, fine. If not, they would find something else for Wilma Harper in Arizona. They decided there was plenty of room in the extra apartment over the four car garage that would serve as home for Jay Morgan and Wilma Harper.

Will returned to the hospital to discuss the move with Wilma. "Mrs. Harper, we would like very much to take you to Arizona and help you mend. Get some good medical help and get you away from your cruel husband, Max."

"Why help me?"

"I've been blessed with abundance and think the good Lord gave it to me to share with others."

"Is there a catch to all this?"

"I would hope when you are well that you could work with Mrs. Brahns, helping with the house maintenance and some administrative assistance. We will pay you when you work. In the meantime the apartment at our home and groceries are free. Is that fair?"

"More than fair," Wilma agreed with huge tears of joy in her eyes.

"Let's talk to the doctor about how soon you can fly to Arizona."

"There are some problems. The apartment we live in is on a year's lease with two months to go. Max probably won't pay the rent."

"Let that be his problem if he wants to continue to live there. If he leaves, then you can let the prepaid months' deposit pay for the time it takes to re-rent it. We'll work that out."

"I don't want to ever, ever live with Max again. But we're married."

"That shouldn't be a problem. A divorce should be easy with the way he treats you and Jay. I'll talk to my attorney. He'll take care of it."

Wilma dry eyed now, stared at Will. "Are you Santa Claus?"

Will answered, "Call me what you like. I know I am blessed even more when I share."

"What a good man you are. I was so lonesome with no man in my life and knew I was getting older and feeling life was running out so I married that bum, Max. He wasn't physically cruel until after we married. The marriage turned into a living hell, I thought I was trapped forever. The worst thing for me was the way he treated Jay."

"Jay thought the most horrible thing was the way he treated you, Mrs. Harper. He was worried about you when he brought the police to find you. You should have heard him telling Patrick about finding you in a pool of blood, laying still. He thought you were dead," Will shared.

"He's a good boy. I don't know what I'd do without him. Will Child Protective Services take him away?"

"Of course not. You have an offer of a good job with us and a chance to take care of him. You'll be there when he gets home from school. You'll see a lot more of him. Teens need that."

"I know."

"Maybe in a way we can be grandparents to him," Will said.

Quietly she whispered, "Thanks. Thank you so much. I'll be forever indebted to you. I'll try to make it up to you."

Jay had sat quietly through the whole conversation. "Don't I get a say about what we do?"

"Oh, yes son. How do you vote?"

"Go! Let's go."

The doctor arrived. Will asked, "How soon do you feel Mrs. Harper will be in condition to fly to Arizona?"

"In four or five days, if all goes well."

Turning to Wilma, "We'll plan on leaving in five days. The police will accompany you and Jay to get your personal belongings. You won't need furniture. Your apartment in Arizona is furnished. Get your clothing and personal books, games, photos etc. Some things may have to be shipped. My plane has limited capacity."

"You have your own plane?" Jay asked.

"Yes. Do you like to fly?"

"I don't know. I've never flown," Jay said with wide eyes.

"Mr. Brahns, why are you so nice to us? We're strangers," Wilma wanted to know.

"You're good people. I like good people. If it is okay with you we will take Jay home to stay with Patrick for the next five days."

"Wonderful. I was worried about him staying at home alone or if Max gets out of prison I sure didn't want Jay with him."

The apartment in Arizona was cheerful and Wilma and Jay adjusted to the loving atmosphere of the Brahns. Wilma healed.

Jay helped wherever and whenever he could around the estate. He loved gardening. He hadn't had the opportunity to work with shrubs and flowers when living in apartments. He blossomed along with the beautiful plants. It was obvious he was thrilled to be away from Max and Maryland. Julian was hired to help through the summer in the garden. He was from South America. He didn't talk much about home. Julian and Jay became fast friends and he taught Jay some Spanish.

Wilma became good friends with Julian through Jay. She even invited Julian to dinner one evening to be friendly. She found Jay to be right. Julian was handsome. He was well read, very gentlemanly and gracious. She thrived on the distraction of a male friend. However, she never wanted to be romantically involved again.

Besides, working for Mrs. Brahns and attending college at Mesa Community College learning more about computers left too little time for Jay. There definitely was not time for a serious romance For the first time in Wilma's life she felt she was in control of her life and progressing in a positive direction.

Will Brahns' appointment to the Senate was up and he had campaigned for re-election. He won in a landslide. It felt good to know the people wanted him.

Vera and Will decided to buy a home instead of leasing in Washington D. C.. If they were to spend more time in the Washington area they wanted their dwelling to be more personal. They planned a trip to Virginia to select a lot and builder to get things rolling for the fall.

It had been two years now since they returned from Paraguay and Lana thought they had settled in, planting some roots. Then General Martin from Washington offered Brian a position to be in charge of DASA NET (Defense Atomic Support Agency Nuclear Emergency Team), located in Albuquerque, New Mexico–an offer too good to refuse. So it was moving time again.

Lana called her father, "Hello, Father dear."

"Lana, how are you? You don't usually call during the day and usually I'm Dad, not Father dear. Is something wrong?"

"I need to talk to you. Bad. How long have you lived in that same house?"

"Let's see, about thirty three years I guess. Why?"

"We are moving again," Lana stated.

"Where?"

"To Albuquerque. We will be nearer when you are in Phoenix, farther when you're in Washington D. C.. It's difficult to move Patrick in school, get settled in a new community and make new friends. I don't know. I'm dreading it."

"I'll send the plane over to pick you up for a visit if you would like."

"Please do. I need to see you. Is Mom at home?"

"No. She is off to some board of directors meeting. But I know she will love having you. Jay and Wilma will be pleased to see you. They're both doing very well."

"Let me talk to Brian, then I'll call you back."

"Call soon. Love you. Bye."

"Bye. You're a jewel. You're always there for me. You're one special father. Love you heaps."

"Dad, it always feels so secure to return home to visit. It's my comfort zone."

"It's good to have you. Patrick has shot up several inches since we last saw him. Wow!" Will observed.

"He's going to be a tall one. He's sure a fine son. For that I'm so thankful. Many parents have problems with their children and we enjoy

Patrick. He acts, talks and thinks like an adult. He's our best friend."

"Maybe that's the secret, Lana. You enjoy him so he doesn't need to get into trouble to get attention. Anyway I'm sure proud of that grandson."

"How is Julian working out? I see he is still here," Lana observed.

"He seems so much more refined than most gardeners. He has worked as an alternate chauffeur. I'm glad we kept him on after his summer commitment. For a while I thought Wilma was interested in him. But that seems to have cooled," Will said.

"Who is that big ugly guy that came up to talk to Julian?" Lana asked.

"I don't know. He has come by a couple of times and he seems to upset Julian each time. Maybe it's a connection to his past in South America."

As the big man turned, Lana saw his gold tooth glistening in the sun and the scar on his forehead. She gasped, grabbed her father's arm and whispered, "That's Poco Loco. The rebel that tried to rape me when I was a prisoner."

"Who?"

"Poco Loco. Remember, the one that tore my blouse off and was going to rape me then Estelle came and rescued me?"

"Are you sure?"

"I'm positive. I couldn't forget an ugly face like that."

Will ran to the phone and dialed 911. "I need help here at the Brahns'. I have a criminal on the premises. Please come immediately."

Poco looked up and saw Lana looking right at him and hit the road on a run.

Will opened the door and yelled, "Stop him Julian. Please stop him."

Julian took off after Poco, but was lost in the dust. When Poco was a good block ahead, Julian stopped, turned and went back to meet Mr. Brahns.

As Will and Julian returned to the breakfast room they saw Lana white and still shaken as a nasty part of her past was made too real once more.

"Julian, how could that bum be part of your life?" Will asked.

"He offered me a way to get to the States and a possible job as a gardener for a year to help make money to pay the other thousand dollars he demanded. You know gardening was my hobby before. I'm a professor of literature."

"Why did he want you to work as a gardener?"

"To work for you and feed him information mostly about your daughter. He wanted to know her schedule. I told him no, but he assured me I would be returned to South America if I didn't cooperate."

"How could you get Lana's schedule?"

"Through Wilma. She's in the house often helping the Señora. I think she could easily have found out. She refused and now will not speak to me. She's very loyal to you and your family."

"Why did he want Lana's schedule?"

"I don't know. But I'm sure it was not for a good reason."

"When my daughter was held prisoner in Paraguay during the coup attempt, Poco tried to rape her. He later rigged a bomb on their car to kill them. Their gardener took the car next so it killed him instead.

"I didn't know. Honestly, I had no idea," Julian responded, shaken by the truth.

"You know where he lives?" Will asked.

"Yes. I'll take you there."

"The police should be here in a few seconds. Please show them the way."

"Señor, when I refused to get the information, Poco said he would be sure my dream of bringing my ill, widowed mother here would never happen. In fact he threatened that if I didn't cooperate, my mother would no doubt have a very unfortunate accident. That I would never see her alive again. I know you've trusted me and I'm very sorry to lose that trust."

The police arrived. "Where's your problem Mr. Brahns?"

"He ran. But Julian will show you where he lives."

"Julian, we need to talk further, after this is settled."

Now that Lana had identified him, Poco was sure that Julian would show the police where he lived. He would outsmart them and not return to his apartment.

Lana didn't know Poco's total fascination with her.

Poco knew she was feisty and probably would never submit willingly, that he would have to take her by force all the way. He was willing to do just that. He wanted Lana and didn't want to be cheated out of his dream of conquest. He would wait until Lana went somewhere and then follow her–catch her and take her. Poco relished the idea of finally getting his revenge–his dues, that he had been cheated of in Paraguay. It had become an obsession with him. Franco had been cooperative in getting Lana Carter's home address and giving it to the rebel leaders..

Poco had been a master at racketeering in Paraguay, like he already was in the United States. It was his game. Do unto others before they can do unto you, was his motto.

Poco didn't have to wait long. Shortly after lunch he saw the Mercedes leave with only Lana inside. He had heard that she didn't like to use the limo and the chauffeur. His bet paid off. Poco gave her ample room, then pulled into the traffic.

Lana started through the countryside heading for her favorite marketplace near Apache Junction to pick up some dates and citrus fruit to take back to Maryland with her. Brian was always so good to pamper her and let her come home to get her emotional batteries charged and ready for the move. She wanted to surprise him with some of his favorite foods.

Thank goodness this car was mister dependable. Her favorite to drive when in town. It was always available for her personal use.

A fairly new Buick pulled up beside her and honked. She ignored it. It honked again. She looked over and saw the man motion to pull off to the side of the road.

She ignored him. He honked again and pulled dangerously close. Then she recognized who was driving. Poco Loco! She saw a strip mall in the distance. She decided she would make a run for that, then stop and run inside and call the police. Lana speeded up.

The Buick pulled so close it bumped her side. Scared, she stepped harder on the gas to out run him. He speeded up and pulled into her lane just in front of her Mercedes, slammed on his brakes and she ran off the road to avoid smashing into the rear of his car..

Lana was still at least a half block from the mall. Poco had pulled right in front of her. She backed up to go around; he immediately pulled sideways in front again. She was blocked. Lana flung open the door and started to run as fast as her legs would take her to get help.

Barely halfway there, Poco caught her and gripped her. “Where are you going so fast, feisty one?”

“To get help.” she screamed between hits and kicks which didn’t seem to faze Poco.

“You’re not going any place except with me.”

“Let me go!” Lana demanded. Feeling helpless in his vicelike grip, She realized she had left her safety zone, the car, in her panic to get help.

“You can go after I am through with you,” Poco threatened.

She stopped fighting and stood frozen.

“What is your game, Poco?”

“I want my just dues.”

"Your what?"

"Come with me to my car and we’ll discuss it there."

"No. I want to discuss it here and now."

"You're still the feisty little tiger. I like that."

"I don't like you, Poco. You have caused a lot of pain in my life. I'm going up to that mall to call for help."

"You're going to need a lot of help."

Poco blocked Lana.

Lana started to walk by Poco and he grabbed her arm twisting it behind her back. "Is that convincing you to come with me?"

"Never. You're ruthless." Lana shouted each word distinctly and slowly. "I'll go down fighting, but I won't quietly submit to you ever."

"The harder you fight, the better I like it. That makes it exciting. Too bad your father isn't here to bail you out. Money should be able to buy anything, even safety for his daughter. Right?"

Lana turned and kicked his shins. He hardly flinched.

Using his old trick,Poco grabbed Lana's hair and pulled her head back and tried to kiss her. She clenched her teeth to be sure his filthy tongue did not enter her mouth. When he started to pull away she again hit him with a vengeance.

"Go ahead and fight harder. I love it."

Poco pushed Lana toward his car. Lana started screaming.

"They'll think your husband has you under control."

"No one would believe I'm married to you. You sleazy bum."

Lana screamed again. "Help! Help me, please!"

The cars whizzed on by and no one paid attention. Some had their windows down–but ignored her plea for help.

Lana was terrified. Poco's car was near and she couldn't break loose. Poco was big and very strong. He opened the door and pushed her in. As he started around the car, Lana quickly exited the car and started running toward the mall.

Poco overtook her in a flash, yelling, "That's enough. Me gusta a fighter, but you're impossible. Another stunt like that and I'll knock ya out 'til I get ya where I want ya."

Poco pushed Lana back toward his car. He heard a siren, looked, and spotted the police car approaching with lights flashing. He grabbed Lana's shoulder and threw her to the ground by the side of the road. He ran and jumped into his car and took off.

"Are you okay?" called the policeman.

"Yes, get him then come back for me!" Lana responded.

The police jammed on the gas and took off, siren wailing.

Lana pulled herself to a sitting position and started brushing off the gravel and dirt from her clothes, hair and face.

Tears streamed down her face. What a monster that Poco was. She thought she was safely back in the States only to be confronted with this horror of her past.

Seconds later Lana's father pulled up and bounded out of his limo to catch Lana in his arms. "How are you, precious one?" Will's brisk business ways always melted to tenderness when it concerned his daughter.

"I'm scared, but okay."

Will confessed, "When Julian returned and said Poco was not at his apartment, fear gripped me. Then Julian reported that he saw Poco in a car on the side street and that he took off right after you did. I decided he was probably following you. I immediately called the police and told them where you were headed."

"It was great to hear their sirens. It scared Poco off."

"Thank goodness."

"When I first saw the empty Mercedes I was scared he had you."

"He did get his clutches on me. I tried to escape. It was the arrival of the police that saved me. Thanks, Dad. You're a quick thinker."

After they were safely home and Vera had settled down from hysteria about her daughter's encounter, Lana tried to call Brian to let him know what was going on. She let the phone ring at least a dozen times. No answer.

Lana decided to wait a while and call again.

After dinner Lana picked up the phone and dialed home to talk to Brian. She needed his comforting encouragement after the horrible afternoon.

Still there was no answer. She remembered there was a lab party. Usually Brian would have called early before going. That was strange because Brian called every evening to chat and this evening there was no call.

Brian went to a party which included most of the people in his research area of the lab. Brian, being a party animal, enjoyed himself dancing the night away.

Elaine, one of the fairly new scientists in the lab, found Brian fascinating. She finally asked, "Where is your charming wife?"

"Arizona, visiting with her father. She's a little upset about our forthcoming move."

"That's right. You have this great offer to head DASA NET in New Mexico. What a wonderful opportunity. Want to trade? You stay here and I'll go there."

"No. I'm excited about the move. However, it's difficult to move Patrick and Lana." Brian was captivated with Elaine's sparkly personality, her charm and on a scale of one to ten she would rate a nine or ten in the looks department.

"You're on an upward mobility path. Doesn't Lana appreciate that?"

"I think so. But it's difficult for her to make new friends and all in a new community. You know--establish yourself when you don't work."

"I wouldn't think twice if you were my husband and had an offer like that."

Brian realized Lana was a bit spoiled and that made it more difficult for her to adjust. She was used to having most things easy. Moves were not easy.

"My, my. You are far away in thought."

"Yeah," Brian replied.

"I'm right here for all it's worth. Congratulations on such an enviable position."

"It's worth a lot. Thanks for the words of encouragement." It was good to hear some positive words of congratulations on the appointment.

"Glad to be helpful," Elaine said.

"Shall we dance?"

"I thought you'd never ask."

Elaine was a great dancer. After a while she snuggled a little closer as the music switched to soft melodic. It sounded romantic and she made it feel very romantic. Brian tightened his grip on her a little and she seemed to fit just right in his arms. As they approached a door to the veranda it seemed quite natural to go out to see the moon and stars and talk.

Standing near the rail of the veranda they had a fabulous view of the city below. Brian slipped his arm around Elaine and looked up at the moon. "Seems romantic and eerie."

"It's romantic for me. Why eerie?" Elaine asked.

"I don't know. Maybe too many crazy movies that portray some sort of mystery with full moons. It is romantic."

"Do you want to stay here until the last dog is hung?"

"Not really. What would you suggest?" Brian asked.

"I don't have my car here to get home. I came right from the lab with Hans to help get things organized. He and Ruth were to take me home. But I would be happy for you to."

"Sounds good to me."

"Wait one. I'll let them know," she said.

At Elaine's apartment she asked, "Would you like to come in for a nightcap?"

Temptation pounded at Brian's door. He weakened. Elaine was Gorgeous, charming, energetic, fun and a supporter. Why not? A night cap and more talk. Maybe more encouragement.

"Sounds good to me."

"That's one of your favorite expressions. I'll know when I'm in tune with you," Elaine said.

As Elaine unlocked the door, Brian had a qualm of guilt as he knew he was flirting with a very dangerous situation. He thought he could handle it.

"Wait one," Elaine called as she disappeared.

When she returned in her flowing gown and sumptuous figure showing delectably through, Brian knew he couldn't handle it. He held out his arms and she glided into them.

Still upset by the day's events, Lana couldn't sleep. She decided to call Brian again. She knew he was probably asleep at one a.m. but she needed to talk and tell him the experiences of the day. She needed to feel his supportive voice and encouragement. Brian had a way of making things seem right. She was desperate to be reassured.

She dialed their number. It rang twenty-four times. No answer. Lana was concerned. Even if he went to the party without her, he should be home by now. They usually wound up by eleven. That was two hours ago.

Weariness and needing to talk to Brian let suspicion creep into Lana's mind. Many friends along the way had commented what a flirt Brian was. She had always trusted him. Was that blind trust because she wanted to believe his flirting was innocent?

She thought of waking up her Dad or Mom to talk. No, she decided, she would go have a cup of hot chocolate and see if that calmed her nerves. Then she would call Brian again.

Will heard her in the kitchen. He joined her. "Today has been a nightmare, hasn't it?"

"Yes. I wanted to talk to Brian about it. But he doesn't seem to be home."

"That's right. He didn't call as usual last night," Will said.

"No. There was a lab party. They usually start early and finish early on a weeknight. So I thought he might call later."

"You're concerned about his safety?"

"I'm not sure."

"Then what?" Will asked.

"Do you think Brian is faithful to me, Dad?"

"I think he idolizes you."

"It's nearly two in the morning and he's not home."

"Maybe he's asleep and didn't hear the phone."

"I let it ring a couple of dozen times and we have a phone right by the head of our bed. I think he would eventually hear it."

"Sounds reasonable."

"This has been one of the most horrible days of my whole life. I need to talk to him. I don't need a new worry."

"Lana, try to get some sleep. Maybe there's a good explanation for his being gone."

"I don't want to be a sucker. Brian's flirting never bothered me as I thought he was overly friendly, but harmless."

Lana picked up the phone and dialed again. Still no answer.

As Brian pulled into their driveway in the early dawn hours he remembered he had forgotten to call Lana. He was heavy with a guilty conscience of the night's activities.

As he entered the house the phone was ringing.

"Brian, where in the world have you been?"

Caught off guard he lied, "Right here."

"You don't sound sleepy. I tried at one to call you. Again at two. No answer even though I let it ring and ring."

"You sound very upset, Lana."

"I am. Yesterday was a nightmare. I needed to talk to you desperately."

"What happened?"

She related the beastly experiences of Poco Loco showing up at her father's estate.

When Lana and Patrick returned to Maryland she found it difficult to be as close to Brian. She still had many unanswered questions about that horrible night that she needed Brian and he wasn't there for her. She decided not to approach the subject right now. With the move she didn't feel equal to coping with what might be in store for her. Honesty was very important to Lana.

Patrick felt the strain, "Mom, are you mad at Dad?"

"Not really. I'm uptight about the move."

"Hey, we can handle it. We've moved a lot. It isn't a coup. You're not a prisoner."

"That's right, Patrick, we can handle it. Do you want to go house hunting with us in Albuquerque?"

"Of course."

Chapter Eleven

The Carters found Albuquerque, New Mexico, a fascinating place to live. The mountains east of the city were beautiful. The relaxed atmosphere was delightful. People were extremely friendly.

They bought a Mediterranean style home sitting up on the mountain toward Sandia Peak, in the northeast part of the city. The huge windows of the living room, dining room and the family room looked up toward the mountain. They could watch a snow storm coming over the mountain and sneak into their back yard. It was a land of enchantment.

In nice weather they could sit in the courtyard in the evening and watch the lights of Albuquerque come alive. They loved their home and Brian's new position.

Another plus about Albuquerque was that it was nearer Phoenix and Lana's parents. Also over the last two years Patrick had become fast friends with Jay Morgan. He felt he had helped save the boy from a disastrous life. It made him feel good.

Albuquerque was also near Durango, Colorado where Brian's parents lived. They enjoyed seeing more of them.

The Carters lived fairly near Brian's office. The wide open space was inviting after the heavy traffic of the east coast. The clear blue sky and bright sun with no haze was welcome also.

Lana located a position as manager of a head hunting group. One morning when driving down Lomas Boulevard, headed for her office, Lana felt almost lightheaded with the beauty of the city before her. It lay in the valley like a glittering jewel in the morning light.

She saw a girl that looked a lot like Tanya. That wasn't unusual. Lana often saw someone with dark curly hair and would think "that looks like Tanya would probably look now." Tanya still dominated many of her thoughts. When this girl turned, Lana could see that without a doubt, it was Tanya! Lana didn't know the lady with her, but it was Tanya. Lana quickly drove ahead of the little girl and pulled over to the curb and got out of the car.

Tanya saw Lana. She broke her hand loose from the woman's and she ran full speed towards Lana. Lana ran towards Tanya. Before they met, Lana bent over, held open her arms and Tanya ran into them, burying her head in Lana's shoulder. How wonderful it felt to hold her again. Lana couldn't speak for a moment.

The sweetness of that hug, sweetness of Tanya obviously remembering Lana and the joy reflected in Tanya's face–how heavenly! They held tight. Tanya exclaimed, "Mama, Mama!"

Lana's heart was singing with joy at seeing and holding Tanya again and being called "'Mama". At the same time, her heart was crying out with pain at all the smiles and hugs she had missed in between through the years. Lana whispered in Spanish, "How are you, little one?"

"I'm not so little now. Look at me." Tanya said in very good English, pulling back and standing tall.

"You look wonderful. No, you're not so little now. But how are you?"

"Bien, (good)."

After the nasty trial, the Arnolds had forbidden the Carters to keep in touch in any way. The last she had heard, Bernie was headed to an assignment in Washington D. C., so it was total shock to see Tanya in Albuquerque, New Mexico. What a wonderful surprise.

Lana turned to who must have been the nanny and asked, "Are you living near?"

She hesitated, looking completely baffled with all that had happened, then answered, "In Santa Fe."

"What are you doing in Albuquerque?"

"Caroline had a meeting and we were killing time and going to catch a cab or bus to Old Town for lunch. We were told it's an interesting place to visit and has excellent Mexican food."

"Please, let me treat you to lunch. I have a favorite restaurant in Old Town. I can change my appointments and spend some time with you two. Please," Lana pleaded.

Tanya also reinforced the request with, "Please, please, Margo."

Margo and Tanya crawled in the car and they headed for Old Town and the Hacienda Restaurant for a wonderful Mexican treat. After they were seated, Tanya commented, "That tree is growing right in the middle of the restaurant."

"Yes, they built the restaurant around it. Isn't that neat?"

"What are they cooking over there?" Tanya asked, pointing to the large vat of boiling oil with a señorita dressed in a mexican blouse and long ruffled skirt, standing in front of it.

"Sopapillas, the delicious hot bread they serve with our meals."

"Can we watch?" Tanya asked.

"Yes. As soon as I find a phone and call the office."

Lana returned to the table as soon as she had changed her appointments for the day. "I'm ready to go watch."

Tanya took her hand and walked over to where they were making the sopapillas. Holding Tanya's hand again made Lana's heart sing. The excitement was indescribable. It brought back so many fond memories of days past.

Tanya watched them fry the bread, fascinated with how it was rolled, cut, and pushed into the large vat of hot oil.

When they returned to the table, Tanya ate a whole basket of warm sopapillas by herself. Some she ate straight, others she poured honey on.

Tanya looked at Lana excitedly and said, "School starts again in two weeks. Did you know Ina is a good artist? Many of her drawings are shown at school."

"Who is Ina?" Lana inquired.

"My sister, silly," she answered giggling. "You remember Ina, don't you?"

"Oh sure, but I thought her name was Ignacia."

"Ina is better, we call her Ina now. It's more American."

"Where is your Dad today?" Lana asked.

"Didn't you know, he was killed?" Tanya answered.

"No. When?"

"When we lived back in Washington D.C. That was a long time ago."

"How was he killed?" Lana asked.

"A drunk driver hit him head on. Totaled his car and him. Mom doesn't drink anymore. She says it's bad."

"I agree. Drinking isn't good. Where is Juan? Do you still call him Juan? Or did you change his name also?"

"We call him Jon now. He and Ina stayed in Santa Fe with friends today. They were going on a hike and picnic. Mom said I was too young, so Margo and I came to Albuquerque with her."

Lana ate as slowly as possible. She didn't want this to ever end. "When did your mother go back to work?"

"After Dad was killed. I don't like her working." Then as Margo got up to go to the restroom Tanya added, "Margo is nice but I miss Mom at home with us. She's too tired to do a lot of the fun things we used to do."

"What are some of the fun things you like to do?"

"Swim. You taught me how to have fun in the water. I like the zoo." After some thought she added, "I like to explore. Mom used to take us places and say we were exploring. I liked those days."

"Maybe Margo could take you exploring."

"It's not the same. Now that you know where we live, will you come to see me? Maybe I could spend some time with you."

Lana sat quiet for a minute and thought how wonderful that would be. To keep in touch and see Tanya grow and mature was better than nothing. "We would like that, Tanya. I must check with Caroline first. I do hope we can."

Tanya told Lana more about the sad news. "It was terrible when Dad was killed. Mom was very sick for awhile. She cried a lot. Went into her bedroom for days and wouldn't come out. Her sister came to live with us and she helped us. She helped Mom, too."

"How nice that family came to your rescue. It's good that you were there for Caroline, Tanya. I'm sure you three were a big comfort to her."

"Mom started to feel better. She was more normal when she went back to work. I guess it's good that she works."

Now Caroline was both mother and father to those three children she had rescued from Paraguay. Lana again admired Caroline and thought how fortunate that she had the children to bring some sunshine into her life–but Lana still resented the way she had obtained Tanya.

When Lana got home from work that evening, the phone was ringing off the hook.

Picking it up she cheerfully said, "Good evening, Carter's." She was still on a high from being with Tanya. Her mood darkened immediately when she heard the angry voice of Caroline on the line. "What do you mean stalking my daughter and stirring up old feelings of loyalty to you. You'll keep her so mixed up. She's had enough to deal with losing her father. Leave us alone!"

"True, I was with Tanya. It was a joy for me to see what a lovely–happy eight year old she is. I admire you for raising that family alone. Maybe we could help out in some way."

"We don't need your help. Bernie was well insured. The children are happy. Leave us alone or I'll get another restraining order to keep you away."

Lana begged, "Caroline, please let us come and visit. That would mean so much to us."

"That would keep her confused and uncertain. Keep away from her."

"Please, it would mean a lot to see Tanya as an aunt or such and see her grow. We wouldn't try to steal her like you did." She regretted saying that as soon as it passed her lips.

"Be nasty if you want, but stay out of our lives," Caroline yelled as she hung up.

Lana realized she had messed up.

Brian came through the door, "You look like someone hit you in the belly."

"I feel like I was blasted." Lana recounted her experiences for the day, happy and sad ones.

CHAPTER TWELVE

Will sent Lana a copy of Phoenix's favorite newspaper. the Arizona Republic with headlines reading, *Rebel Leader from South America* Convicted. The paper told of Poco Loco's many atrocities in drug dealing, prostitution, and human slavery of individuals he had illegally brought into the United States. The story continued to tell of the many atrocities and horrors that were allegedly committed by this man while in Asunción. How he was pursued by the police there and had somehow gotten out of the country after the coup attempt and relocated in Arizona. He admitted selecting Arizona because he knew Lana's parents lived there and he was determined to make trouble for Lana. He held a grudge for being cheated out of what he called his "just dues."

Lana was relieved that the trial was over and that the sentence had been handed down. She hated having to relive those horrible days of the civil war in Paraguay when she testified.

She picked up the phone to thank her father for his help in getting Poco Loco convicted. "Dad, thanks for the newspaper. That's great news."

"I knew you would be happy with the results," Will said.

"Yes, I left as soon as possible after my testimony."

"Our lives are gaining some normality again. How about you?"

"Yes, thank goodness. What happened to Julian?" Lana inquired.

"We helped him straighten out his life. He is going to teach at Arizona State University in Tempe come fall. In the meantime he is still working for me. I took into account if it were my mother, how I would feel and decided forgiveness was right. Wilma is even speaking to him again now that she knows the whole story."

"That's good. Julian is a good man. A handsome educated man and very much a gentleman. Wilma could do worse–especially since Jay and Julian are such good friends."

Wilma still lived at the Brahns' apartment and paid rent since she no longer worked for them. After completing college the administrative offices at the college offered her a position. Wilma loved the work. It was more interesting and rewarding than work at the shoe factory.

Will Brahns treated Jay as a grandson with love and respect, taking him on a flight occasionally, or to a ball game to sit in his big private box. Jay now called Mr Brahns "Grandpa Will" . He learned what family love was and felt secure for the first time in his life. Jay didn't feel as close to Vera and still addressed her as Mrs. Brahns. He loved and respected her, but she hadn't spent a lot of time with him–one on one.

Vera helped Wilma in her educational pursuit and taught her social graces. Vera even let Wilma co-hostess a couple of parties.

Wilma longed to be in a good relationship again, with a dynamic man who had the world by the tail.

Brian came home with news that some of the NDL people from Maryland were visiting DASA NET for the week and he thought it would be nice if the Carters took them out to dinner and reminisced.

Lana agreed, but she decided to have a party in their home and share with them the beautiful view of the city and Sandia Mountains. She thought that was a better idea.

There were seven in the group–five men and two ladies.

"Who came?" Lana asked.

"The top notch leaders at the lab."

Lana had forgotten how devastatingly beautiful Elaine was. It was great to see the old crowd.

Rita was the down-to-earth Jewish lady who had always been no nonsense and dependable.

The men had not changed at all. Lana realized how much she missed this group, the ones who had helped the Carters get some normalcy in their lives after their South America escapades. Brian often referred to them as the old comfortable crowd.

As the evening progressed Lana could not help but notice the closeness that Elaine and Brian shared. It bothered her a lot. Maybe that was where Brian was when she tried to call. She still had not forgotten that awful night with no response when she needed him desperately.

"How do you like Albuquerque?" Hans asked.

"It's a wonderful city. We love it. Skiing is close and our parents are fairly near," Brian replied.

"We miss you two in Maryland," Hans said.

"We miss you and Maryland," Lana said. "This is a marvelous opportunity for Brian in his career. He loves his work here."

"That's obvious," Elaine said.

After the Maryland group left, Lana looked Brian straight in the eye and asked, "Were you with Elaine the night I called and called and couldn't get you?"

Brian immediately looked away and struggled for an answer. Finally he admitted, "Yes."

"Brian, I am so disappointed. I needed you that night and you weren't there for me. Now to find out you were with another woman, I feel devastated and betrayed." Lana was too angry to cry. She waited for Brian to make the next move.

The silence was deafening. No one spoke for ages.

Finally Brian weakly offered, "Lana, for what it is worth I have regretted that night many times. I know I betrayed your trust. I want that trust again."

"You didn't seem too remorseful tonight. It was obvious you're still drawn to her and she kindled a fire in you. That's how I knew."

"It's crazy, I know. But she does make me feel like king of the mountain; like I could do anything. But you're the one I love and care for and want for my constant companion."

"You can't have it both ways, Brian."

"I don't want Elaine; I want only you. How can we start over?"

"I'm not sure we can. You not only betrayed my trust, but you lied to me. You told me you were home all night when I called."

"I'm so sorry. You're the only one I love and want, Lana."

"Right now I'm too crushed to think about it. Let's talk more in the morning. I'm too angry to cry. Yelling won't help."

"Can't we talk more now? One big mistake by me can't wipe out all that we feel for each other, can it?" Brian asked as he tried to put his arm around Lana.

"Leave me alone. I'm too upset," Lana responded as she turned and headed for the bedroom to gather her clothes and go to the guest room. She knew she could not share the bed with him that night. She hoped Patrick hadn't heard any of their conversation.

Lana and Brian slept apart for a week and shared very little communication, her tension was mounting.

As she stared at Brian across the table she wondered why he would turn to another woman? Hadn't she always supported him in his crazy notions of adventure? Did he love her or was he more enamored with her background, and her parents' wealth?

Brian suggested, "Let's go to dinner tonight and have some privacy with no interruptions. I can't stand this quiet wall you've put between us."

"That I have put between us? Who was unfaithful and lied? Have there been others, Brian?"

"No," he lied. If she was having so much trouble dealing with this, he couldn't chance her being able to handle more.

"Is it me or my rich parents that keep you in our relationship?"

"You."

"I'm hurt and I'm angry. I've always trusted you completely. Now I feel when you flirt with others you're testing the water."

"Lana, I don't mean to flirt. I'm a friendly guy."

"I used to think that and it didn't bother me. Now it bothers me a lot," Lana admitted.

"Patrick feels the tension and we've got to get this resolved."

"I know. I think I'll go to Phoenix for a visit."

"Does your father know?"

"Not yet. Does that matter?"

"No. Well, yes. I guess I don't want him to know. I don't want him angry at me too."

"I need some space. I'll take Patrick with me. It's a couple of weeks before school starts."

"Can't you at least try to forgive me for my horrible mistake. Elaine offered understanding and praise for my great opportunity with DASA NET. Yes, she is very attractive and charming, but the encouragement she gave was what meant a lot."

"Talking, dancing, having fun is always all right with me. But to spend the night and break your vow of fidelity is not a trivial matter to me–then to lie to me on top of that. I'm trying to see it from your side. But I've never been tempted to go to bed with anyone else. No, I don't understand."

"I didn't mean to. I went in to have a nightcap and talk. It happened. One too many champagnes."

"If you knew you were vulnerable, why did you go in?"

"Temptation got me."

"Where is all that strength you're supposed to have?" Lana asked.

"It left me for that night," Brian admitted.

"How do I know it won't leave again and again when you have had a few drinks and I'm out of town?"

"If I promise not to go to parties without you, will that help?"

"I don't want to control you. I want you to be faithful because of your great love for me. I want you to not even think of betraying my trust. This has been a giant battle for me."

"What can I do to help? I love you, Lana. I want you in my bed again. I miss you and don't sleep well without you near. My whole life is you. I'm a nervous wreck. My work is suffering; I'm suffering. My world is crazy."

They went out to dinner and danced. Brian held Lana close and again sparked the fire in her for his companionship. He whispered in her ear, "This feels so good to have you near again. You fit in my arms. You don't know how much I've missed you."

Lana snuggled and they danced on.

That night Lana slipped back into their room and into bed with Brian. He held out his arms to welcome her. He stroked her hair, ran his hand lovingly along her cheek. It was a glorious reunion.

It was now 1967. Years passed and the Carters moved to California.. Brian had an offer he couldn't refuse again for a new exciting position in leadership for a new corporation. He hoped it would be challenging, but more important, an opportunity to use newfound management skills. He was confident this corporation was going places, and he would be a dynamic driving force making it happen as Executive Vice President.

Lana didn't like moves. They always upset her organized life, tore her away from friends and now it would take her far from Tanya. Even though she couldn't go visit her, she knew she was near. It had been so many years since Lana had seen her in Albuquerque and spent that glorious day in Old Town. Tanya would be a teen now.

Lana couldn't help wondering what she looked like and if she was interested in boys or what subjects she liked best in school.

Patrick was ready for college and had been accepted at UCLA, to study pre-med. It would be nice to be close to him. Patrick was one of their dearest friends, so enjoyable on the golf course, at the movies and on traveling excursions that Lana was pleased not to have to abort all activities with him.

The Carters seldom mentioned Tanya. All three of them had gotten over most of that terrible longing they felt for her. At least they didn't verbalize it. Deep in her heart Lana still had many thoughts of that sad-eyed little girl, now a young lady. Tanya still tugged at Lana's heart strings.

Julian was wrapped up in his teaching position at Arizona State University in Tempe. He reveled in being back in his profession. He felt at peace with himself. He now owned a nice home with a yard, enabling him to enjoy his hobby of gardening. Often he wondered if all this and freedom was real. He feared that he would wake up and find he was back in South America.

However, he had not forgotten Wilma and Jay and wanted them to meet his sweet mother who had joined him in the States. On a whim he called, "Wilma, this is Julian."

"Hello there. How are you?"

"Never been better. I have my mother safely with me. She would love to meet you–and I'm anxious to see you again."

"Julian, how nice not to be forgotten."

"Would Friday night be a good night to take you and Jay out to dinner? I know he loves the Green Gables with their knight on the white steed to meet you and people in the old English costumes."

Wilma was surprised at how excited she was with the promise of spending an evening with Julian. Jay would be delighted. Julian always brought out the best in Jay.

California was good for the Carters. Lana was soon managing a head hunting organization similar to the one in Albuquerque. They advertised in the local paper as well as national publications for people to fill positions.

Her next appointment that afternoon was with a librarian looking for an opportunity with more promise than her present position in a school library. She was attractive but seemed distant–calculating in fact. Lana thought she was judging what Lana wanted to hear, so she could expound on that. She definitely was not relaxed. The lady opened her purse and pulled out three photographs. She laid them carefully on the corner of Lana's desk facing her. "Do you recognize any of these?"

Lana's heart skipped a beat. She gasped. It was Tanya as a teen. Even though she had not seen Tanya for years, she knew it was Tanya, those same eyes and smile. There were others also in the photo. Lana was stunned.

"How did you get these photos?"

"They are photos of children my sister, Caroline, adopted."

Lana took in a deep breath and tried in vain to keep her professional stance. Then the sob escaped and memories flooded her mind.

Lana laid her head on her arms and struggled with those yearnings to hold Tanya and to know more about her. Minutes later with red eyes and a tear-stained face, Lana lifted her head and sat there bewildered not knowing what to say or do.

When she thought she was in control again she asked, "Where does Caroline live now?"

"Over in Pacific Grove."

"How is Tanya?"

"She's a lovely young lady. Quite a handful for Caroline."

"You made this appointment on purpose to check me out, didn't you?"

"Yes, as a matter of fact I did. We saw your name advertised in the paper with job opportunities and wondered if it was the same Lana Carter that Caroline had known in Paraguay."

"Are you interested in the position?" Lana asked.

"Yes, I am. Did I blow it with this escapade?"

"No. This is a business and if your qualifications are the best or one of the best we'll set up an interview for you. Please give me Caroline's phone number so I can call her."

"No, she asked me not to give it to you. If you want to give me your home phone, I'll give her a message and your phone number."

"I'd appreciate that." Lana wrote her home phone on the back of one of her business cards.

"I'll be sure she gets this."

"Thanks. Please tell Caroline how grateful I would be to have them over to dinner or be permitted to take Tanya for lunch and enjoy her for an hour or so."

"I'll tell her. Caroline is struggling with three teens right now. Ina is ready for college. Jon is in the community college here in Monterey. He is doing pretty well, but still yearns to go back and see his homeland and his brothers who live in Paraguay."

"Does Caroline know?"

"Yes, she is considering giving him a round trip airline ticket to return and visit his older brothers for Christmas. Hoping that will satisfy him and he'll return and be serious about his studies. She knows that the opportunities are much better for Jon here in the States."

"Do you think he will return after his visit?" Lana asked.

"He has this notion that he needs to go back and connect with his past. Ina seems content here and Tanya doesn't even mention Paraguay. The brothers keep in touch. Caroline has been good to that whole family."

"Yes, she has. How is Tanya doing in school?"

"Good most of the time."

"Please tell Caroline we would love to see her."

Two days later, Lana returned from work and removed her jacket to start dinner, when the phone rang. Lana hurriedly picked it up.

"Hello, Carter's."

"This is Caroline. I'd like to talk to you about Tanya."

Bewildered is not strong enough to describe Lana's emotions when she heard Caroline's friendly voice and a request to talk about Tanya. Her voice was pleasant, not unhappy and screaming like the last time she had called. Caroline was pleasant, much like old times when they were close friends.

"Sure. Gladly."

"Tanya is in her teen years now and I'm having a rotten time trying to manage her. She's rebellious and sometimes nasty."

"What can we do to help?"

"Ina and Tanya are very competitive. Maybe that's part of the problem. Without Bernie to help in this parenting business it seems overwhelming at times. I've been thinking, I've probably been very unfair with you over the years and maybe you wouldn't mind taking Ina or Tanya for a short while. The one you take would have a home with both a mom and a dad."

"Of course. We would love to have either one, but would especially love to have Tanya. How long would you like us to keep her?"

"Maybe we could work out something where she stayed with you during the week and here with me and her family on the weekends. That would give me a breather. It might help her to adjust."

"Sounds terrific to me. The schools here are wonderful and I can take some time off work to be here in the afternoon when she comes home from school. We would enjoy her."

"Would you mind if we started next week?"

"We'll have her room ready and waiting. Are her favorite colors still yellow and purple?"

"What a memory you have, yes."

"Shall we pick her up?"

"No, I have a business appointment in Monterey. Which part of the city do you live in?"

"We overlook Monterey Bay, up on the hill near town."

"My appointment is not too far from you. I'll drop her off on my way. Would you go to school with her and get her registered and started. I'll send information about her courses."

"I'd love to. About what time?"

"Is eight a.m. too early?"

"Of course not. I'm an early bird." Lana gave Caroline their street address and instructions on how to find their house.

Lana called Brian. "You won't believe who called and what she wanted! Caroline wants us to keep Tanya during the week for awhile and help her through a rough time."

"Would you please repeat that? I can't believe what I'm hearing," Brian said.

"True. It's true. She'll be here Monday to stay until Friday afternoon then she will go back to Caroline's for the weekends."

The biggest guest room was transformed with mellow yellow carpeting and purple bedspread and drapes and bright yellow pillows on the bed. A vase of long stemmed yellow roses were placed on the table near the bed. It looked great! Tanya's eyes shone when Lana showed her to her room.

"You haven't forgotten how I love yellow roses. I used to beg Franco to cut all the big yellow roses so I could have them in the house with me. You even put one in my hair once when I wore that white dress trimmed in yellow. And that purple dress that you said was not my color, but you bought the material and had it made for me anyway because I loved the picture of the dress so much."

"You are a part of us always, Tanya and we remember with fondness the time you lived with us in Asunción. You know we fought a long hard battle to get you back?"

"Yes. But the Arnolds were very nice to me, too. Mom has changed a lot since Dad died."

"Maybe because she has a lot more strain on her now that she is being both Mom and Dad."

"We don't get along."

"She loves you a lot, Tanya, or she wouldn't eat humble pie and let you come stay with us. That was very difficult for her."

"I know. But I begged," Tanya said.

"You did?"

"Yes, I remembered the happiness in your home and there is so much bickering in our home now that it's crazy."

"Maybe you can help to change that. Caroline needs your love and understanding in a big way now. We're thrilled to have you here and we'll enjoy every second with you."

"It's so good to be here. It seems Mom and I get into a fight over nothing and when it starts, it's hard to stop. What should I call you now?"

"Probably Lana would be the best and Brian. We don't want Caroline to feel we are stealing her rightful place in your life. Does that sound all right to you?"

"It'll take some adjusting. I still think of you as Mama and Brian as Papa but I think you're right."

The Carters were thrilled to have Tanya in the home again.

Patrick came home for Thanksgiving. Since Caroline had a convention out of town for that week, she let Tanya spend Thanksgiving with the Carters. That was a special bonus. They had time to watch the old home movies of Patrick and Tanya in Paraguay as they chased Shadow, the dog, picked fruit from the trees, played in the pool, and did a lot of acting silly.

Patrick commented how nice it was to all be together again. Lana realized that in her own loneliness she hadn't realized what a void he had felt.

Brian radiated a warmth seeing his son and daughter happy and content.

The Carters couldn't help feeling like Tanya was their daughter. They were the first to take her home and clean her up and teach her how to laugh. Even though she now reserved the title of Mom for Caroline, in Lana's heart she secretly felt she still deserved it.

Thanksgiving day was rewarding. With a big delicious meal spread before them, they talked about all the little things in their lives. Patrick told them, "University life is great. I particularly like the Gorgeous girls on campus."

Brian queried, "Anyone special?"

"Yes, her name is Megan and I want you to meet her soon."

"Why don't you bring her home for Christmas? We would love to meet her. Tell us more about Megan."

"She is not only drop dead beautiful, she's thoughtful and understanding."

"We'll look forward to Christmas being another special holiday and meeting your Megan, Patrick. In the meantime, please send us a photo," Lana said.

Then, as was their tradition, after the main meal was served and eaten and the table cleared, they took a breather and each shared what had been their very special blessings for the past year. They recorded it all on a tape and later transcribed it into the family journal for a keepsake. When Brian, Patrick and Lana had listed their blessings, Tanya said, "I know I'm not exactly part of this family, but I would like to add my two cents worth."

"You are most certainly a very important part of this family," Lana assured her.

"Thank you. I've missed each of you. I missed the fun and laughter that go with this family. It's sweet to be back in your home. I wish I could stay here always and go back to Caroline's to visit once in a while."

"We love having you, but your legal family is Caroline," Lana managed to say without crying. "Let's not forget that."

Patrick jumped up to help serve dessert and fill drink glasses. Lana reached up and put her arm around him and squeezed, saying, "Hey I've missed your helping hands around here, Patrick. I always appreciated it when I came home from work tired and you would come in and offer to set table and help. I miss you and I miss the great talks we had while you were helping. Those special sharing times were even more important to me than the assistance."

Christmas was approaching and Tanya was to go home for the holidays. It was going to be rough not having her around for more than two weeks.

Patrick got home from UCLA Thursday. His special friend Megan, was to follow the next Tuesday for a few days. The Carters decided to have an early mini-Christmas together before Tanya left. They sang Christmas carols, ate a special prime rib dinner and exchanged a few gifts.

As Caroline pulled into the driveway to pick up Tanya the next day, Lana sensed the sadness underlying the happy countenance of Tanya. She reluctantly went to get her suitcase and join Caroline.

Thank goodness they had a small package for Caroline. Perhaps it would rekindle the friendship of yesteryear and bridge that awful gap of years of hostility. Caroline seemed sad. Lana knew holidays for widows are always difficult. Lana yearned to put her arm around Caroline like old times, but she hesitated. They visited in the courtyard for a few minutes then Caroline said, "We must get home and finish holiday preparations." She climbed in the driver's side of the car.

Before reaching the car, Tanya turned and ran back to the Carters, threw her arms around Lana's neck and said, "I want to spend Christmas here with you and Papa."

Caroline was stunned, as were the Carters. Then Caroline's face clouded up and she demanded, "Get in this car."

Lana loosened Tanya's arms and pushed her toward the waiting car with, "Better go be with your family."

"You're my family," she declared. Running to Brian and tightly wrapping her arms around his neck feeling he would defend her.

They all stood there without words for a few seconds then Brian pulled Tanya's arms loose from his neck and guided her to Caroline's car. "Caroline is your mother and your family is in Pacific Grove, Tanya. Caroline has cared for you, nurtured you and is only letting us borrow you on occasion. For this we are grateful. But that is your family."

Tanya looked at Brian like he was betraying her. Lana knew Tanya wanted him to say he wanted her to stay. Of course he couldn't. Brian opened the car door and she slid in, pouting like it was against her every wish.

On New Year's Day the dreaded phone call came.

Caroline said, "Tanya's counselor and I both agree that splitting her living arrangements has also split her feelings of loyalty and security. We feel it best that she stay here and attend school."

"When will we see her again?"

"Never. It's best for you not to contact her at all. No phone calls. No letters and of course, no visits."

"That's not fair."

"It's what we feel is right for Tanya." With that Caroline hung up without a simple good-bye.

Lana and Brian decided they would deal with their disappointment later. Patrick had a plane to catch the next day. They didn't want to mar this special time with him. Lana held back the huge, unshed tears and pasted a smile on her face as Patrick entered the room. "What a joy it is to have you with us, Son. You put the sunshine in our lives."

"Mom, there is no place like home. It's the comfort zone. I love being here."

Those kind words eased Lana's heavy heart. Lana was grateful for her son and the joy he brought to the home.

Brian decided to accept a position in the New York area and it was moving time again. From one coast to the other, a great distance from Patrick and Tanya. Lana rang Patrick.

"Your Dad has accepted a position in the New York City area."

"He mentioned he might. Are you glad?" Patrick asked.

"Not really. I hate moving. I especially don't like being so far from you."

"Via plane it isn't far, Mom," Patrick reminded her.

"Too far to come for a week-end with you and Megan, or a bonus long weekend of exploring with you."

"Mom, you'll adjust. Give it a try. Dad seems to think it's a good career move."

"I'll try."

It was going to be terrible to have Patrick so far away.

Lana thought about Tanya. We never get to see her anyway–well, practically never. Tanya had managed to sneak away a few times to visit. Lana was ashamed to admit she encouraged the visits.

Tanya was nearly ready for college and Lana wanted to get word to her that they were moving and where she could contact them if she ever needed them. After all, Bernie was dead and if anything happened to Caroline, Tanya needed to know how to get in touch. Caroline was older.

So Lana took a chance and called. She was lucky, Tanya answered.

"Tanya, Brian has accepted a position back east."

"When are you leaving?" Tanya asked.

"Next week. Did you get the national honor scholarship?"

"No, I've decided to go to UCLA. I'll work this summer, then Mom is going to pay what I don't earn."

"What do you plan to study?"

"Science, microbiology probably, then I'll plan on teaching and doing research after I get a graduate degree, hopefully a Ph.D. Wish me luck."

"Tanya, you know you're always in our thoughts and prayers. That's why I had to call and let you know we were moving. There was that long void where we didn't keep in touch and I need to know you're all right."

"I know. I wish I could see you before you leave."

"Could we arrange a lunch in Carmel on Thursday? I would bring you Brian's new work address and let you know how to get in touch with us if you ever need us. You know we'll always be there for you if you need anything."

"I know," Tanya said.

"I could make it Friday, too, if Thursday is not good for you."

"Thursday is fine. At the Clam Box?"

"Great, that's one of my favorite restaurants."

That afternoon with Tanya was wonderful.

"I'd like to be able to keep in touch. It's months before you leave for University. Let me rent a post office box in Carmel."

"That would be great, Lana. Then we could write."

"I think of you often and wonder what's happening in your life. I want to be kept up-to-date on studies, friends and activities."

Once the Carters decided on a house to buy, Lana wrote her first letter to Tanya.

Dear Tanya,

The move has been a challenge partly because of

leaving both you and Patrick on the west coast. It seems so far away. I miss you both very much.

We have found a charming home that overlooks the ocean. It's not right on the beach. You have to walk a couple of blocks to the ocean but the view is wonderful and we can watch the ships come and go.

When does University start?

Will you go home for the Thanksgiving holiday? I hope so. The first few months at college are lonely. I hope you can go home and connect with Caroline, Ina and Jon for turkey day.

I'm anxious to hear from you. Letters are next best to hearing your voice on the phone or seeing you. Please call if you get a chance and let us know what your phone number is in your room once you're settled at college. Feel free to call collect.

The hustle here in the Big Apple is maddening at times but we are getting acquainted with some of our neighbors and find them friendly.

Brian loves his work. He travels a lot so I may go back to work to keep busy and not be too lonesome.

Have you kept your hair short, or are you letting it grow long and sensational again? You mentioned last time we talked you thought it looked better long. It's wonderful either way. The short cut is very sophisticated and it enhances your facial features. As a rule men like long hair so if you are in the mood to lure men your way, that might be best.

Speaking of men, will you keep us posted when you meet Mr. Right at college or any man that you are interested in? If you meet someone special, please send us a photo of him. We want to share your hopes and dreams.

Our new address and phone number are on the enclosed card for your address book.

Love,

Lana and Brian

After ten days Lana started watching the mailbox for a reply from Tanya. Each day disappointment filled her soul as no word came. After three weeks Lana wrote again. The days, weeks and months went by with not a single letter.

Lana wrote again and again. Tanya never answered. Thanksgiving came and went. Still no word from Tanya.

Lana wondered what could have happened to her. Did she tell her Mom? Was Caroline reading the letters? After nearly a year Lana quit writing. It was too painful running to the mailbox each day when she got home from work to see if Tanya had written. Never a single word. The big question was if Tanya was all right?

Thank goodness Patrick wrote or called regularly and he shared his dreams and relationships with them. He and Megan, the charming blond, were busy planning their wedding. Lana and Brian were thrilled. They loved Megan.

Patrick had never been one of those rotten ill-tempered teens. He had been a good friend enjoying activities and life with his parents. They felt so blessed to have such a marvelous son. He was not only fun to be with he was very intelligent and graduated magna cum laude from UCLA pre med.

Lana decided to take an adventurous step and write directly to Caroline and see if she would answer. She was so concerned about Tanya.

> Dear Caroline,
>
> What is the latest on Tanya? We would be so grateful for some word of how she is doing and what is happening in both of your lives–in fact all four of your lives? Did Ina finish college? Did Jon go back to Paraguay? Did he go and return, or stay and live?
>
> Are you planning to retire soon?
>
> A note or a call would be very much appreciated.. I'm enclosing a card with our new address, phone number and Brian's work number.

Fondly,
Lana

Lana did not receive an answer.

A Christmas card to Caroline was returned with a notation that she had moved. Now Lana felt completely severed. Nearly five years had passed with no word.

Lana found out after many long distance phone calls that Caroline had retired and they kept track of their retired staff. Lana immediately sat down and wrote a long pleading letter asking Caroline to at least acknowledge that Tanya was well. The corporation would not give out addresses but assured Lana they would see that Caroline got the letter.

However, Lana received no answer.

One of Lana's fondest dreams was about to come true. Brian was to be baptized. When Patrick was baptized the only glitch in the day was that Brian could not participate as he did not belong to the church. Lana yearned for her family to be one in their faith and hopes for a future together both in worship and in aspiration.

Brian had finally read enough of the church literature and prayed for verification to gain a testimony and make a commitment. Will and Vera planned on coming for the glorious occasion. Hopefully, Patrick and Megan could also come.

Brian sat with Bishop Nelson, discussing his baptizm. It was explained to Brian that baptism washed away former sins. How comforting that was.

Bishop Nelson explained, "If offense have been committed and not reconciled, you must go to that person and confess and ask forgiveness and then ask the Lord to forgive you also."

Brian felt empty. He had never asked for forgiveness from Lana about his infidelity in Las Vegas when he had been there for testing so long ago, early in their marriage. Actually, he had lied to Lana, declaring no other betrayals when the Elaine affair happened. This would be tough.

"If it was long ago and I have changed, could the waters of baptism still be as effective?"

"We are told you should make all things right as you come before the Lord in humility. Is there something you want to talk about?"

"Not really. But maybe I should. In early marriage I was unfaithful to my wife and she doesn't know about it. Why should I open up a new wound?"

"That does take courage. But your relationship will be stronger after you make the confession and ask for forgiveness. If you truly repent, you will find new strength in yourself."

"I don't know. She's not quick to forgive a breach in trust."

"Brian, it is better to be honest in all things. The Lord knows your heart and will help you if you trust him and do what is right."

Lana and Brian excitedly talked about the forthcoming baptism. Brian gathered all his courage and followed Bishop Nelson's advice.

"Lana, before I get baptized I want to be completely honest with you."

With fear Lana asked, "Is this confession time?"

"Yes, I suppose it is. It was long ago. Before we went to South America, I betrayed your trust by having a short two day affair with one of the scientists that was attending the test site near Las Vegas."

Stunned, Lana replied in a low voice, "But you assured me that there weren't others when you slept with Elaine."

"I feared I would lose you if I told the truth. I'm sorry I lied."

“It is more than your lying, Brian, it is more than being unfaithful, it is more than shaking my faith in you. It's lousy!”

"Lana, I didn't have to tell you. You would never have known. I wanted to start fresh and honest. Honest for the rest of my life. Can't you understand that?"

"No, I cannot. I only understand that there has been more infidelity. I was thrilled with this new step forward in your life. Now I'm shaken to the core," Lana stormed.

Brian shouted, "You know you are a spoiled brat, like my mother said when we told her we were marrying. You expect everything to be picture perfect. If it isn't, you can't handle it. Maybe that's why I need some realism in my life occasionally."

"Realism, like another woman?" Lana shouted as she threw the book she was holding onto the table.

"Forget it. You wouldn't understand." He turned to walk away.

"That's right, Brian. Drop this bomb, say nasty things, then walk away."

"We are both angry and hurt, let's not say more we'll regret later."

Brian walked outside and thought the Bishop had certainly given him a bum steer. How dumb could he be to do this?

He did have a testimony and wanted to enter the waters of baptism. Was it worth this?

Lana again transferred to the guest room to have her space and think about Brian's lie, his infidelity and his nasty remarks about her being a spoiled brat. She was deeply hurt. Lana stared at the ceiling in the dark, unable to sleep, unable to feel anything except disappointment and anger. She had been on a high, now she was in the bottom of the pit.

Next morning Lana called her dad, "I would like to come for a visit. Is now a good time for you and Mom?"

"You sound very troubled, Lana, want to talk about it?"

"Yes, when I get there. Is it okay if I come today?"

"Sure we'd love to have you. Want me to send the plane over to pick you up?"

"No, I'll catch a commercial flight."

"Sure you don't want to talk?" Will encouraged.

She gave in to the emotional strain and her voice caught before a sob escaped. "Dad, I can't talk now. I have so much to tell you and so much to ask you. I need some of your wisdom."

"I thought there was to be a big celebration this weekend for Brian's baptism. We're planning to be there."

"Maybe yes and maybe no," Lana answered.

On Saturday Bishop Nelson called to see that all was in order for Brian and the big event the next day.

"You really messed up my life with your great advice, Bishop."

"How is that?"

"I was honest with Lana and she took off the next morning to see Daddy. She couldn't handle the truth."

"How would you have felt if you hadn't given her the opportunity to handle it?"

"Better."

"Look into your heart, Brian. Would you have felt true and honest?"

"I don't know. She took off and isn't even here for the day that I thought would be special for both of us. I wanted most of all to share this time with Lana. My life seems so empty without her."

"She probably needs time to think," the Bishop said.

"We both said some pretty ugly things before she left. I think I goofed big time. I didn't just tell her, I lost my temper. I was ugly."

"That wasn't smart when she needed encouragement and understanding. She was going to feel betrayed and hurt. It would have helped if you had been comforting to help her."

"I know. I messed up."

"Where do we go from here?"

"Do you mean about tomorrow?" Brian asked.

"Yes, do you want to wait for Lana or go on as planned?"

"Better not wait for Lana; she might never be here again."

After telling her dad about Las Vegas and about Elaine, Lana felt better. It helped to have him listen.

"You sound hurt and angry," Will said.

"Yes, I am."

"Have you thought about how difficult it was for Brian? He didn't have to tell you this time. You guessed about Elaine. But you didn't have a clue about Las Vegas and he wanted to wipe the slate clean."

"He wiped me right out of his life with his confession. How can I ever trust him again?"

"Maybe you can trust him even more now that you know he is completely honest."

"Dad, you would never do such a rotten thing. I expect my husband to rise to your standards–to be as true and honest as you are."

There was a long silence. Will didn't remark, swallowed hard, looked his daughter in the eye, tried to smile.

Lana felt uneasy, "You have never been a rotten skunk have you, Dad?"

Will sat quietly, thinking about his adorable daughter who had such unshakable faith in her father.

"Dad, have you?" Lana demanded.

"Yes and I didn't have the courage to tell Vera for fear I would lose my Queenie. Brian had the courage to tell you. That should be worth something."

"You? I can't believe it. You have always been so devoted to Mom. How could you?"

"I made a very big mistake. Once only and I realized I had jeopardized the relationship most precious to me. I have carried that guilt with me all through the years. Maybe it's time I was finally honest with your mother."

"When were you unfaithful, Dad?"

"When we were engaged."

"But you hadn't taken the vow of fidelity yet."

"Yes, I had. I had promised my heart and soul to Vera. Then on a skiing trip to the Alps which had been planned for ages, Vera couldn't come because of a big trip her parents had already planned to France and Switzerland. We laughed that it was our last separate adventure. It was quite an adventure for me."

"What happened?"

"Rowena was pretty, in fact gorgeous. She was great on skis, laughed a lot and she didn't make any bones about finding me desirable. It went to my head."

"Did she know you were engaged?"

"Absolutely. Ken told her many times she was wasting her time. I was solidly promised. She would laugh and say, 'the knot isn't tied yet'."

"What happened?" Lana found it difficult to believe this was her father talking. It sounded so strange to hear him talk about anyone but Vera, her mother. She was the center of his existence. He adored her, respected her and always sang her praises.

"I went to Rowena's room one evening after a marvelous day on the slopes. We talked, we laughed, then one thing led to another and the next thing I knew–I succumbed."

"You went to bed with her? Dad, going to her room was flirting with danger."

"Yes, I know. Afterwards we got up and sipped hot chocolate together. She coyly looked at me and whispered, "I knew that knot wasn't tied yet. You're mine aren't you, Will?"

"Boy, she was a self-confident gal," Lana said.

"Yes, she was. I sat still for a few minutes until the impact of what I had done hit me like a ton of bricks. Then I answered, Rowena, I'm Vera's if she'll still have me. She's the love of my life."

"How did she take that?"

"Rowena sat there and looked at me and challenged, 'Will, you can't tell me tonight meant nothing to you. You were loving and lovable. It had to mean something.'"

"I answered, I was drawn to your beauty and to your wonderful personality. But try to understand this, I love Vera with all my heart and soul," Will declared.

"I can't believe you men are all alike. Given a beautiful woman, you fall in bed with her. You're all a bunch of lousy rats–insincere, lying scoundrels," Lana flung at her father as she fled from the room with a solid slam of the door. Going to her own room she sat in one of the large chairs facing a round table.

Will hesitated, then followed her. "You don't understand the great penalty I have paid for that one unfortunate night, Lana. It has weighed heavily on my heart always. Many times I wanted to be honest with Vera, but I was always a coward."

"Dad, why should men be so tempted? I've never once been tempted to make love with another man. Brian is my whole romantic life. When I dream of intimacy, it's with Brian."

"I don't know the answer to that. I do know I have never betrayed Vera's trust again. Haven't you ever been drawn to other men?"

"No. Are you still tempted by other women?"

"Oh, yes, but I know better now. Lana, be honest, hasn't some gorgeous man along the way brought your romantic desires to the surface and tempted you for a minute?"

"Oh, I like many men's voices; they intrigue me. Or I think he is a wonderful specimen of manhood, good looking and a leader. But those are the very things I love and admire about Brian–his strong, but mellow voice, his wonderful erect walk that looks like he has a purpose in life, his charm. I feel drawn only to his arms when it comes to bedroom activities. I look forward to our beautiful moments together."

"I'm so proud of you, Lana. That's good," Will confirmed as he sank into the other chair, almost facing Lana.

"When it was over, how did you feel after betraying Mom?"

"I went back to my room and sat on the bed, stared into space and then I started to cry. I cried because I was so disappointed in myself." Will hesitated, then continued, "I cried because I was so sad at the thought of jeopardizing my relationship with my true love, Vera. I cried because I was devastated at seeing my weakness. I cried because I couldn't undo what I had done."

"Did Mom ever guess everything was not right?"

"No. I'm glad because I was so afraid of losing her. The next morning was horrible! I had this huge knot in my stomach. A huge ache in my heart. The rest is history."

"Did Rowena still pursue you?"

"Yes, but I quickly turned away each time. I didn't leave room for temptation to move in."

"Did you ever see Rowena again?"

"No. I didn't see her, but she scared the tar out of me. Rowena called with her wonderful laughing way a couple of months later. She announced that we had made a baby that night and she wanted to know what I was going to do about that."

"She was pregnant?" Lana asked.

"She led me to believe she was. While I was stewing in my juice and reeling over what I had done, she again laughed and said to relax. There was no baby. She wanted to know what I would do if there was one."

"What a weird woman."

Lana sat there in disbelief. She couldn't accept that her own father had been such a rat–her wonderful father–and her mother didn't even know.

"How could you, Dad?"

"Weakness. I never put myself in that vulnerable place again. I learned it was not worth a few minutes of excitement to have to live with the guilt the rest of my life. Many times others tempted me, I don't deny it. But I never gave them room to move in."

Lana slowly got up and went to her father, knelt beside him, reached up and put her arms around him. "Thanks for your honesty."

"Can you still respect me, Lana?"

"Of course. I love you, too."

The baptism did not hold the excitement Brian had dreamed of with Lana and her parents not there. They had all planned to share such a wonderful experience with each other and with good friends and family. The plans included a huge get together at the Carter's after the baptism. Brian was concerned about handling it alone. However, he did want to celebrate this new step forward in his life. Most of the celebration was being catered. It would work.

The congregation didn't understand why Lana was not present. A couple of people asked where she was and Brian avoided answering as best he could. It was tough. Each time someone asked, he felt his stomach tighten. He tried to smile and go forward realizing that he might be without Lana permanently. He loved Lana. If he could only have another chance to let her know how very important she was to him.

Brian decided to call Lana as soon as the baptism was over and apologize for the rotten nasty words he had spoken. He wanted so much to be forgiven for his horrible mistakes of the past and let Lana know she had his complete dedication from this day forward and always. Maybe that had been part of his terrible mistake. He had taken her and their happiness for granted. He wanted a chance to prove he deserved her love.

After a song, the opening prayer and Karen Nelson's wonderful talk on the meaning and need of baptism, the door in the back of the chapel opened. Bishop Nelson looked to see who was joining them so late. His grin spread over his whole face and everyone turned to see what made him so happy.

Entering was Lana, her parents and Patrick and Megan. Brian stood up and rushed to her side. They embraced. Brian led them to the front; people moved over to make room for all. Brian sat with his arm around Lana.

It was 1988. Lana nearly gave up ever getting word of Tanya. She couldn't help but think of Tanya often and wonder if she had married. Did she have children? Most of all Lana wondered why all these years Tanya had never kept in touch. The day at the Clam Box had seemed so perfect. Lana thought Tanya shared the special bond she felt. Why had there been no communication?

No letters, phone calls, or visits followed through the years. Had something happened to Tanya? Lana wondered if she had been killed in a car wreck or some other tragedy. Surely if she was well she would have contacted them.

As it neared Tanya's birthday, Lana thought maybe that would pull on Caroline's heart strings and she would answer. After all, Caroline and Lana had been best friends in the past and she had renewed that friendship a bit while they had lived in California. Maybe Caroline had mellowed in her senior years. It was worth a chance. Lana took up pen and wrote a long letter.

> Dear Caroline,
>
> We are retiring and going to enjoy those golden years. Before we settle down completely however, we are going to go to Australia for eighteen months to serve a mission for our church. Then if all goes as planned, we'll come back and settle in Cincinnati, Ohio near Patrick, his wife, Megan and our grandchildren. We have two lovely grandchildren and a third on the way. We want to be a part of their lives and share in their growing up.
>
> Has Tanya Married? Does she have children?

It would mean a great deal to us to know what is happening in her life.

Has Ina married? How many grandchildren do you have now? Did Jon go back to Paraguay? Is he married?

I understand you have retired. What are you doing exciting in retirement? Do you travel a lot? Have you been back to Paraguay recently?

Where is Ina living?

Please, please drop us a note or call. We'll be at this current address for two more weeks before we pack up and put things in storage while we are in Australia. We have sold our home here. Any word or correspondence would be very much appreciated. I've enclosed a card with Patrick's address and phone number on it. You can always contact us through him.

Fondly,

Lana

The letter was addressed to headquarters with a plea to forward it to Caroline immediately. Many days passed and still no word.

Maybe Caroline had finally remarried. Maybe she was dead. The silence was terrible. It left a cloud over everything else. Did Caroline plan it that way? Maybe this was her revenge.

As passports were readied and clothes packed, Lana thought, "Australia is really the other side of the world, not across the United States. If Tanya needs us, we won't be there."

Lana went to lunch with one of her best friends and they chatted much longer than expected. It was way past time for her to be home with Brian's car. Lana had already sold her car with the upcoming move to Australia. She called to tell Brian she would be late.

When he answered the phone he blurted, "You would never guess who called."

"Who?"

"Caroline!"

"For real? I missed the call! What luck! What did she say?"

"Don't worry, she left a lot of information. She's living in Tacoma, Washington now and Tanya is quite ill. She has breast cancer. She has had surgery and is now undergoing all the wretched treatments that follow, chemotherapy, radiation and all. Caroline said Tanya has been married and has two daughters. She is now divorced. She gave me her phone number and address but I thought I'd wait until you got here to call. I knew you would have a lot of questions that I didn't ask. Caroline seemed friendly. Can you believe it? All these years of silence and now she opens the window and lets us peek in."

"What rotten timing. We're ready to go to Patrick's for a final farewell before flying to Australia. We have two days of jammed schedule before leaving. Life is full of challenges. I want to go directly to Tanya and hold her hand and reassure her life can be rosy again. What can we do?"

"Let's talk to her on the phone and then decide."

As soon as Lana got home, they called Tanya and had a marvelous talk. Tanya was full of hope and promise. She was thrilled that the Carters cared and even happier that they called.

They decided that they would go visit Tanya as soon as they returned from Australia. She agreed she would like that. Tanya assured the Carters that everything was going well and that she was happy–tired and weak, but fine. The doctors hoped that she was free of the cancer. She would have the periodic checks for five years to be sure the cancer was completely gone.

Australia was a marvelous experience. The Carters loved the Auzzies. The cockatoo birds, the parrots, the fields of wild flowers were all beautiful. The Carters often drove up to the blue mountains on weekends to drink in the beauty from walking paths.

They rode a crazy train straight up and down the mountain. They always stopped at their favorite hotel, Hydro Majestic, located between Sydney and the blue mountains for at least one meal, sometimes breakfast on the way up, other times for lunch or dinner on the way back. The hotel furnishings were elegant, reflecting an era of the past. The history of the hotel was fascinating. It was a grand baroque style building. The service was five star.

They didn't see many wild kangaroos until they went into the outback area. Then the poor wallabies and kangaroos were road killed by the dozens beside the road.

Driving to Canberra, the capital of Australia, in the spring was one of the most beautiful sights in the world. Acres of blue wild flowers with the Gorgeous white cockatoo birds flying above. It was breathtaking to see as they drove by one field after another.

They traveled to many of the Pacific islands, but New Zealand was the Carter's favorite. They were mesmerized by the beautiful countryside and the marvelous, loving people. The country ranged from snow-covered mountains to mud pots, to waterfalls and green hillsides dotted with white sheep.

There was one little problem. Lana yearned to go home and see Patrick and his family. They hadn't had a chance to hold their new granddaughter, Becky, who looked so adorable in her pictures.

Letters from Tanya were comforting. It was great to be in touch with her again. She confided she had a new love, Mark. He was one of the doctors at the cancer clinic. A date had been set for their wedding. Lana wanted to be at Tanya's wedding, but couldn't. It was before they returned to the USA. Lana enjoyed the mission, however, she still had an occasional day of being homesick yearning for her family.

When they landed at Cincinnati International Airport , Lana was so excited she could hardly wait her turn to exit. There they stood. Their handsome son Patrick, his beautiful wife, Megan, adorable little Becky and nine-year-old Andrew, tall and grinning. They hugged all around. Andrew didn't even mind. Steven, their oldest, missed the homecoming.

As Lana approached Becky and tried to make friends, Patrick said, "Mom, we think she looks a lot like you."

Lana looked at Becky and saw both Patrick and Megan's resemblance, none of herself. Lana still loved the thought and cherished it. Becky's parents had briefed Becky on who was coming and showed her photos so she warmed up to Brian and Lana in a hurry. They were grateful for that.

Since they had sold their home and both cars before leaving the States,

Patrick and Megan invited them to make their place headquarters while they hunted for a home and cars.

Luckily they located a house in the same neighborhood with Patrick and Megan. The house was open and lovely, perfect for the two of them.

Next item on the agenda was to make plans to visit Tanya. Lana couldn't wait to see her as an adult and a mother. The Clam Box in Carmel, California was their last time together, many years ago.

Lana had her address book open looking up Tanya's phone number when the phone rang. Caroline's voice was stressed and tired. She had kept the card with Patrick's phone number and he had given her Lana's present phone number. Caroline sounded desperate. "Lana, it's bad news. Tanya is in her final hours of life. The cancer came back with a vengeance and it's terminal. There's nothing we can do about it."

"I thought she had been given a clean slate after the chemo and radiation treatments."

"We thought so too and then she started to have problems but didn't tell us. She had remarried and I think it was a case of denial. She didn't want anything to be wrong. She thought if she ignored it, it would go away."

"What happened?" Lana asked.

"The pain and problems became so intense she had to go to the doctor and sure enough, the cancer had spread to many places and now it's a matter of time."

"How much time?"

"Very little, a matter of days I imagine," Caroline answered.

"We'll come immediately and visit her."

"No. It's only family now," Caroline said.

"We are family. Who discovered her in the orphanage? Caroline, you have to let us come."

"I doubt if she would know you if you did come. I don't think she would last until you get here. I don't want any further stress on her. Don't come. I had to let you know the latest development, heaven knows why. But don't come."

"Caroline this isn't fair."

"Fair or not, it's right. Ina and Jon came from Paraguay last week to visit and she was so weak she could hardly talk to them. I felt I had to bring them back for one last visit with Tanya. They seemed thrilled to see both of us and relayed the love of her other brothers in Paraguay. You knew both Ina and Jon have returned to Paraguay didn't you?"

"No. Remember there has been no communication for years."

"I know. It's been difficult, Lana."

"I'm trying to understand. I wish you had called sooner."

"It was painful to call now. I know about the deception of the mailbox in California and the letters. I don't really know why I'm calling. I felt so betrayed. I wanted to never see or speak to you again. The very idea that you would sneak behind my back with Tanya. You've hurt me so much through the years. I've felt threatened by you, especially since that Christmas back in California when Tanya wanted to spend Christmas with you and not her family. It seemed you were always stealing her loyalty and love."

"This is no time to fight over the past, Caroline. I made mistakes. I'm sorry. We're happy you've made such a loving home for Tanya. Happy, too, that you brought her sister and brother here to keep that much of the family together as they grew up. We think that's admirable and realize you have a huge wonderful heart and have done so much for Tanya and her whole family. Florentina told us you sent money to the brothers in Paraguay on a regular basis to help them. So let's not talk about old problems between us. I'm glad you called to let us know. We'll keep her in our prayers."

"Thanks," Caroline said.

"Would you mind if I dropped her a note?" Lana asked.

After a long hesitation she answered, "No. She's at the Tacoma General Hospital, Room 505, 1301 Highlands Parkway, Tacoma, Wa. 98406. I don't know if she can read it. I've had to read her letters to her the last two visits. She knows the end is near and yesterday I reminded her that her biological mother would be waiting in heaven for her and that she would have a glorious reunion with her. You know what she said?"

"What?" Lana asked with a knot in her stomach.

"You're my real mother. I've forgotten completely about the one that gave me birth. You're the one who has cared for me and raised me. It made me feel great to know Tanya felt that way. Go ahead and write if you want to."

"I'll feel better sending it even if she never gets it. Thanks. We're sorry you're having to go through this terrible crisis. What can we do to help?"

"Nothing. Mark, Tanya's new husband is very attentive and is trying to be brave. Her two daughters, Amy and Chris, are both with her. That helps her a lot. Actually, I don't think Tanya would last long enough for you to come." Lana could tell Caroline was mellowing, as she added,"Tanya is very weak."

"Thanks again for letting us know. We're very sad. Sad to see Tanya's bubbly personality end so soon. Sad at not seeing her for so long. Sad for you and her family," Lana said.

Again Caroline hung up without saying good-bye–that old habit that Lana detested.

Lana knew Brian was listening on the other phone even though he hadn't said a word. He came in, opened his arms and Lana fell into them, letting the tears flow. When Lana got herself under control, she headed for her desk to write a long, loving letter to Tanya.

Then Lana looked up the phone number of her favorite florist, Covenant Gardens and called in an order to have one dozen yellow roses with six white roses in a huge vase delivered to Tanya's room with a short note: "Love, roses and prayers, from your Carter family. Letter follows."

The flowers and letter were small satisfaction. Lana yearned to go and be with Tanya and hold her in her arms one last time and assure her of the bright cheerful light she had brought into their home. Lana wanted her to know how dear she was–and always would be to them.

Lana searched for Brian, saw him in a bush bed at the back of the house digging around the rose bushes with tears rolling down his face.

She walked to where he knelt. Putting her hand on his shoulder, "Let's talk a minute," Lana requested.

"Let's. I had hoped that someday Tanya would come here and visit, that we could cut these beautiful yellow roses and put them in a vase in her room. I had hoped she would return if only for a few days."

"I know. Me too," Lana agreed.

"How could Caroline deny us a last visit? Even if Tanya doesn't know us, we could spend some time with her and meet her daughters and get to know her new husband," Brian said.

"It's unfair. I feel the same way. Why don't we go?" Lana declared, knowing she had to see Tanya even if she didn't know who they were. It was for Lana's good at this point, not Tanya's.

"You heard Caroline. Only family allowed to visit."

"I'm going to call the hospital and see if that's valid. I want to go. So many things have stood in our way. It's now or never; let's make it now."

"See what you can find out," Brian agreed.

Lana called the hospital. "This is Lana Carter, could I please speak to Tanya's doctor?"

"What is Tanya's last name?"

"Richardson. She is in room 505."

"You're not listed as part of her family."

"No. I'm not. Just a very close friend."

"I'll put you through to Ruth, Tanya's private nurse."

"Thank you." The phone clicked. There was a short wait and then, "Hello, I'm Ruth."

"How aware of visitors is Tanya now? Does she know people?"

"Most of the time she recognizes her immediate family. Only family are permitted to visit her."

"Is she in a lot of pain?" Lana asked, feeling pain herself for what Tanya was experiencing.

"We are trying to keep that under control. She has a specialist that is doing a great job. Who are you?"

"We are relatives from back east: We're the Carter's."

"Oh yes, the ones who sent the yellow and white roses. I'll tell her you called. She is lucid at times. Actually today has been one of her really good days."

"Thanks for your information, Ruth. We will probably call back to keep in touch. What's your extension?"

"I'd prefer you get information from her husband or mother. We try to discourage too many calls to the hospital."

"Okay," Lana agreed.

The afternoon was long and the evening longer. Caroline had

forbidden the Carters to visit Tanya. Lana still wanted to go. Lana found Brian at his desk with his head in both hands.

Lana stood in the doorway staring at him. He felt her look and responded. "I was trying to write a letter to Tanya. It's so hard to put my thoughts on paper. How do you explain those deep down feelings that go straight to your heart?"

"Tough isn't it? I had the same problem. I did the best I could. I want to go to Washington. I need to see Tanya. We must go. At lease I must go," Lana declared as she realized she would never forgive herself if she didn't.

"You what? Caroline will be furious. Maybe it won't be good for Tanya either."

"I know. I still have to go."

"Tanya probably won't know us when we get there. We may not be permitted to go in to see her."

"We know her room number and I don't plan to ask permission. We will walk right in and sit with her, hold her hand or talk or whatever. I have to go, Brian."

"Lana, think about this until morning. I don't want a scene at the hospital." He hesitated, then added, "I know Tanya would be glad to see us."

"Me too. I'm going to call for plane tickets for tomorrow. Then I'll sleep on it. Time is slipping away."

"If you have your heart set on going, I'll go too. Make those reservations for two."

Lana called Tanya's room. She sounded drugged. It was late and she already had her pain killer and sleep medication, but she was still alive. "Tanya, this is Lana Carter."

"Yes, I know, I recognized your voice."

"We have airline tickets for early in the morning to come see you. Would you like that?"

"Oh yes, please come. I'll hold on. I want to see you again."

"I'm so glad you recognized my voice. I know life is very challenging for you now. But I need to hold you and tell you many things."

"Today has been one of my best days in the whole month. I even sat up for a while this afternoon when Chris came. She was amazed. I have much to tell you, also."

"See you soon. Love you heaps!"

"Love you too, bye," Tanya said.

When the phone was hung up there was no doubt the Carters would use those reservations.

Lana always wore high heels, but that didn't stop them from running through the airport following the signs to the Avis rental counter. After signing car rental papers , they stopped long enough to ask for a map and directions for the shortest and fastest route to the hospital. They realized there would still be some rush hour traffic, luckily not much.

Reaching the hospital, they parked the car, then ran for the lobby. Brian spotted the elevator and again Lana's high heels made a staccato noise as they ran that direction. Would Tanya still be alive? Could they sneak into her room undetected? Would she be strong enough to speak to them?

With Washington state being three hours behind east coast time they arrived early. It was a few minutes before nine in the morning. They hoped the family would not be there yet and they could sneak into room 505 and visit for a few minutes with Tanya before others arrived. Following the signs after getting off the elevator they easily located Tanya's room. As they started to enter the room, a nurse held up her hand and said, "No visitors are allowed here."

"We have traveled several thousand miles to give a precious friend a hug. Please?"

Tanya heard Lana's voice, "Ruth, it's family and I need to see them."

Ruth reluctantly stood aside and Lana rushed by. She stood drinking in mature, beautiful Tanya to treasure in her heart. Tanya looked tired and she was thin. Lana opened both arms and rushed to Tanya's bedside, folding her into a huge bear hug. Tanya whispered into Lana's hair, the old familiar title of, "Mama." How sweet the word sounded to Lana. With tears streaming down both of Lana's cheeks, she stepped back so Brian could greet Tanya.

Tanya and Brian held in a tearful embrace. "I knew if you found out I was sick you'd come."

"Of course," Brian assured her.

"Your voice sounded so good on the phone," Tanya whispered.

"It was marvelous to be recognized after all this time. I thought you had forgotten us for sure," Lana lamented.

"I tried. But I couldn't. It's been ages. So much has happened since I last saw you. I have so much to tell you and explain to you."

"Tanya, it's all okay. We needed to be with you, see you, hold you and let you know how much happiness you brought to us. Has my letter arrived?"

"Yes, it was delivered early this morning before all our morning routine started. Now that I'm bathed, Ruth was going to read it to me. Thanks for the beautiful roses. They really brightened up the room and they were special 'cause I knew when I saw them that you remembered I loved yellow roses. Would you please read the letter to me?"

"First let me sit beside you, hold your hand and visit. I'll try to convey all the emotion that I packed into that letter. Brian brought a letter too, but we may not need them now that we can tell you."

"It's wonderful to see you one last time, I know it's a final goodbye and my end is near. Sometimes I'm at peace and sometimes I'm scared."

"That's natural," Lana said.

"Mostly I'm at peace. It's hard to leave my daughters and husband. They are good people and I've missed them so much while here in the hospital. I hate to leave Mom, too. She is nearly eighty. She needs me and I am leaving her."

"She understands. You've brought her so much happiness, Tanya. She will have many fond memories. I want you to know you brought a very special ray of sunshine into my life. The first time you laughed out loud my heart sang so loud I thought it might drown out the music of your laughter." Lana hesitated, then asked, "Why did you pick me to follow at the orphanage?"

"I don't know. There was a special feeling I had when you smiled at me as I sat there on the log. I was lonely and you walked in with a big smile. I thought, this lady is happy. She can teach me how to be happy . You did."

Brian added, "You brought happiness into our home, too. The first time I saw you with Lana in that little red outfit, my heart jumped for joy. Then later when Patrick shared his dog with you and let you into our intimate family circle, that was a special time for me. I could see our family and love expanding."

"You'll never know how grateful I was to be driven away from that horrible Sanitario. Actually I didn't know how pitiful it was until I spent a few days in your home. Then when I went back I told everyone about you, your home, and how wonderful it was. They told me I was dreaming to think I might be a permanent part of that. In a way I was. I thought you might come back and rescue me for good. You did! That was the sweetest moment of my life when you drove me away for keeps, I thought."

"We thought it was for always, also. We did everything we could to make it final. We thought you were ours forever. Even when we were forced to leave you behind in Paraguay, we thought it was temporary."

"Me too. I counted the days until I came back to you. Then everything started to change. Caroline saying she wanted to keep me permanently and that she was planning to take Ina too. The whole fight was a nightmare. Do you know how painful that day in court was for me?"

"I guess I understand a little. I saw you were sobbing. I knew it was a painful choice for you."

"When I was asked by the judge where I wanted to live, even though I was very young I felt old for my years and I knew if Caroline and Bernie would bring Ina and maybe Jon to the states and give them a good life, I had to chose the Arnolds. I looked at you two there pleading with your eyes, 'Choose us.' Then I looked behind you and I could see my sister and brother pleading 'Keep us together and give us a chance.' Lana, you only know part of the orphanage story. You saw the pitiful bathroom facilities. You fixed that through your club. But you didn't see that we slept two and three in those small beds meant to hold one. Some of the very sick or ugly ones were forced to sleep on the floor or in the yard on the ground. I think they hoped they would die. As young as I was, I knew many things were not right. There were other horrible things happening too. I couldn't stand to have my sister who was not too pretty, treated so shabbily. I had to make that choice and give my sister and brother a chance at a decent life."

"Of course you did, I understand. You're weak, why don't you rest?" Lana agreed as it opened anew an old painful wound.

"No. I've wanted to tell you for so long what's in my heart. I could never make it real on paper. I wanted to tell you in person. That court decision was very difficult for me because I never felt as strong a love for Caroline. I always considered you two my parents and the Arnolds temporary even though she cared for me and gave me a wonderful home. In my mind, I was there until I came back to you."

"We felt that way too. But it turned out for the best Tanya. After all, the Arnolds did bring Ina and Jon."

"I know. As I've looked back on my life, I've realized many things. I'm so ashamed to admit that I resented having to give up my dream of returning to you to give my brother and sister a chance at life. It was so selfish. But I did resent it. I compared Mom to you and I gave her all kinds of problems. I was sure I had made the great self-sacrifice for my family. I took it out on Caroline. Do you know that until I went away to college I never really appreciated Mom? She has been wonderful to me and my whole family. I'm ashamed to admit that for years I felt so sorry for myself I didn't see that."

"It's okay, Tanya, Caroline understands, I'm sure. I do."

"I often compared the happy noises and joyful feeling in your home and would think I would rather be with you. I thought it was heaven on earth at your house and I only remembered the good and wonderful times. When I went away to college, I started to appreciate the many sacrifices that Caroline made, not just for me, but for my whole family. What unconditional love she always gave. Even when I was a miserable brat, she gave love and understanding. I realized what a great Mom I had and how unfair I had been to her. Did you know she sent money to Pedro and Paulo, my older brothers regularly?" Tanya asked.

"Yes. Florentina told me. That was very unselfish of her. I really admire her for that," Lana agreed.

"Did you know Mom and I went back to Paraguay and she rescued my oldest brother Pedro and his wife and Paulo from Chaco-Land and bought them a nice comfortable home in a decent area of Asunción. Pedro named his first child after Mom. It was a girl and she is their Carolina."

"No, I didn't know that," Lana admitted. "But, we too, are grateful. Caroline is a wonderful woman and has a huge, generous heart. She was one of my best friends. That's the reason I asked her to keep you; I knew she would be good to you, because she was a good woman. Caroline told us you brought new happiness into their home. That's why she wanted to keep you. Thank goodness you were there for her when Bernie was killed. She would have been all alone."

"When I saw your heart nearly break when I made that choice in court, it hurt me way down deep and I felt like a traitor. But I had to do it. I had to give Jon and Ina a chance too. It hurt to see them in that awful orphanage and me in a nice loving home."

"Tanya, you were brave to make that choice. It was the right choice."

“Do you remember the Christmas I didn’t want to return home with Mom for the holidays?”

Brian stepped forward and answered, “Yes. It nearly broke my heart to have to pull your clenched arms from around my neck and command you to get in the car with Caroline. I wanted you to stay with us. But I knew you couldn’t.”

“Even though I went home with Mom, I gave her a fit for many days. I desperately wanted to be with you and share when you had your annual Christmas party. Your home was decorated so beautifully and I knew the joyous spirit and feeling that would be there over the holidays. Instead I pouted at home, rebelled every chance I got, screamed and yelled at everyone making life miserable. One evening after I had pitched a real temper tantrum, Mom came to my room and lovingly said, ‘I know you’re frustrated with life Tanya, but I love you dearly. Try to see my side.’ With that she squeezed my shoulder and left the room before I could reply.”

“What unconditional love,” Lana said. She moved closer and took Tanya’s hand.

“Yes, it was. It helped me soften a little. However, I didn't understand how much it must have hurt Mom to see me not want to return home that Christmas until I got divorced and my own daughter wanted to spend Christmas with her father and stepmother in Texas instead of with me. It was painful and I remembered the hurt I gave Mom. I know I have hurt you too. Can you try to understand and forgive me?" Tanya continued.

"Of course. You made the right choice in choosing the Arnolds. If we had been smarter and more mature, we too, would have brought your family to the United States. All of them. But we were barely thirty years old and life looked very different to me. We wanted a daughter, a sister for Patrick, and didn't feel we could take on such a humongous task of five more. Florentina did suggest that we bring at least you three, but we said no. Now we know better. We've both learned a lot through life haven't we?" Lana asked.

“Thanks for coming. I now think of Caroline as my real mother, she has been so great to me during my divorce and all my illness. But you two will always have a very special place in my heart and I will look forward to our reunion later. You can meet my biological mother."

"We'll look forward to that," Brian said.

"Sometimes when I'm medicated I'm not sure if I am having visions of what's to come or if I am hallucinating, but I feel the sweetness and joy of the next world. I feel so peaceful and know I can handle what's coming. Do you believe in another life after this?" Tanya asked as she pushed her hair behind her left ear in the old familiar way.

"Yes, definitely and that there was life before. Maybe we knew each other in the pre-mortal existence, Tanya. Maybe that's why there was that bond between us right away. I only regret that I didn't have an opportunity to share in your growing up to become such a wonderful adult. I'm grateful Caroline was there for you."

Brian stepped forward. Lana relinquished Tanya's hand and the seat next to her bed and he slipped into the chair. He picked up her hand, looked into her eyes, "Tanya, when we saw little dark-haired girls with sparkly brown eyes we would think, that must be about Tanya's size now. I wonder what Tanya looks like? What is she doing? Then every real contact with you, even though few and far between, would bring us up-to-date and we would refuel our emotional batteries to go forward again."

Tanya turned to Lana and she went forward to take her hand.

"You must have felt betrayed again when I didn't write from California. Did you hate me?"

"Of course not. I wondered why. I thought maybe you had been in an accident or some horrible thing."

"I made the mistake of trusting Ina with the privileged information of the post office box. Mom took me to UCLA early and I was anxious to get your letter. I asked Ina to pick up the letters and forward them to me. I lost the card with your new address that you gave me when you left. I think Mom found it and destroyed it. She was so devastated when she found out about our meeting and the mail box. I could see how hurt she was, way down deep and I felt so ashamed that I had caused that hurt. I had started to appreciate Mom and understand her better by then," Tanya said. She was becoming breathless from the excitement and strain.

"Did she forward my letters to you?" Lana asked.

"No. She said you didn't write. I never received a single letter. Ina told Mom about the post office box and there was all hell to pay. Mom felt both you and I had betrayed her. When I saw her hurting so much over the whole thing, I realized how wrong I had been. I realized how unfair I had been to her all those years. It had been unfair to want to be with you instead of her and to make her pay for my unhappiness. I made the choice, but I made her pay. It took years to sort that out. I turned over a new leaf and I tried to make her happy and I tried to forget you."

"I did write repeatedly, Tanya. I knew there must be a good reason why you didn't answer," Lana assured her.

"I'm glad to know you wrote. I knew you would. But Mom and Ina both declared there was never a letter. I missed you so much through the years, Mama. It's like I had three mothers. One gave me birth, one got me out of that horrible orphanage and one raised me." Tanya was smiling. "Mama, I love you."

Hearing Tanya call her Mama again was heavenly music to Lana's ears. She bent over and gave Tanya a loving hug and kiss on the cheek.

"It's so good to see your smile still bright and your eyes sparkly. They are your hallmark, Tanya. Keep smiling," Brian said.

"Remember, that's what you said when you left Paraguay. I always remembered your request when I felt down. I..." Her eyes looked different, they looked distant.

The smile faded from her lips and she slowly closed her eyes. Her hand slackened its grip. The nurse ran into the room. The monitor at the nurses' station had alerted them to trouble. The Carters quickly slipped out of the room.

"Better call Tanya's doctor," Ruth yelled to the other nurse. "We are losing her fast. Caroline should be here any minute but in case she was detained, call her, too. She'll want to be with Tanya. Call Mark, I know her husband will want to be with her."

Brian and Lana proceeded down the hall to the elevator. As they waited to get on, Lana thought of Caroline and how difficult this must be for her. When the doors of the elevator opened, there stood Caroline.

Lana and Caroline were both speechless for a minute, staring at each other. Then Caroline accused, "I knew you would come even though I told you not to. I knew when I gave you the hospital address to write to that you would come." Caroline took a deep breath then added, "Let's talk for a minute."

"You better go to Tanya. The nurse was concerned–Tanya's monitor indicated problems. We'll wait over there until you get back."

Caroline turned and dashed to Tanya's room.

Brian and Lana found chairs in the waiting area and settled in. Knowing Caroline was going through a rough time spending the last few minutes of mortality with her beloved daughter touched Lana's heart and she worried what dialogue would follow when Caroline returned. Lana didn't want this to be unpleasant.

It seemed hours before Caroline returned. Actually it was only minutes, about forty-five. Caroline's eyes were swollen and red. She announced, "She's dead. Tanya's dead. Mark didn't get there until she was nearly gone. But in time to give her a final hug."

Lana slipped her arm around Caroline's shoulder as they stood in the middle of the room. Caroline began to sob.

"Did she rally and talk when you got to her?" Lana asked quietly.

"Yes, enough to squeeze my hand and tell me she loved me. Her final whisper was thanks for everything, everything I had done for her and her family. Tanya always was so appreciative."

"You gave her an opportunity for a great life, gave her a home and family and you brought her joy and happiness, Caroline," Lana said.

"Death seems so final even though I believe in another life to follow.

That life seems vague now."

Lana guided Caroline to the sofa and they sat. Lana reached and took Caroline's hand in both of hers.

Lana remembered the closeness Caroline and she shared when they were young, some thirty years ago back in Paraguay. How they were family for each other when so far from biological families. Caroline was the one who took Tanya when they had to leave Paraguay immediately, making a home for her so they didn't have to put Tanya back in that horrible orphanage.

Lana was so thankful Tanya, Ina and Jon had all been rescued. Lana didn't know where to start, or exactly how.

Then Caroline spoke softly, "I'm glad she's out of pain. Tanya has suffered so much these last few months. But it's going to leave such an emptiness in my life. I used to worry about being old when I adopted her and then, with Bernie gone, I wondered, if I died who would be there for her? Ina and Jon have gone their own way, returning to Paraguay. Who would be there for Tanya?"

That was something Lana had been worried about, too. Lana took one hand away from Caroline's and slipped her arm around Caroline's shoulders to let her know she cared.

Lana's resentment and feeling of betrayal by Caroline taking Tanya from them was replaced with appreciation for all she had done, not only for Tanya, but her whole family. The old hurt of the many intervening years slipped away. Lana truly appreciated this fine noble lady–her "sister" from yesteryear.

Brian had been pacing the floor. Hands in his pockets and his head slightly bent–reliving his conversation with Tanya.

He stopped pacing, and came and stood in front of Caroline as if to speak to her. Instead he listened.

It was as if a plug in the bath tub had been pulled and the anger and hurt, like water, drained slowly out. Brian saw and felt Caroline's intense pain. As he listened to her, his face softened.

It had been a long road back from resentment, to love and understanding, then appreciation. Brian stopped pacing and slipped into the chair on the other side of Caroline

He put his arm around Caroline. He bent his head so his forehead touched Caroline's. She reached out and took his other hand.

END